SELECTED SHORT STORIES

OF FRANZ KAFKA

SELECTED

short stories

OF

franz kafka

TRANSLATED BY *Willa and Edwin Muir*

INTRODUCTION BY *Philip Rahv*

THE MODERN LIBRARY · NEW YORK

Library of Congress Catalog Card Number: 52–9771

Distributed in Canada
by Random House of Canada Limited, Toronto

———

THE MODERN LIBRARY
is published by RANDOM HOUSE, INC.

Manufactured in the United States of America by H. Wolff

Contents

Contents

Introduction

BY PHILIP RAHV

THOUGH THE WORK of Franz Kafka has but lately been made available to readers, his name is today firmly linked in the literary mind to such names as Joyce and Proust and Yeats and Rilke and Eliot—the "sacred untouchables," as they have been rightly called, of the modern creative line. Among them he is exceptional in that he enjoyed no public recognition of consequence during his lifetime, for he withheld his longer narratives from publication and was scarcely known beyond a narrow circle of German writers. His posthumous world-fame came to him only in the past two decades.

The first translation of one of his books appeared in this country in 1930, six years after his death. That book was *The Castle,* a novel that ranks high in the Kafka canon. Few readers were then able to gauge its true worth, and even as late as 1937, when *The Trial* was brought out here, it was chiefly Kafka's apparent mystifications rather than his pattern of meaning and basic motives that aroused interest. Readers were astonished by him but hardly convinced of his importance. Since then his idiosyncratic but powerful sensibility has en-

tered into the bloodstream of twentieth-century literature. He has been made the subject of numerous critical
studies in many languages; and everywhere the more
sensitive younger writers, conscious of the static condition of the prevailing fictional techniques and seeking a
creative renewal through mythic and symbolic concep-
tions, have taken his example to heart. There can be
little doubt any longer of his stature as an artist in the
metaphysical mode, whose concern is with the ultimate
structure of human existence, or of his surpassing origi-
nality as an innovator in creative method. Like Rilke
in the *Duino Elegies* he asked the supreme question:
Was war wirklich im All? ("What was real in the
world?").

A master of narrative tone, of a subtle, judicious and
ironically conservative style, Kafka combines within one
framework the recognizable and mysterious, extreme
subjectivity of content with forms rigorously objective,
a lovingly exact portrayal of the factual world with a
dreamlike and magical dissolution of it. By unifying
those contrary elements he was able to achieve no less
than a new mutation in the art of prose fiction. This
much can be said, I think, without attempting to give
an integrated critical estimate of his work, which at this
time may well be premature. The analysis and descrip-
tion of some of its qualities will suffice. Thus it is clear
that if Kafka so compellingly arouses in us a sense of
immediate relatedness, of strong even if uneasy identification, it is because of the profound quality of his feeling for the experience of human loss, estrangement,

guilt and anxiety—an experience increasingly dominant in the modern age.

That Kafka is among the most neurotic of literary artists goes without saying. It accounts, mainly, for the felt menace of his fantastic symbolism and for his drastic departure from the well-defined norms of the literary imagination. For all its obviousness, however, the fact of Kafka's neuroticism presents a danger, if not a vulgar temptation, to the unliterary mind, which tends to confuse a fact so patent with critical judgment and appraisal. No greater error is possible in our approach to literary art. To avoid that common error it is above all necessary to perceive that Kafka is something more than a neurotic artist; he is also an artist of neurosis, that is to say, he succeeds in objectifying through imaginative means the states of mind typical of neurosis and hence in incorporating his private world into the public world we all live in. Once that is accomplished, the creative writer has performed the essential operation which is the secret of his triumph as an artist, if not as a man; he has exorcised his demon, freed himself of his personal burden, converting us into his accomplices. And we, as good readers, as willing accomplices, have no real reason to complain. Neurosis may be the occasion, but literature is the consequence. Moreover, the creative writer is the last person we may look to if our concern is with drawing a line between the normal and the abnormal. For whatever the practicing psychologist may make of that crude though useful distinction, the artist cannot attend to it without inhibiting his sense of life in its full concreteness and complexity.

The novelist Graham Greene has remarked that "every creative writer worth our consideration, every writer who can be called in the wide use of the term a poet, is a victim: a man given over to an obsession." Kafka's obsession was an inordinate sense of inadequacy, failure and sinfulness—a sinfulness corresponding to nothing he had actually done or left undone, but lodged in the innermost recesses of his being. "The state in which we find ourselves is sinful, quite independently of guilt," he wrote in his notebook. The clue to *The Trial* is in the reflection that "only our concept of time makes it possible for us to speak of the Day of Judgment by that name; in reality it is a summary court in perpetual session." And in the same sequence of reflection we find the perfectly typical sentence: "The hunting dogs are playing in the courtyard, but the hare will not escape them, no matter how fast it may be flying already through the woods." The identification here is plainly with the hare; and with the hunting dogs, too, insofar as they represent the hare's longing for self-punishment, his inner wish to be cornered, to be hurt, to be torn to pieces so as to atone for the guilt that fills him from top to bottom. In this one short sentence about the hare and the hunting dogs you have the gist of the typical Kafkan narrative, the obsessive theme, the nuclear fable concerning the victim of an unappeasable power to which he returns again and again, varying and complicating its structure with astonishing resourcefulness, and erecting on so slender a foundation such marvelous superstructures as that of the myth of the Old Commander in *In the Penal Colony*, the myth of the Law in

The Trial and of the celestial bureaucracy in *The Castle*.

The simplicity of the nuclear fable in Kafka should not lead us, however, to disregard the qualities that make him one of the most enigmatic figures in world literature. It does no good to speak of him as an author of religious allegories. Unlike such religious allegorists as Dante or Bunyan he does not depend on the definitive logic of a generally known system of theology; his creative mode presupposes no body of knowledge external to itself; he is not allegorical in any accepted sense but rather an innovator so deeply individualistic as to fit none of the familiar categories. Also, the difficulty of understanding him is on a different plane from that encountered in reading a novelist like James Joyce, for example. Whereas the obscurities of the latter are inherent in the elaborate stylization of his material and in his complex structural designs, in Kafka's case it is the meaning alone that baffles us. Both in language and construction he is elementary compared to Joyce, yet many readers have been mystified by his fictions. But the mystification is gradually cleared up once we learn to listen attentively to his tone and become accustomed to the complete freedom with which he suspends certain conventions of storytelling when it suits his symbolic purpose. Thus when we read in the first sentence of *The Metamorphosis* that the clerk Gregor Samsa awoke one morning to find himself changed into a gigantic insect, it is a mistake to think that by means of this bold stroke Kafka intends to call into question the laws of nature. What he calls into question, rather, is the convention that the laws of nature are at all times to be observed in fiction; and having suspended that convention in the very first paragraph of the story, from that point on he develops it in a logical and realistic manner. The clerk's metamorphosis is a multiple symbol of his alienation from the human state, of his "awakening" to the full horror of his dull, spiritless existence, and of the desperate self-disgust of his unconscious fantasy-life, in which the wish to displace the father and take over his authority in the family is annulled by the guilt-need to suffer a revolting punishment for his presumption.

Another type of symbolism, far less psychologically charged, is found in stories like *The Great Wall of China*. What is the Great Wall? It is likewise a multiple symbol—of human solidarity, of earthly fulfillment and of mankind's effort to obtain supernatural guidance. But why was the wall built in a piecemeal fashion, thus permitting the nomads of the North to slip through the gaps? The reply is that it is in the nature of man to achieve only limited ends. He cannot comprehend the Whole; his vision is discontinuous, his security always incomplete; his aims he can realize only in fragmentary fashion. No doubt the "high command" is ultimately responsible for the apparently inexpedient method of the wall's construction, yet it would never do to question its decrees. Not that such questioning is blasphemous in itself, but rather that in the long run it is useless. Logic can bring us up only to a certain point. Beyond that an answer of a sort is given by the beautiful parable of the river in spring. And as the story continues the theme of the wall is dialectically converted into a series of poetic speculations concerning the relationship between the Chinese and the imperial court at Pekin, that is between God and man. While in *Investigations of a Dog* the remoteness of God is represented as a remoteness in time, in this story the imagery is chiefly spacial. Pekin is so far away from the villagers of the South that they can hardly imagine its existence. They worship dynasties long since dead; news arriving from the imperial court is obsolete by the time it reaches them. This inability of the "Chinese" to possess their Emperor in his vital contemporaneity appears to be a reflection on the idea of God as known to modern man—an idea ill-defined, nebulous and, above all, archaic. Man is now unaware of the real powers that govern his life; insofar as he has any knowledge of divinity it is as of something purely historical.

The quarrel between the religious and the psychoanalytic interpreters of Kafka is of no great moment, as his work is sufficiently meaningful to support some of the "truths" of both schools. Thus the father who condemns his son to death by drowning (in *The Judgment*) can be understood as the tyrannical father of Freudian lore and at the same time as the God of Judgment rising in His wrath to destroy man's illusion of self-sufficiency in the world. At bottom there is no conflict between the two interpretations. For one thing, they are not really mutually exclusive; for another, the reading we give the story depends as much on our own outlook—within certain limits, of course—as on that of the author. There was in Kafka's character an element of radical humility not permitting him to set out to "prove" any given attitude toward life or idea about it. This he plainly tells us in some of the aphorisms that he wrote about himself in the third person: "He proves nothing but himself, his sole proof is himself, all his opponents overcome him at once, not by refuting him (he is irrefutable) but by proving themselves."

That Kafka was a man of religious temper I have no doubt. Though the creator of a surpassing imagery of human failure and frustration, inclined to feel imprisoned on this earth, afflicted with "the melancholy, the impotence, the sicknesses, the feverish fancies of the captive," he never abandons his trust in the spirituality of existence, in the "indestructible," and is disheartened by his literary effort because he wants his writing to attain the power of lifting the world into the realm of "the pure, the true, the immutable." Yet there is nothing either in his private papers or in his fiction to warrant the claim that he was a believer in a personal God who gave his assent to any of the dogmatic systems associated with institutional religion. Even original sin, the dogma closest to the thematic center of his work, he interprets speculatively as "consisting of the complaint, which man makes and never ceases making, that a wrong had been done to him, that the original sin was committed upon him." From the standpoint of the theologian that is sheer heresy, gentle, self-incriminating heresy, to be sure, but heresy nevertheless. The German critic Franz Blei, who was personally acquainted with Kafka, speaks of him as "the servant of a God not believed in." A piety so paradoxical, so immune to cate-

gorical definition, so removed from the fixed and traditional, refusing the consolation of revealed religion yet
intent on winning through to "a faith like a guillotine,
as heavy, as light," could never have found expression
in general ideas or logical thought but only in the
language of art, the one language capable of offering
everything while claiming nothing, asserting nothing,
proving nothing.

Born in Prague in 1883 of middle-class Jewish parents, Kafka appears to have lost his self-confidence early
in life, exchanging for it, as he himself put it, "a
boundless sense of guilt." Moods of loss and failure,
and the idea of the insolubility even of the most ordinary human problems, depressed his youth and later
inspired his art. Because of this unceasing distrust in
himself he tended to regard with astonishment and
inordinate admiration all examples of constructive will,
of the ability of men to discover their true calling and
achieve that integration in the community to which he
attached the highest value but which he believed to be
beyond his own reach. His constant plaint was the same
as that of that character in Hawthorne's story, *The Intelligence Office,* who never ceases to cry out: "I want
my place, my own place, my proper sphere, my thing
to do, which nature intended me to perform when she
fashioned me thus awry, and which I have vainly sought
all my lifetime!"

In the center of Kafka's life stands the father, a figure
fully corresponding to that Freudian terror, the Primal
Sire. Energetic, overbearing, capricious, successful, respectable, the father, not so much by malicious inten-

tion as by being simply what he was, exposed to ridicule his son's impractical inclinations and spiritual wanderings. The mother, though solicitous for her son, was far too much absorbed in her husband to play an independent role; and young Franz was thus driven to extremes of loneliness and introspection that continually negated themselves in the idea of integration through marriage, children and the practice of an honorable profession ("a true calling . . . the right vocation"). The effect on him of his father was such that though he usually talked exceedingly well, in the presence of the formidable parent he took to stuttering. "For me," he wrote to his father in later life, "you began to have that mysterious quality which all tyrants have, whose privilege is based on their personality, not on reason." It is clear that the source of the principle of authority so characteristic of his art is to be traced to his ambivalent attitude to his father, an attitude of strong repulsion as well as identification. Constructed out of elements of his own personality, the protagonist of his major fictions is coerced by extranatural powers who are continually justified and exalted even as they are made to manifest themselves in the guise of a menacing and arbitrary bureaucracy. Max Brod, Kafka's lifelong friend, biographer and editor of his posthumous writings, relates that in many talks he attempted to demonstrate to him the foolishness of his self-contempt and chronic overestimation of his father. These talks were useless, for Kafka produced a "torrent of arguments" that shattered and repelled his friend, who soon realized that only from the standpoint of an outsider could it be asked: "What difference could his father's approval make to Kafka?" His need for that approval was obviously "an innate, irrefutable feeling" that lasted to the end of his life.

In 1906 he took his degree in law at the German University in Prague and soon afterwards obtained a post in an accident-insurance office. But his real interest was in writing, which he approached with the utmost moral earnestness, regarding it as a sacred expenditure of energy, an effort at communion with one's fellowmen, the reflected splendor of religious perception. However, it could never serve as his means of livelihood; aside from his objection in principle to turning literary talent into a source of material benefits, there were other obstacles. He wrote at a pace altogether his own, filled with a raging discontent; at the same time there was the drastic need to stand on his own feet, to win immediate independence from the family. Yet the work at the insurance office disintegrated him; the two occupations were incompatible.

In his letters he writes of literature as his only hope for happiness and fulfillment; and telling of trancelike states when he felt himself at the boundary of the human, he adds that they lacked the serenity of inspiration and were not conducive to the best writing. He speaks of himself as having been on the way to create "a new secret doctrine, a Kabala," but his replies as to the meaning of that doctrine are as diverse as they are contradictory. (His precision, Brod rightly says, was moral, not intellectual.) "I represent," we read in his diary, "the negative elements of my age . . . Unlike

Kierkegaard, I was not guided in life by the now heavily sinking hand of Christianity, nor have I caught hold, like the Zionists, of one of the ends of the flying prayer-shawl of the Jews." The one break in his relationship with Brod seems to have been caused by his coolness to Zionism. "What have I in common with the Jews," he wrote, "when I have scarcely anything in common with myself?" In later years, however, he developed a lively interest in the aspirations of the Zionists, studied Jewish folk-literature, the Hebrew language and read the Talmud (to which his style, by the way, in its reasoning, argumentative quality, in its movement through assertion and contradiction, statement and refutation, bears some resemblance).

It was in 1912—a fateful year in his life—that he met Felice B., the young woman from Berlin whom he wanted to marry but was forced to renounce, suffering terrible anguish in twice breaking his engagement to her. He felt that for a man in his uprooted condition, lacking independent status and a secure orientation in life, marriage was an impossible task. But that was the year, too, in which his literary intentions and continual probing of his own predicament came together in a way enabling him to forge decisively ahead in his work. Compared to what he wrote in the fall of that year everything he had written previously seems sketchy and unfinished. On the night of September 22nd of that seminal fall he wrote *The Judgment* in one sitting, remarking afterwards that during that long stretch between ten o'clock in the evening and six o'clock the next morning he more than once carried his weight on his own back. *The Judgment* is the first Kafkan story which is all of a piece and the first in which the characteristic theme of the struggle between father and son is sounded to the depths. That same month and the next he wrote the long opening chapter of *Amerika,* his first novel, and in November he completed *The Metamorphosis,* certainly his greatest story, in which he achieves an overpowering effect through his consummate handling of the factual detail that supports and actualizes the somber fantasy of the plot. This story is the very embodiment of that quality of the exigent and the extreme, that sense of a human being hemmed in by his own existence and absolutely committed to it, which touches us so deeply in Kafka because it is at once method and content, entreaty and response, the goal and the way. It is mainly through this "existential" quality that Kafka *substantiates* his world for us, imparting the unmistakable appeal of reality to those elements in it that might otherwise appear to be little more than the products of a bizarre or erratic imagination. In *The Metamorphosis,* I would say, Kafka for the first time fully realized his own innermost conception of writing—a conception of inexpressible urgency and inwardness. Long before the composition of the story, he attempted to explain what writing meant to him when he said in a letter to his friend Oskar Pollak that "the books we need are of the kind that act upon us like a misfortune, that make us suffer like the death of someone we love more than ourselves, that make us feel as though we were on the verge of suicide, or lost in a forest remote from all human habitation—a book should serve as the ax for the frozen sea within us."

In October of that same year Max Brod notes in his diary: "Kafka in ecstasy. Writes all night long. . . ." And again: "Kafka in incredible ecstasy." There is something more to this ecstatic state than elation and the sense of freedom a writer normally experiences when making visible progress in his work. The patently compulsive nature of *The Judgment* and *The Metamorphosis,* no less than Kafka's own comment upon them in his diaries, suggest that these stories served as "the ax for the frozen sea" within him—in other words, that the process of their creation involved a breakthrough to layers of repressed material which had heretofore proven inaccessible. It is as if in these psychodynamic fictions the neurotic sufferer in Kafka and the artist in him locked hands and held on for dear life. Precisely of works such as these one can say with Yeats that "the more unconscious the creation the more powerful."

The movement of Kafka's narrative art is from psychology to experimental mythology, from the immediate appropriation of personal states to their projection into the world at large. Thus the principle of authority in which his work is centered is at the outset, as in *The Judgment* and *The Metamorphosis,* represented in the figure of a "real" father, a father whom it is not very difficult to identify in terms of the Freudian "family romance," while in the later and longer works the father is no longer recognizable as a figure in the world we know. He has been removed from the family circle and generalized into an institutional power—hierarchic, remote, mysterious—such as the Law, the Court and the order of officials that resides in the Castle.

In respect to this line of development *In the Penal Colony* can be regarded as a transitional story. It was written in November, 1914, when Kafka had already begun working on *The Trial*. Perhaps because it shows the influence of Kierkegaard, upon whom Kafka first came in 1913, the religious analogues of this story are clearer than in the earlier tales. The Old Commander, whose dread memory is invoked in *In the Penal Colony*, retains some of the individual traits of the "real" father, at the same time as he is mythicized in the manner of the images of authority projected in the later novels.

But in the long run the early breakthrough in his writing to the deeper layers of his psychic life failed to free Kafka of his nerve-destroying fears and sense of unworthiness. He continued to quarrel with himself, plotting self-punishment, thinking even of suicide. "Balzac carried a cane on which was carved the legend: I smash every obstacle; my legend reads: Every obstacle smashes me." The constant seesaw between writing and his job affected his health. He suffered from headaches and insomnia, finally tuberculosis set in and he was compelled to spend years in sanitariums. His illness he considered to be psychically determined—"My head conspired with my lung behind my back." It was not until 1923, when he met Dora Dymant, a girl brought up in an orthodox Jewish family in Poland, and he found himself well enough to move with her to Berlin, that he at long last realized his longing for independence. But, as it turned out, it was already too late to obtain the restitution he sought for the lost years of sickness and misery. In June, 1924, at the age of forty-one, he died in a hospital near Vienna of laryngeal tuberculosis.

During his lifetime he published only some of his shorter works, and never quite finished any of his three novels. Before his death he wrote to Max Brod requesting him to burn all the manuscripts he was leaving behind. Fortunately, his friend took upon himself the honorable responsibility of disregarding that desperate last instruction.

The stories in this volume are printed in the approximate order of their composition. All but *The Hunter Gracchus, A Common Confusion, The Great Wall of China, The Burrow* and *Investigations of a Dog,* appeared during their author's lifetime; and of the five posthumous pieces only *A Common Confusion* is complete; the last pages of the other stories are either missing or were never written.

New York
June, 1952

SELECTED SHORT STORIES

OF FRANZ KAFKA

The Judgment

It was a Sunday morning in the very height of spring. Georg Bendemann, a young merchant, was sitting in his own room on the first floor of one of a long row of small, ramshackle houses stretching beside the river which were scarcely distinguishable from each other except in height and coloring. He had just finished a letter to an old friend of his who was now living abroad, had put it into its envelope in a slow and dreamy fashion, and with his elbows propped on the writing table was gazing out of the window at the river, the bridge and the hills on the farther bank with their tender green.

He was thinking about his friend, who had actually run away to Russia some years before, being dissatisfied with his prospects at home. Now he was carrying on a business in St. Petersburg, which had flourished to begin with but had long been going downhill, as he always complained on his increasingly rare visits. So he was wearing himself out to no purpose in a foreign country; the unfamiliar full beard he wore did not quite conceal the face Georg had known so well since childhood, and his skin was growing so yellow as to indicate some latent disease. By his own account he had no regular connection with the colony of his fellow countrymen out there and almost no social intercourse with Russian families, so that he was resigning himself to becoming a permanent bachelor.

What could one write to such a man, who had obviously run off the rails, a man one could be sorry for but could not help? Should one advise him to come home, to transplant himself and take up his old friendships again—there was nothing to hinder him—and in general to rely on the help of his friends? But that was as good as telling him, and the more kindly the more offensively, that all his efforts hitherto had miscarried, that he should finally give up, come back home, and be gaped at by everyone as a returned prodigal, that only his friends knew what was what and that he himself was just a big child who should do what his successful and home-keeping friends prescribed. And was it certain, besides, that all the pain one would have to inflict on him would achieve its object? Perhaps it would not even be possible to get him to come home at all—he said himself that he was now out of touch with commerce in his native country—and then he would still be left an alien in a foreign land embittered by his friends' advice and more than ever estranged from them. But if he did follow their advice and then didn't fit in at home—not out of malice, of course, but through force of circumstances —couldn't get on with his friends or without them, felt humiliated, couldn't be said to have either friends or a country of his own any longer, wouldn't it have been better for him to stay abroad just as he was? Taking all this into account, how could one be sure that he would make a success of life at home?

For such reasons, supposing one wanted to keep up correspondence with him, one could not send him any real news such as could frankly be told to the most distant acquaintance. It was more than three years since his last visit, and for this he offered the lame excuse that the political situation in Russia was too uncertain, which apparently would not permit even the briefest absence of a small business man while it allowed hundreds of thousands of Russians to travel peacefully abroad. But during these three years Georg's own position in life had changed a lot. Two years ago his mother had died, since when he and his father had shared the household together, and his friend had of course been informed of that and had expressed his sympathy in a letter phrased so dryly that the grief caused by such an event, one had to conclude, could not be realized in a distant country. Since that time, however, Georg had applied himself with greater determination to the business as well as to everything else.

Perhaps during his mother's lifetime his father's insistence on having everything his own way in the business had hindered him from developing any real activity of his own, perhaps since her death his father had become less aggressive, although he was still active in the business, perhaps it was mostly due to an accidental run of good fortune—which was very probable indeed —but at any rate during those two years the business had developed in a most unexpected way, the staff had had to be doubled, the turnover was five times as great, no doubt about it, further progress lay just ahead.

But Georg's friend had no inkling of this improvement. In earlier years, perhaps for the last time in that letter of condolence, he had tried to persuade Georg to emigrate to Russia and had enlarged upon the prospects of success for precisely Georg's branch of trade. The figures quoted were microscopic by comparison with the range of Georg's present operations. Yet he shrank from letting his friend know about his business success, and if he were to do it now retrospectively that certainly would look peculiar.

So Georg confined himself to giving his friend unimportant items of gossip such as rise at random in the memory when one is idly thinking things over on a quiet Sunday. All he desired was to leave undisturbed the idea of the home town which his friend must have built up to his own content during the long interval. And so it happened to Georg that three times in three fairly widely separated letters he had told his friend about the engagement of an unimportant man to an equally unimportant girl, until indeed, quite contrary to his intentions, his friend began to show some interest in this notable event.

Yet Georg preferred to write about things like these rather than to confess that he himself had got engaged a month ago to a Fräulein Frieda Brandenfeld, a girl from a well-to-do family. He often discussed this friend of his with his fiancée and the peculiar relationship that had developed between them in their correspondence.

"So he won't be coming to our wedding," said she, "and yet I have a right to get to know all your friends." "I don't want to trouble him," answered Georg. "Don't misunderstand me, he would probably come, at least I think so, but he would feel that his hand had been forced and he would be hurt, perhaps he would envy me and certainly he'd be discontented and without being able to do anything about his discontent he'd have to go away again alone. Alone—do you know what that means?" "Yes, but may he not hear about our wedding in some other fashion?" "I can't prevent that, of course, but it's unlikely, considering the way he lives." "Since your friends are like that, Georg, you shouldn't ever have got engaged at all." "Well, we're both to blame for that; but I wouldn't have it any other way now." And when, breathing quickly under his kisses, she still brought out: "All the same, I do feel upset," he thought it could not really involve him in trouble were he to send the news to his friend. "That's the kind of man I am and he'll just have to take me as I am," he said to himself, "I can't cut myself to another pattern that might make a more suitable friend for him."

And in fact he did inform his friend, in the long letter he had been writing that Sunday morning, about his engagement, with these words: "I have saved my best news to the end. I have got engaged to a Fräulein Frieda Brandenfeld, a girl from a well-to-do family, who only came to live here a long time after you went away, so that you're hardly likely to know her. There will be time to tell you more about her later, for today let me just say that I am very happy and as between you and me the only difference in our relationship is that instead of a quite ordinary kind of friend you will now have in me a happy friend. Besides that, you will acquire in my fiancée, who sends her warm greetings and will soon write you herself, a genuine friend of the opposite sex, which is not without importance to a bachelor. I know that there are many reasons why you can't come to see us, but would not my wedding be precisely the right occasion for giving all obstacles the go-by? Still, however that may be, do just as seems good to you without regarding any interests but your own."

With this letter in his hand Georg had been sitting a long time at the writing table, his face turned towards the window. He had barely acknowledged, with an absent smile, a greeting waved to him from the street by a passing acquaintance.

At last he put the letter in his pocket and went out of his room across a small lobby into his father's room, which he had not entered for months. There was in fact no need for him to enter it, since he saw his father daily at business and they took their midday meal together at an eating house; in the evening, it was true, each did as he pleased, yet even then, unless Georg—as mostly happened—went out with friends or, more recently, visited his fiancée, they always sat for a while, each with his newspaper, in their common sitting room.

It surprised Georg how dark his father's room was even on this sunny morning. So it was overshadowed as much as that by the high wall on the other side of the narrow courtyard. His father was sitting by the window in a corner hung with various mementoes of Georg's dead mother, reading a newspaper which he held to one side before his eyes in an attempt to overcome a defect of vision. On the table stood the remains of his breakfast, not much of which seemed to have been eaten.

"Ah, Georg," said his father, rising at once to meet him. His heavy dressing gown swung open as he walked and the skirts of it fluttered round him.—"My father is still a giant of a man," said Georg to himself.

"It's unbearably dark here," he said aloud.

"Yes, it's dark enough," answered his father.

"And you've shut the window, too?"

"I prefer it like that."

"Well, it's quite warm outside," said Georg, as if continuing his previous remark, and sat down.

His father cleared away the breakfast dishes and set them on a chest.

"I really only wanted to tell you," went on Georg, who had been vacantly following the old man's movements, "that I am now sending the news of my engagement to St. Petersburg." He drew the letter a little way from his pocket and let it drop back again.

"To St. Petersburg?" asked his father.

"To my friend there," said Georg, trying to meet his father's eye.—In business hours he's quite different, he was thinking. How solidly he sits here with his arms crossed.

"Oh, yes. To your friend," said his father, with peculiar emphasis.

"Well, you know, Father, that I wanted not to tell him about my engagement at first. Out of consideration for him, that was the only reason. You know yourself he's a difficult man. I said to myself that someone else might tell him about my engagement, although he's such a solitary creature that that was hardly likely—I couldn't prevent that—but I wasn't ever going to tell him myself."

"And now you've changed your mind?" asked his father, laying his enormous newspaper on the window sill and on top of it his spectacles, which he covered with one hand.

"Yes, I've been thinking it over. If he's a good friend of mine, I said to myself, my being happily engaged should make him happy too. And so I wouldn't put off telling him any longer. But before I posted the letter I wanted to let you know."

"Georg," said his father, lengthening his toothless mouth, "listen to me! You've come to me about this business, to talk it over with me. No doubt that does you honor. But it's nothing, it's worse than nothing, if you don't tell me the whole truth. I don't want to stir up matters that shouldn't be mentioned here. Since the death of our dear mother certain things have been done that aren't right. Maybe the time will come for mentioning them, and maybe sooner than we think. There's many a thing in the business I'm not aware of, maybe it's not done behind my back—I'm not going to say that it's done behind my back—I'm not equal to things any longer, my memory's failing, I haven't an eye for so many things any longer. That's the course of nature in the first place, and in the second place the death of our dear mother hit me harder than it did you.—But since we're talking about it, about this letter, I beg you, Georg, don't deceive me. It's a trivial affair, it's hardly worth mentioning, so don't deceive me. Do you really have this friend in St. Petersburg?"

Georg rose in embarrassment. "Never mind my friends. A thousand friends wouldn't make up to me for my father. Do you know what I think? You're not taking enough care of yourself. But old age must be taken care of. I can't do without you in the business, you know that very well, but if the business is going to undermine your health, I'm ready to close it down tomorrow for-ever. And that won't do. We'll have to make a change in your way of living. But a radical change. You sit here in the dark, and in the sitting room you would have plenty of light. You just take a bite of breakfast instead of prop-erly keeping up your strength. You sit by a closed win-dow, and the air would be so good for you. No, Father! I'll get the doctor to come, and we'll follow his orders. We'll change your room, you can move into the front room and I'll move in here. You won't notice the change, all your things will be moved with you. But there's time for all that later. I'll put you to bed now for a little; I'm sure you need to rest. Come, I'll help you to take off your things, you'll see I can do it. Or if you would rather go into the front room at once, you can lie down in my bed for the present. That would be the most sensible thing."

Georg stood close beside his father, who had let his head with its unkempt white hair sink on his chest.

"Georg," said his father in a low voice, without mov-ing.

Georg knelt down at once beside his father. In the

old man's weary face he saw the pupils, over-large, fix-
edly looking at him from the corners of the eyes.

"You have no friends in St. Petersburg. You've always
been a leg-puller and you haven't even shrunk from
pulling my leg. How could you have a friend out there!
I can't believe it."

"Just think back a bit, Father," said Georg, lifting his
father from the chair and slipping off his dressing gown
as he stood feebly enough, "it'll soon be three years since
my friend came to see us last. I remember that you used
not to like him very much. At least twice I kept you
from seeing him, although he was actually sitting with
me in my room. I could quite well understand your
dislike of him, my friend has his peculiarities. But then,
later, you got on with him very well. I was proud because you listened to him and nodded and asked him
questions. If you think back you're bound to remember.
He used to tell us the most incredible stories of the
Russian Revolution. For instance, when he was on a
business trip to Kiev and ran into a riot, and saw a priest
on a balcony who cut a broad cross in blood on the palm
of his hand and held the hand up and appealed to the
mob. You've told that story yourself once or twice
since."

Meanwhile Georg had succeeded in lowering his
father down again and carefully taking off the woollen
drawers he wore over his linen underpants and his socks.
The not particularly clean appearance of this underwear made him reproach himself for having been neglectful. It should have certainly been his duty to see

that his father had clean changes of underwear. He had not yet explicitly discussed with his bride-to-be what arrangements should be made for his father in the future, for they had both of them silently taken it for granted that the old man would go on living alone in the old house. But now he made a quick, firm decision to take him into his own future establishment. It almost looked, on closer inspection, as if the care he meant to lavish there on his father might come too late.

He carried his father to bed in his arms. It gave him a dreadful feeling to notice that while he took the few steps towards the bed the old man on his breast was playing with his watch chain. He could not lay him down on the bed for a moment, so firmly did he hang on to the watch chain.

But as soon as he was laid in bed, all seemed well. He covered himself up and even drew the blankets farther than usual over his shoulders. He looked up at Georg with a not unfriendly eye.

"You begin to remember my friend, don't you?" asked Georg, giving him an encouraging nod.

"Am I well covered up now?" asked his father, as if he were not able to see whether his feet were properly tucked in or not.

"So you find it snug in bed already," said Georg, and tucked the blankets more closely round him.

"Am I well covered up?" asked the father once more, seeming to be strangely intent upon the answer.

"Don't worry, you're well covered up."

"No!" cried his father, cutting short the answer, threw

the blankets off with a strength that sent them all flying in a moment and sprang erect in bed. Only one hand lightly touched the ceiling to steady him.

"You wanted to cover me up, I know, my young sprig, but I'm far from being covered up yet. And even if this is the last strength I have, it's enough for you, too much for you. Of course I know your friend. He would have been a son after my own heart. That's why you've been playing him false all these years. Why else? Do you think I haven't been sorry for him? And that's why you had to lock yourself up in your office—the Chief is busy, mustn't be disturbed—just so that you could write your lying little letters to Russia. But thank goodness a father doesn't need to be taught how to see through his son. And now that you thought you'd got him down, so far down that you could set your bottom on him and sit on him and he wouldn't move, then my fine son makes up his mind to get married!"

Georg stared at the bogey conjured up by his father. His friend in St. Petersburg, whom his father suddenly knew too well, touched his imagination as never before. Lost in the vastness of Russia he saw him. At the door of an empty, plundered warehouse he saw him. Among the wreckage of his showcases, the slashed remnants of his wares, the falling gas brackets, he was just standing up. Why did he have to go so far away!

"But attend to me!" cried his father, and Georg, almost distracted, ran towards the bed to take everything in, yet came to a stop halfway.

"Because she lifted up her skirts," his father began to flute, "because she lifted her skirts like this, the nasty creature," and mimicking her he lifted his shirt so high that one could see the scar on his thigh from his war wound, "because she lifted her skirts like this and this you made up to her, and in order to make free with her undisturbed you have disgraced your mother's memory, betrayed your friend and stuck your father into bed so that he can't move. But he can move, or can't he?"

And he stood up quite unsupported and kicked his legs out. His insight made him radiant.

Georg shrank into a corner, as far away from his father as possible. A long time ago he had firmly made up his mind to watch closely every least movement so that he should not be surprised by any indirect attack, a pounce from behind or above. At this moment he recalled this long-forgotten resolve and forgot it again, like a man drawing a short thread through the eye of a needle.

"But your friend hasn't been betrayed after all!" cried his father, emphasizing the point with stabs of his forefinger. "I've been representing him here on the spot."

"You comedian!" Georg could not resist the retort, realized at once the harm done and, his eyes starting in his head, bit his tongue back, only too late, till the pain made his knees give.

"Yes, of course I've been playing a comedy! A comedy! That's a good expression! What other comfort was left to a poor old widower? Tell me—and while you're answering me be you still my living son—what else was left to me, in my back room, plagued by a disloyal staff, old to the marrow of my bones? And my son strutting through the world, finishing off deals that I had

prepared for him, bursting with triumphant glee and
stalking away from his father with the closed face of a
respectable business man! Do you think I didn't love
you, I, from whom you are sprung?"

Now he'll lean forward, thought Georg. What if he
topples and smashes himself! These words went hissing
through his mind.

His father leaned forward but did not topple. Since
Georg did not come any nearer, as he had expected, he
straightened himself again.

"Stay where you are, I don't need you! You think you
have strength enough to come over here and that you're
only hanging back of your own accord. Don't be too
sure! I am still much the stronger of us two. All by myself I might have had to give way, but your mother has
given me so much of her strength that I've established a
fine connection with your friend and I have your customers here in my pocket!"

"He has pockets even in his shirt!" said Georg to himself, and believed that with this remark he could make
him an impossible figure for all the world. Only for a
moment did he think so, since he kept on forgetting
everything.

"Just take your bride on your arm and try getting in
my way! I'll sweep her from your very side, you don't
know how!"

Georg made a grimace of disbelief. His father only
nodded, confirming the truth of his words, towards
Georg's corner.

"How you amused me today, coming to ask me if you
should tell your friend about your engagement. He

knows it already, you stupid boy, he knows it all! I've been writing to him, for you forgot to take my writing things away from me. That's why he hasn't been here for years, he knows everything a hundred times better than you do yourself, in his left hand he crumples your letters unopened while in his right hand he holds up my letters to read through!"

In his enthusiasm he waved his arm over his head. "He knows everything a thousand times better!" he cried.

"Ten thousand times!" said Georg, to make fun of his father, but in his very mouth the words turned into deadly earnest.

"For years I've been waiting for you to come with some such question! Do you think I concern myself with anything else? Do you think I read my newspapers? Look!" and he threw Georg a newspaper sheet which he had somehow taken to bed with him. An old newspaper, with a name entirely unknown to Georg.

"How long a time you've taken to grow up! Your mother had to die, she couldn't see the happy day, your friend is going to pieces in Russia, even three years ago he was yellow enough to be thrown away, and as for me, you see what condition I'm in. You have eyes in your head for that!"

"So you've been lying in wait for me!" cried Georg.

His father said pityingly, in an offhand manner: "I suppose you wanted to say that sooner. But now it doesn't matter." And in a louder voice: "So now you know what else there was in the world besides yourself, till now you've known only about yourself! An innocent child, yes, that you were, truly, but still more truly have you been a devilish human being!—And therefore take note: I sentence you now to death by drowning!"

Georg felt himself urged from the room. The crash with which his father fell on the bed behind him was still in his ears as he fled. On the staircase, which he rushed down as if its steps were an inclined plane, he ran into his charwoman on her way up to do the morning cleaning of the room. "Jesus!" she cried, and covered her face with her apron, but he was already gone. Out of the front door he rushed, across the roadway, driven towards the water. Already he was grasping at the railings as a starving man clutches food. He swung himself over, like the distinguished gymnast he had once been in his youth, to his parents' pride. With weakening grip he was still holding on when he spied between the railings a motor-bus coming which would easily cover the noise of his fall, called in a low voice: "Dear parents, I have always loved you, all the same," and let himself drop.

At this moment an unending stream of traffic was just going over the bridge.

The Metamorphosis

I

As Gregor Samsa awoke one morning from uneasy dreams he found himself transformed in his bed into a gigantic insect. He was lying on his hard, as it were armor-plated, back and when he lifted his head a little he could see his dome-like brown belly divided into stiff arched segments on top of which the bed quilt could hardly keep in position and was about to slide off completely. His numerous legs, which were pitifully thin compared to the rest of his bulk, waved helplessly before his eyes.

What has happened to me? he thought. It was no dream. His room, a regular human bedroom, only rather too small, lay quiet between the four familiar walls. Above the table on which a collection of cloth samples was unpacked and spread out—Samsa was a commercial traveler—hung the picture which he had recently cut out of an illustrated magazine and put into a pretty gilt frame. It showed a lady, with a fur cap on and a fur stole, sitting upright and holding out to the spectator a huge fur muff into which the whole of her forearm had vanished!

Gregor's eyes turned next to the window, and the overcast sky—one could hear rain drops beating on the window gutter—made him quite melancholy. What about sleeping a little longer and forgetting all this nonsense, he thought, but it could not be done, for he was accustomed to sleep on his right side and in his present condition he could not turn himself over. However violently he forced himself towards his right side he always rolled on to his back again. He tried it at least a hundred times, shutting his eyes to keep from seeing his struggling legs, and only desisted when he began to feel in his side a faint dull ache he had never experienced before.

Oh God, he thought, what an exhausting job I've picked on! Traveling about day in, day out. It's much more irritating work than doing the actual business in the office, and on top of that there's the trouble of constant traveling, of worrying about train connections, the bed and irregular meals, casual acquaintances that are always new and never become intimate friends. The devil take it all! He felt a slight itching up on his belly; slowly pushed himself on his back nearer to the top of the bed so that he could lift his head more easily; identified the itching place which was surrounded by many small white spots the nature of which he could not understand and made to touch it with a leg, but drew the leg back immediately, for the contact made a cold shiver run through him.

He slid down again into his former position. This getting up early, he thought, makes one quite stupid. A man needs his sleep. Other commercials live like harem women. For instance, when I come back to the hotel of a morning to write up the orders I've got, these others are only sitting down to breakfast. Let me just try that with my chief; I'd be sacked on the spot. Anyhow, that might be quite a good thing for me, who can tell? If I didn't have to hold my hand because of my parents I'd have given notice long ago, I'd have gone to the chief and told him exactly what I think of him. That would knock him endways from his desk! It's a queer way of doing, too, this sitting on high at a desk and talking down to employees, especially when they have to come quite near because the chief is hard of hearing. Well, there's still hope; once I've saved enough money to pay back my parents' debts to him—that should take another five or six years—I'll do it without fail. I'll cut myself completely loose then. For the moment, though, I'd better get up, since my train goes at five.

He looked at the alarm clock ticking on the chest. Heavenly Father! he thought. It was half-past six o'clock and the hands were quietly moving on, it was even past the half-hour, it was getting on toward a quarter to seven. Had the alarm clock not gone off? From the bed one could see that it had been properly set for four o'clock; of course it must have gone off. Yes, but was it possible to sleep quietly through that car-splitting noise? Well, he had not slept quietly, yet apparently all the more soundly for that. But what was he to do now? The next train went at seven o'clock; to catch that he would need to hurry like mad and his samples weren't even packed up, and he himself wasn't feeling particularly fresh and active. And even if he did catch the train he wouldn't avoid a row with the chief, since the firm's porter would have been waiting for the five o'clock train and would have long since reported his failure to turn up. The porter was a creature of the chief's, spineless and stupid. Well, supposing he were to say he was sick? But that would be most unpleasant and would look suspicious, since during his five years' employment he had not been ill once. The chief himself would be sure to come with the sick-insurance doctor, would reproach his parents with their son's laziness and would cut all excuses short by referring to the insurance doctor, who of course regarded all mankind as perfectly healthy malingerers. And would he be so far wrong on this occasion? Gregor really felt quite well, apart from a drowsiness that was utterly superfluous after such a long sleep, and he was even unusually hungry.

As all this was running through his mind at top speed without his being able to decide to leave his bed —the alarm clock had just struck a quarter to seven— there came a cautious tap at the door behind the head of his bed. "Gregor," said a voice—it was his mother's —"it's a quarter to seven. Hadn't you a train to catch?" That gentle voice! Gregor had a shock as he heard his own voice answering hers, unmistakably his own voice, it was true, but with a persistent horrible twittering squeak behind it like an undertone, that left the words in their clear shape only for the first moment and then rose up reverberating round them to destroy their sense, so that one could not be sure one had heard them rightly. Gregor wanted to answer at length and explain everything, but in the circumstances he confined himself to saying: "Yes, yes, thank you, Mother, I'm getting up now." The wooden door between them must have kept the change in his voice from being noticeable outside, for his mother contented herself with this statement and shuffled away. Yet this brief exchange of words had made the other members of the family aware that Gregor was still in the house, as they had not expected, and at one of the side doors his father was already knocking, gently, yet with his fist. "Gregor, Gregor," he called, "what's the matter with you?" And after a little while he called again in a deeper voice: "Gregor! Gregor!" At the other side door his sister was saying in a low, plaintive tone: "Gregor? Aren't you well? Are you needing anything?" He answered them both at once: "I'm just ready," and did his best to make his voice sound as normal as possible by enunciating the words very clearly and leaving long pauses between them. So his father went back to his breakfast, but his sister whispered: "Gregor, open the door, do." However, he was not thinking of opening the door, and felt thankful for the prudent habit he had acquired in traveling of locking all doors during the night, even at home.

His immediate intention was to get up quietly without being disturbed, to put on his clothes and above all eat his breakfast, and only then to consider what else was to be done, since in bed, he was well aware, his meditations would come to no sensible conclusion. He remembered that often enough in bed he had felt small aches and pains, probably caused by awkward postures, which had proved purely imaginary once he got up, and he looked forward eagerly to seeing this morning's delusions gradually fall away. That the change in his voice was nothing but the precursor of a severe chill, a standing ailment of commercial travelers, he had not the least possible doubt.

To get rid of the quilt was quite easy; he had only to inflate himself a little and it fell off by itself. But the next move was difficult, especially because he was so uncommonly broad. He would have needed arms and hands to hoist himself up; instead he had only the numerous little legs which never stopped waving in all directions and which he could not control in the least. When he tried to bend one of them it was the first to stretch itself straight; and did he succeed at last in making it do what he wanted, all the other legs meanwhile waved the more wildly in a high degree of unpleasant agitation. "But what's the use of lying idle in bed," said Gregor to himself.

He thought that he might get out of bed with the lower part of his body first, but this lower part, which he had not yet seen and of which he could form no clear conception, proved too difficult to move; it shifted so slowly; and when finally, almost wild with annoyance, he gathered his forces together and thrust out recklessly, he had miscalculated the direction and bumped heavily against the lower end of the bed, and the stinging pain he felt informed him that precisely this lower part of his body was at the moment probably the most sensitive.

So he tried to get the top part of himself out first, and cautiously moved his head towards the edge of the bed.

That proved easy enough, and despite its breadth and mass the bulk of his body at last slowly followed the movement of his head. Still, when he finally got his head free over the edge of the bed he felt too scared to go on advancing, for after all if he let himself fall in this way it would take a miracle to keep his head from being injured. And at all costs he must not lose consciousness now, precisely now; he would rather stay in bed.

But when after a repetition of the same efforts he lay in his former position again, sighing, and watched his little legs struggling against each other more wildly than ever, if that were possible, and saw no way of bringing any order into this arbitrary confusion, he told himself again that it was impossible to stay in bed and that the most sensible course was to risk everything for the smallest hope of getting away from it. At the same time he did not forget meanwhile to remind himself that cool reflection, the coolest possible, was much better than desperate resolves. In such moments he focused his eyes as sharply as possible on the window, but, unfortunately, the prospect of the morning fog, which muffled even the other side of the narrow street, brought him little encouragement and comfort. "Seven o'clock already," he said to himself when the alarm clock chimed again, "seven o'clock already and still such a thick fog." And for a little while he lay quiet, breathing lightly, as if perhaps expecting such complete repose to restore all things to their real and normal condition.

But then he said to himself: "Before it strikes a quarter past seven I must be quite out of this bed, without fail. Anyhow, by that time someone will have come from the office to ask for me, since it opens before seven." And he set himself to rocking his whole body at once in a regular rhythm, with the idea of swinging it out of the bed. If he tipped himself out in that way he could keep his head from injury by lifting it at an acute angle when he fell. His back seemed to be hard and was not likely to suffer from a fall on the carpet. His biggest worry was the loud crash he would not be able to help making, which would probably cause anxiety, if not terror, behind all the doors. Still, he must take the risk.

When he was already half out of the bed—the new method was more a game than an effort, for he needed only to hitch himself across by rocking to and fro—it struck him how simple it would be if he could get help. Two strong people—he thought of his father and the servant girl—would be amply sufficient; they would only have to thrust their arms under his convex back, lever him out of the bed, bend down with their burden and then be patient enough to let him turn himself right over on to the floor, where it was to be hoped his legs would then find their proper function. Well, ignoring the fact that the doors were all locked, ought he really to call for help? In spite of his misery he could not suppress a smile at the very idea of it.

He had got so far that he could barely keep his equilibrium when he rocked himself strongly, and he would have to nerve himself very soon for the final decision since in five minutes' time it would be a quarter past seven—when the front doorbell rang. "That's someone from the office," he said to himself, and grew almost rigid, while his little legs only jigged about all the faster. For a moment everything stayed quiet. "They're not going to open the door," said Gregor to himself, catch, ing at some kind of irrational hope. But then of course the servant girl went as usual to the door with her heavy tread and opened it. Gregor needed only to hear the first good morning of the visitor to know immediately who it was—the chief clerk himself. What a fate, to be condemned to work for a firm where the smallest omis· sion at once gave rise to the gravest suspicion! Were all employees in a body nothing but scoundrels, was there not among them one single loyal devoted man who, had he wasted only an hour or so of the firm's time in a morning, was so tormented by conscience as to be driven out of his mind and actually incapable of leaving his bed? Wouldn't it really have been sufficient to send an apprentice to inquire—if any inquiry were necessary at all—did the chief clerk himself have to come and thus indicate to the entire family, an innocent family, that this suspicious circumstance could be investigated by no one less versed in affairs than himself? And more through the agitation caused by these reflections than through any act of will Gregor swung himself out of bed with all his strength. There was a loud thump, but it was not really a crash. His fall was broken to some ex- tent by the carpet, his back, too, was less stiff than he thought, and so there was merely a dull thud, not so very startling. Only he had not lifted his head carefully enough and had hit it; he turned it and rubbed it on the carpet in pain and irritation.

"That was something falling down in there," said the

chief clerk in the next room to the left. Gregor tried to
suppose to himself that something like what had happened to him today might some day happen to the
chief clerk; one really could not deny that it was possible. But as if in brusque reply to this supposition the
chief clerk took a couple of firm steps in the next-door
room and his patent-leather boots creaked. From the
right-hand room his sister was whispering to inform
him of the situation: "Gregor, the chief clerk's here."
"I know," muttered Gregor to himself; but he didn't
dare to make his voice loud enough for his sister to
hear it.

"Gregor," said his father now from the left-hand
room, "the chief clerk has come and wants to know why
you didn't catch the early train. We don't know what to
say to him. Besides, he wants to talk to you in person.
So open the door, please. He will be good enough to
excuse the untidiness of your room." "Good morning,
Mr. Samsa," the chief clerk was calling amiably meanwhile. "He's not well," said his mother to the visitor,
while his father was still speaking through the door,
"he's not well, sir, believe me. What else would make
him miss a train! The boy thinks about nothing but
his work. It makes me almost cross the way he never
goes out in the evenings; he's been here the last eight
days and has stayed at home every single evening. He
just sits there quietly at the table reading a newspaper
or looking through railway timetables. The only amusement he gets is doing fretwork. For instance, he spent
two or three evenings cutting out a little picture frame:
you would be surprised to see how pretty it is; it's hang-

ing in his room; you'll see it in a minute when Gregor
opens the door. I must say I'm glad you've come, sir; we
should never have got him to unlock the door by ourselves; he's so obstinate; and I'm sure he's unwell,
though he wouldn't have it to be so this morning."
"I'm just coming," said Gregor slowly and carefully,
not moving an inch for fear of losing one word of the
conversation. "I can't think of any other explanation,
madam," said the chief clerk. "I hope it's nothing serious. Although on the other hand I must say that we men
of business—fortunately or unfortunately—very often
simply have to ignore any slight indisposition, since
business must be attended to." "Well, can the chief
clerk come in now?" asked Gregor's father impatiently,
again knocking on the door. "No," said Gregor. In the
left-hand room a painful silence followed this refusal;
in the right-hand room his sister began to sob.

Why didn't his sister join the others? She was probably newly out of bed and hadn't even begun to put on
her clothes yet. Well, why was she crying? Because he
wouldn't get up and let the chief clerk in, because he
was in danger of losing his job, and because the chief
would begin dunning his parents again for the old
debts? Surely these were things one didn't need to worry
about for the present. Gregor was still at home and not
in the least thinking of deserting the family. At the
moment, true, he was lying on the carpet and no one
who knew the condition he was in could seriously expect
him to admit the chief clerk. But for such a small dis-
courtesy, which could plausibly be explained away
somehow later on, Gregor could hardly be dismissed on

the spot. And it seemed to Gregor that it would be much more sensible to leave him in peace for the present than to trouble him with tears and entreaties. Still, of course, their uncertainty bewildered them all and excused their behavior.

"Mr. Samsa," the chief clerk called now in a louder voice, "what's the matter with you? Here you are, barricading yourself in your room, giving only 'yes' and 'no' for answers, causing your parents a lot of unnecessary trouble and neglecting—I mention this only in passing—neglecting your business duties in an incredible fashion. I am speaking here in the name of your parents and of your chief, and I beg you quite seriously to give me an immediate and precise explanation. You amaze me, you amaze me. I thought you were a quiet, dependable person, and now all at once you seem bent on making a disgraceful exhibition of yourself. The chief did hint to me early this morning a possible explanation for your disappearance—with reference to the cash payments that were entrusted to you recently—but I almost pledged my solemn word of honor that this could not be so. But now that I see how incredibly obstinate you are, I no longer have the slightest desire to take your part at all. And your position in the firm is not so unassailable. I came with the intention of telling you all this in private, but since you are wasting my time so needlessly I don't see why your parents shouldn't hear it too. For some time past your work has been most unsatisfactory; this is not the season of the year for a business boom, of course, we admit that, but a season of the

year for doing no business at all, that does not exist,
Mr. Samsa, must not exist."

"But, sir," cried Gregor, beside himself and in his agitation forgetting everything else, "I'm just going to open
the door this very minute. A slight illness, an attack of
giddiness, has kept me from getting up. I'm still lying
in bed. But I feel all right again. I'm getting out of bed
now. Just give me a moment or two longer! I'm not
quite so well as I thought. But I'm all right, really. How
a thing like that can suddenly strike one down! Only last
night I was quite well, my parents can tell you, or rather
I did have a slight presentiment. I must have showed
some sign of it. Why didn't I report it at the office! But
one always thinks that an indisposition can be got over
without staying in the house. Oh, sir, do spare my parents! All that you're reproaching me with now has no
foundation; no one has ever said a word to me about it.
Perhaps you haven't looked at the last orders I sent in.
Anyhow, I can still catch the eight-o'clock train, I'm
much the better for my few hours' rest. Don't let me
detain you here, sir; I'll be attending to business very
soon, and do be good enough to tell the chief so and to
make my excuses to him!"

And while all this was tumbling out pell-mell and
Gregor hardly knew what he was saying, he had reached
the chest quite easily, perhaps because of the practice
he had had in bed, and was now trying to lever himself
upright by means of it. He meant actually to open the
door, actually to show himself and speak to the chief
clerk; he was eager to find out what the others, after all

their insistence, would say at the sight of him. If they were horrified then the responsibility was no longer his and he could stay quiet. But if they took it calmly, then he had no reason either to be upset, and could really get to the station for the eight-o'clock train if he hurried. At first he slipped down a few times from the polished surface of the chest, but at length with a last heave he stood upright; he paid no more attention to the pains in the lower part of his body, however they smarted. Then he let himself fall against the back of a near-by chair, and clung with his little legs to the edges of it. That brought him into control of himself again and he stopped speaking, for now he could listen to what the chief clerk was saying.

"Did you understand a word of it?" the chief clerk was asking; "surely he can't be trying to make fools of us?" "Oh dear," cried his mother, in tears, "perhaps he's terribly ill and we're tormenting him. Grete! Grete!" she called out then. "Yes, Mother?" called his sister from the other side. They were calling to each other across Gregor's room. "You must go this minute for the doctor. Gregor is ill. Go for the doctor, quick. Did you hear how he was speaking?" "That was no human voice," said the chief clerk in a voice noticeably low beside the shrillness of the mother's. "Anna! Anna!" his father was calling through the hall to the kitchen, clapping his hands, "get a locksmith at once!" And the two girls were already running through the hall with a swish of skirts—how could his sister have got dressed so quickly?—and were tearing the front door open. There was no sound of its closing again; they had evidently left

it open, as one does in houses where some great misfortune has happened.

But Gregor was now much calmer. The words he
uttered were no longer understandable, apparently, although they seemed clear enough to him, even clearer
than before, perhaps because his ear had grown accustomed to the sound of them. Yet at any rate people now
believed that something was wrong with him, and were
ready to help him. The positive certainty with which
these first measures had been taken comforted him. He
felt himself drawn once more into the human circle and
hoped for great and remarkable results from both the
doctor and the locksmith, without really distinguishing
precisely between them. To make his voice as clear as
possible for the decisive conversation that was now imminent he coughed a little, as quietly as he could, of
course, since this noise too might not sound like a human cough for all he was able to judge. In the next room
meanwhile there was complete silence. Perhaps his parents were sitting at the table with the chief clerk, whispering, perhaps they were all leaning against the door
and listening.

Slowly Gregor pushed the chair towards the door,
then let go of it, caught hold of the door for support—
the soles at the end of his little legs were somewhat
sticky—and rested against it for a moment after his efforts. Then he set himself to turning the key in the lock
with his mouth. It seemed, unhappily, that he hadn't
really any teeth—what could he grip the key with?—but
on the other hand his jaws were certainly very strong;
with their help he did manage to set the key in motion,

heedless of the fact that he was undoubtedly damaging them somewhere, since a brown fluid issued from his mouth, flowed over the key and dripped on the floor. "Just listen to that," said the chief clerk next door; "he's turning the key." That was a great encouragement to Gregor; but they should all have shouted encouragement to him, his father and mother too: "Go on, Gregor," they should have called out, "keep going, hold on to that key!" And in the belief that they were all following his efforts intently, he clenched his jaws recklessly on the key with all the force at his command. As the turning of the key progressed he circled round the lock, holding on now only with his mouth, pushing on the key, as required, or pulling it down again with all the weight of his body. The louder click of the finally yielding lock literally quickened Gregor. With a deep breath of relief he said to himself: "So I didn't need the locksmith," and laid his head on the handle to open the door wide.

Since he had to pull the door towards him, he was still invisible when it was really wide open. He had to edge himself slowly round the near half of the double door, and to do it very carefully if he was not to fall plump upon his back just on the threshold. He was still carrying out this difficult manoeuvre, with no time to observe anything else, when he heard the chief clerk utter a loud "Oh!"—it sounded like a gust of wind—and now he could see the man, standing as he was nearest to the door, clapping one hand before his open mouth and slowly backing away as if driven by some invisible steady pressure. His mother—in spite of the chief clerk's being there her hair was still undone and sticking up in all directions—first clasped her hands and looked at his father, then took two steps towards Gregor and fell on the floor among her outspread skirts, her face quite hidden on her breast. His father knotted his fist with a fierce expression on his face as if he meant to knock Gregor back into his room, then looked uncertainly round the living room, covered his eyes with his hands and wept till his great chest heaved.

Gregor did not go now into the living room, but leaned against the inside of the firmly shut wing of the door, so that only half his body was visible and his head above it bending sideways to look at the others. The light had meanwhile strengthened; on the other side of the street one could see clearly a section of the endlessly long, dark-gray building opposite—it was a hospital—abruptly punctuated by its row of regular windows; the rain was still falling, but only in large singly discernible and literally singly splashing drops. The breakfast dishes were set out on the table lavishly, for breakfast was the most important meal of the day to Gregor's father, who lingered it out for hours over various newspapers. Right opposite Gregor on the wall hung a photograph of himself on military service, as a lieutenant, hand on sword, a carefree smile on his face, inviting one to respect his uniform and military bearing. The door leading to the hall was open, and one could see that the front door stood open too, showing the landing beyond and the beginning of the stairs going down.

"Well," said Gregor, knowing perfectly that he was the only one who had retained any composure, "I'll put my clothes on at once, pack up my samples and start off. Will you only let me go? You see, sir, I'm not obstinate, and I'm willing to work; traveling is a hard life, but I couldn't live without it. Where are you going, sir? To the office? Yes? Will you give a true account of all this? One can be temporarily incapacitated, but that's just the moment for remembering former services and bearing in mind that later on, when the incapacity has been got over, one will certainly work with all the more industry and concentration. I'm loyally bound to serve the chief, you know that very well. Besides, I have to provide for my parents and my sister. I'm in great difficulties, but I'll get out of them again. Don't make things any worse for me than they are. Stand up for me in the firm. Travelers are not popular there, I know. People think they earn sacks of money and just have a good time. A prejudice there's no particular reason for revising. But you, sir, have a more comprehensive view of affairs than the rest of the staff, yes, let me tell you in confidence, a more comprehensive view than the chief himself, who, being the owner, lets his judgment easily be swayed against one of his employees. And you know very well that the traveler, who is never seen in the office almost the whole year round, can so easily fall a victim to gossip and ill luck and unfounded complaints, which he mostly knows nothing about, except when he comes back exhausted from his rounds, and only then suffers in person from their evil consequences, which he can no longer trace back to the original causes. Sir, sir, don't go away without a word to me to show that you think me in the right at least to some extent!"

But at Gregor's very first words the chief clerk had already backed away and only stared at him with parted lips over one twitching shoulder. And while Gregor was speaking he did not stand still one moment but stole away towards the door, without taking his eyes off Gregor, yet only an inch at a time, as if obeying some secret injunction to leave the room. He was already at the hall, and the suddenness with which he took his last step out of the living room would have made one believe he had burned the sole of his foot. Once in the hall he stretched his right arm before him towards the stair-case, as if some supernatural power were waiting there to deliver him.

Gregor perceived that the chief clerk must on no account be allowed to go away in this frame of mind if his position in the firm were not to be endangered to the utmost. His parents did not understand this so well; they had convinced themselves in the course of years that Gregor was settled for life in this firm, and besides they were so preoccupied with their immediate troubles that all foresight had forsaken them. Yet Gregor had this foresight. The chief clerk must be detained, soothed, persuaded and finally won over; the whole future of Gregor and his family depended on it! If only his sister had been there! She was intelligent; she had begun to cry while Gregor was still lying quietly on his back. And no doubt the chief clerk, so partial to ladies, would have been guided by her; she would have shut the door of the flat and in the hall talked him out of his horror. But she was not there, and Gregor would have to handle the situation himself. And without remembering that he was still unaware what powers of movement he possessed, without even remembering that his words in all possibility, indeed in all likelihood, would again be unintelligible, he let go the wing of the door, pushed himself through the opening, started to walk towards the chief clerk, who was already ridiculously clinging with both hands to the railing on the landing; but immediately, as he was feeling for a support, he fell down with a little cry upon all his numerous legs. Hardly was he down when he experienced for the first time this morning a sense of physical comfort; his legs had firm ground under them; they were completely obedient, as he noted with joy; they even strove to carry him forward in whatever direction he chose; and he was inclined to believe that a final relief from all his sufferings was at hand. But in the same moment as he found himself on the floor, rocking with suppressed eagerness to move, not far from his mother, indeed just in front of her, she, who had seemed so completely crushed, sprang all at once to her feet, her arms and fingers outspread, cried: "Help, for God's sake, help!" bent her head down as if to see Gregor better, yet on the contrary kept backing senselessly away; had quite forgotten that the laden table stood behind her; sat upon it hastily, as if in absence of mind, when she bumped into it; and seemed altogether unaware that the big coffee pot beside her was upset and pouring coffee in a flood over the carpet.

"Mother, Mother," said Gregor in a low voice, and looked up at her. The chief clerk, for the moment, had quite slipped from his mind; instead, he could not resist snapping his jaws together at the sight of the streaming coffee. That made his mother scream again. She fled from the table and fell into the arms of his father, who hastened to catch her. But Gregor had now no time to spare for his parents; the chief clerk was already on the stairs; with his chin on the banister he was taking one last backward look. Gregor made a spring, to be as sure as possible of overtaking him; the chief clerk must have divined his intention, for he leaped down several steps and vanished; he was still yelling "Ugh!" and it echoed through the whole staircase.

Unfortunately, the flight of the chief clerk seemed completely to upset Gregor's father, who had remained relatively calm until now, for instead of running after the man himself, or at least not hindering Gregor in his pursuit, he seized in his right hand the walking stick which the chief clerk had left behind on a chair, together with a hat and greatcoat, snatched in his left hand a large newspaper from the table and began stamping his feet and flourishing the stick and the newspaper to drive Gregor back into his room. No entreaty of Gregor's availed, indeed no entreaty was even understood; however humbly he bent his head his father only stamped on the floor the more loudly. Behind his father his mother had torn open a window, despite the cold weather, and was leaning far out of it with her face in her hands. A strong draught set in from the street to the staircase, the window curtains blew in, the newspapers on the table fluttered, stray pages whisked over the floor. Pitilessly Gregor's father drove him back, hissing and crying "Shoo!" like a savage. But Gregor was quite unpracticed in walking backwards, it really was a slow business. If he only had a chance to turn round he could get back to his room at once, but he was afraid of exasperating his father by the slowness of such a rotation and at any moment the stick in his father's hand might hit him a fatal blow on the back or on the head. In the end, however, nothing else was left for him to do since to his horror he observed that in moving backwards he could not even control the direction he took; and so, keeping an anxious eye on his father all the time over his shoulder, he began to turn round as quickly as he could, which was in reality very slowly. Perhaps his father noted his good intentions, for he did not interfere except every now and then to help him in the manoeuvre from a distance with the point of the stick. If only he would have stopped making that unbearable hissing noise! It made Gregor quite lose his head. He had turned almost completely round when the hissing noise so distracted him that he even turned a little the wrong way again. But when at last his head was fortunately right in front of the doorway, it appeared that his body was too broad simply to get through the opening. His father, of course, in his present mood was far from thinking of such a thing as opening the other half of the door, to let Gregor have enough space. He had merely the fixed idea of driving Gregor back into his room as quickly as possible. He would never have suffered Gregor to make the circumstantial preparations for standing up on end and perhaps slipping his way through the door. Maybe he was now making more noise than ever to urge Gregor forward, as if no obstacle impeded him; to Gregor, anyhow, the noise in his rear sounded no longer like the voice of one single father; this was really no joke, and Gregor thrust himself—come what might—into the doorway. One side of his body rose up, he was tilted at an angle in the doorway, his flank was quite bruised, horrid blotches stained the white door, soon he was stuck fast and, left to himself, could not have moved at all, his legs on one side fluttered trembling in the air, those on the other were crushed painfully to the floor—when from behind his father gave him a strong push which was literally a deliverance and he flew far into the room, bleeding freely. The door was slammed behind him with the stick, and then at last there was silence.

II

NOT UNTIL it was twilight did Gregor awake out of a deep sleep, more like a swoon than a sleep. He would certainly have waked up of his own accord not much later, for he felt himself sufficiently rested and well-slept, but it seemed to him as if a fleeting step and a cautious shutting of the door leading into the hall had aroused him. The electric lights in the street cast a pale sheen here and there on the ceiling and the upper surfaces of the furniture, but down below, where he lay, it was dark. Slowly, awkwardly trying out his feelers, which he now first learned to appreciate, he pushed his way to the door to see what had been happening there. His left side felt like one single long, unpleasantly tense scar, and he had actually to limp on his two rows of legs. One little leg, moreover, had been severely damaged in the course of that morning's events—it was almost a miracle that only one had been damaged—and trailed uselessly behind him.

He had reached the door before he discovered what had really drawn him to it: the smell of food. For there stood a basin filled with fresh milk in which floated little sops of white bread. He could almost have laughed with joy, since he was now still hungrier than in the morning, and he dipped his head almost over the eyes straight into the milk. But soon in disappointment he withdrew it again; not only did he find it difficult to feed because of his tender left side—and he could only feed with the palpitating collaboration of his whole body— he did not like the milk either, although milk had been his favorite drink and that was certainly why his sister had set it there for him; indeed it was almost with repulsion that he turned away from the basin and crawled back to the middle of the room.

He could see through the crack of the door that the gas was turned on in the living room, but while usually at this time his father made a habit of reading the afternoon newspaper in a loud voice to his mother and occasionally to his sister as well, not a sound was now to be heard. Well, perhaps his father had recently given up this habit of reading aloud, which his sister had mentioned so often in conversation and in her letters. But there was the same silence all around, although the flat was certainly not empty of occupants. "What a quiet life our family has been leading," said Gregor to himself, and as he sat there motionless staring into the darkness he felt great pride in the fact that he had been able to provide such a life for his parents and sister in such a fine flat. But what if all the quiet, the comfort, the contentment were now to end in horror? To keep himself from being lost in such thoughts Gregor took refuge in movement and crawled up and down the room.

Once during the long evening one of the side doors was opened a little and quickly shut again, later the other side door too; someone had apparently wanted to come in and then thought better of it. Gregor now stationed himself immediately before the living-room door, determined to persuade any hesitating visitor to come in or at least to discover who it might be; but the door was not opened again and he waited in vain. In the early morning, when the doors were locked, they had all wanted to come in; now that he had opened one door and the other had apparently been opened during the day, no one came in and even the keys were on the other side of the doors.

It was late at night before the gas went out in the living room, and Gregor could easily tell that his parents and his sister had all stayed awake until then, for he could clearly hear the three of them stealing away on tiptoe. No one was likely to visit him, not until the morning, that was certain; so he had plenty of time to meditate at his leisure on how he was to arrange his life afresh. But the lofty, empty room in which he had to lie flat on the floor filled him with an apprehension he could not account for, since it had been his very own room for the past five years—and with a half-unconscious action, not without a slight feeling of shame, he scuttled under the sofa, where he felt comfortable at once, although his back was a little cramped and he could not lift his head up, and his only regret was that his body was too broad to get the whole of it under the sofa.

He stayed there all night, spending the time partly in a light slumber, from which his hunger kept waking him up with a start, and partly in worrying and sketching vague hopes, which all led to the same conclusion, that he must lie low for the present and, by exercising patience and the utmost consideration, help the family to bear the inconvenience he was bound to cause them in his present condition.

Very early in the morning, it was still almost night, Gregor had the chance to test the strength of his new resolutions, for his sister, nearly fully dressed, opened the door from the hall and peered in. She did not see him at once, yet when she caught sight of him under the sofa—well, he had to be somewhere, he couldn't have flown away, could he?—she was so startled that without being able to help it she slammed the door shut again. But as if regretting her behavior she opened the door again immediately and came in on tiptoe, as if she were visiting an invalid or even a stranger. Gregor had pushed his head forward to the very edge of the sofa and watched her. Would she notice that he had left the milk standing, and not for lack of hunger, and would she bring in some other kind of food more to his taste? If she did not do it of her own accord, he would rather starve than draw her attention to the fact, although he felt a wild impulse to dart out from under the sofa, throw himself at her feet and beg her for something to eat. But his sister at once noticed, with surprise, that the basin was still full, except for a little milk that had been spilt all around it, she lifted it immediately, not with her bare hands, true, but with a cloth and carried it away. Gregor was wildly curious to know what she would bring instead, and made various speculations about it. Yet what she actually did next, in the goodness of her heart, he could never have guessed at. To find out what he liked she brought him a whole selection of food, all set out on an old newspaper. There were old, half-decayed vegetables, bones from last night's supper covered with a white sauce that had thickened; some raisins and almonds; a piece of cheese that Gregor would have called uneatable two days ago; a dry roll of bread, a buttered roll, and a roll both buttered and salted. Besides all that, she set down again the same basin, into which she had poured some water, and which was apparently to be reserved for his exclusive use. And with fine tact, knowing that Gregor would not eat in her presence, she withdrew quickly and even turned the key, to let him understand that he could take his ease as much as he liked. Gregor's legs all whizzed towards the food. His wounds must have healed completely, moreover, for he felt no disability, which amazed him and made him reflect how more than a month ago he had cut one finger a little with a knife and had still suffered pain from the wound only the day before yesterday. Am I less sensitive now? he thought, and sucked greedily at the cheese, which above all the other edibles attracted him at once and strongly. One after another and with tears of satisfaction in his eyes he quickly devoured the cheese, the vegetables and the sauce; the fresh food, on the other hand, had no charms for him, he could not even stand the smell of it and actually dragged away to some little distance the things he could eat. He had long finished his meal and was only lying lazily on the same spot when his sister turned the key slowly as a sign for him to retreat. That roused him at once, although he was nearly asleep, and he hurried under the sofa again. But it took considerable self-control for him to stay under the sofa, even for the short time his sister was in the room, since the large meal had swollen his body somewhat and he was so cramped he could hardly breathe. Slight attacks of breathlessness afflicted him and his eyes were starting a little out of his head as he watched his unsuspecting sister sweeping together with a broom not only the remains of what he had eaten but even the things he had not touched, as if these were now of no use to anyone, and hastily shoveling it all into a bucket, which she covered with a wooden lid and carried away. Hardly had she turned her back when Gregor came from under the sofa and stretched and puffed himself out.

In this manner Gregor was fed, once in the early morning while his parents and the servant girl were still asleep, and a second time after they had all had their midday dinner, for then his parents took a short nap and the servant girl could be sent out on some errand or other by his sister. Not that they would have wanted him to starve, of course, but perhaps they could not have borne to know more about his feeding than from hearsay, perhaps too his sister wanted to spare them such little anxieties wherever possible, since they had quite enough to bear as it was.

Under what pretext the doctor and the locksmith had been got rid of on that first morning Gregor could not discover, for since what he said was not understood by the others, it never struck any of them, not even his sister, that he could understand what they said, and so whenever his sister came into his room he had to content himself with hearing her utter only a sigh now and then and an occasional appeal to the saints. Later on, when she had got a little used to the situation—of course she could never get completely used to it—she sometimes threw out a remark which was kindly meant or could be so interpreted. "Well, he liked his dinner today," she would say when Gregor had made a good clearance of his food; and when he had not eaten, which gradually happened more and more often, she would say almost sadly: "Everything's been left standing again."

But although Gregor could get no news directly, he overheard a lot from the neighboring rooms, and as soon as voices were audible, he would run to the door of the room concerned and press his whole body against it. In the first few days especially there was no conversation that did not refer to him somehow, even if only indirectly. For two whole days there were family consultations at every mealtime about what should be done; but also between meals the same subject was discussed, for there were always at least two members of the family at home, since no one wanted to be alone in the flat and to leave it quite empty was unthinkable. And on the very first of these days the household cook—it was not quite clear what and how much she knew of the situation— went down on her knees to his mother and begged leave to go, and when she departed, a quarter of an hour later, gave thanks for her dismissal with tears in her eyes as if for the greatest benefit that could have been conferred on her, and without any prompting swore a solemn oath that she would never say a single word to anyone about what had happened.

Now Gregor's sister had to cook too, helping her mother; true, the cooking did not amount to much, for they ate scarcely anything. Gregor was always hearing one of the family vainly urging another to eat and getting no answer but: "Thanks, I've had all I want," or something similar. Perhaps they drank nothing either. Time and again his sister kept asking his father if he wouldn't like some beer and offered kindly to go and fetch it herself, and when he made no answer suggested that she could ask the concierge to fetch it, so that he need feel no sense of obligation, but then a round "No" came from his father and no more was said about it.

In the course of that very first day Gregor's father explained the family's financial position and prospects to both his mother and his sister. Now and then he rose from the table to get some voucher or memorandum out of the small safe he had rescued from the collapse of his business five years earlier. One could hear him opening the complicated lock and rustling papers out and shutting it again. This statement made by his father was the first cheerful information Gregor had heard since his imprisonment. He had been of the opinion that nothing at all was left over from his father's business; at least his father had never said anything to the contrary, and of course he had not asked him directly. At that

time Gregor's sole desire was to do his utmost to help
the family to forget as soon as possible the catastrophe
which had overwhelmed the business and thrown them
all into a state of complete despair. And so he had set
to work with unusual ardor and almost overnight had
become a commercial traveler instead of a little clerk,
with of course much greater chances of earning money,
and his success was immediately translated into good
round coin which he could lay on the table for his
amazed and happy family. These had been fine times,
and they had never recurred, at least not with the same
sense of glory, although later on Gregor had earned so
much money that he was able to meet the expenses of
the whole household and did so. They had simply got
used to it, both the family and Gregor; the money was
gratefully accepted and gladly given, but there was no
special uprush of warm feeling. With his sister alone had
he remained intimate, and it was a secret plan of his that
she, who loved music, unlike himself, and could play
movingly on the violin, should be sent next year to study
at the Conservatorium, despite the great expense that
would entail, which must be made up in some other way.
During his brief visits home the Conservatorium was
often mentioned in the talks he had with his sister, but
always merely as a beautiful dream which could never
come true, and his parents discouraged even these innocent references to it; yet Gregor had made up his
mind firmly about it and meant to announce the fact
with due solemnity on Christmas Day.

Such were the thoughts, completely futile in his present condition, that went through his head as he stood

clinging upright to the door and listening. Sometimes out of sheer weariness he had to give up listening and let his head fall negligently against the door, but he always had to pull himself together again at once, for even the slight sound his head made was audible next door and brought all conversation to a stop. "What can he be doing now?" his father would say after a while, obviously turning towards the door, and only then would the interrupted conversation gradually be set going again.

Gregor was now informed as amply as he could wish —for his father tended to repeat himself in his explanations, partly because it was a long time since he had handled such matters and partly because his mother could not always grasp things at once—that a certain amount of investments, a very small amount it was true, had survived the wreck of their fortunes and had even increased a little because the dividends had not been touched meanwhile. And besides that, the money Gregor brought home every month—he had kept only a few dollars for himself—had never been quite used up and now amounted to a small capital sum. Behind the door Gregor nodded his head eagerly, rejoiced at this evidence of unexpected thrift and foresight. True, he could really have paid off some more of his father's debts to the chief with this extra money, and so brought much nearer the day on which he could quit his job, but doubtless it was better the way his father had arranged it.

Yet this capital was by no means sufficient to let the family live on the interest of it; for one year, perhaps, or at the most two, they could live on the principal, that was all. It was simply a sum that ought not to be touched and should be kept for a rainy day; money for living expenses would have to be earned. Now his father was still hale enough but an old man, and he had done no work for the past five years and could not be expected to do much; during these five years, the first years of leisure in his laborious though unsuccessful life, he had grown rather fat and become sluggish. And Gregor's old mother, how was she to earn a living with her asthma, which troubled her even when she walked through the flat and kept her lying on a sofa every other day panting for breath beside an open window? And was his sister to earn her bread, she who was still a child of seventeen and whose life hitherto had been so pleasant, consisting as it did in dressing herself nicely, sleeping long, helping in the housekeeping, going out to a few modest entertainments and above all playing the violin? At first whenever the need for earning money was mentioned Gregor let go his hold on the door and threw himself down on the cool leather sofa beside it, he felt so hot with shame and grief.

Often he just lay there the long nights through without sleeping at all, scrabbling for hours on the leather. Or he nerved himself to the great effort of pushing an armchair to the window, then crawled up over the window sill and, braced against the chair, leaned against the windowpanes, obviously in some recollection of the sense of freedom that looking out of a window always used to give him. For in reality day by day things that were even a little way off were growing dimmer to his sight; the hospital across the street, which he used to execrate for being all too often before his eyes, was now quite beyond his range of vision, and if he had not known that he lived in Charlotte Street, a quiet street but still a city street, he might have believed that his window gave on a desert waste where gray sky and gray land blended indistinguishably into each other. His quick-witted sister only needed to observe twice that the armchair stood by the window; after that whenever she had tidied the room she always pushed the chair back to the same place at the window and even left the inner casements open.

If he could have spoken to her and thanked her for all she had to do for him, he could have borne her ministrations better; as it was, they oppressed him. She certainly tried to make as light as possible of whatever was disagreeable in her task, and as time went on she succeeded, of course, more and more, but time brought more enlightenment to Gregor too. The very way she came in distressed him. Hardly was she in the room when she rushed to the window, without even taking time to shut the door, careful as she was usually to shield the sight of Gregor's room from the others, and as if she were almost suffocating tore the casements open with hasty fingers, standing then in the open draught for a while even in the bitterest cold and drawing deep breaths. This noisy scurry of hers upset Gregor twice a day; he would crouch trembling under the sofa all the time, knowing quite well that she would certainly have spared him such a disturbance had she found it at all possible to stay in his presence without opening the window.

On one occasion, about a month after Gregor's metamorphosis, when there was surely no reason for her to be still startled at his appearance, she came a little earlier than usual and found him gazing out of the window, quite motionless, and thus well placed to look like a bogey. Gregor would not have been surprised had she not come in at all, for she could not immediately open the window while he was there, but not only did she retreat, she jumped back as if in alarm and banged the door shut; a stranger might well have thought that he had been lying in wait for her there meaning to bite her. Of course he hid himself under the sofa at once, but he had to wait until midday before she came again, and she seemed more ill at ease than usual. This made him realize how repulsive the sight of him still was to her, and that it was bound to go on being repulsive, and what an effort it must cost her not to run away even from the sight of the small portion of his body that stuck out from under the sofa. In order to spare her that, therefore, one day he carried a sheet on his back to the sofa —it cost him four hours' labor—and arranged it there in such a way as to hide him completely, so that even if she were to bend down she could not see him. Had she considered the sheet unnecessary, she would certainly have stripped it off the sofa again, for it was clear enough that this curtaining and confining of himself was not likely to conduce to Gregor's comfort, but she left it where it was, and Gregor even fancied that he caught a thankful glance from her eye when he lifted the sheet carefully a very little with his head to see how she was taking the new arrangement.

For the first fortnight his parents could not bring

themselves to the point of entering his room, and he often heard them expressing their appreciation of his sister's activities, whereas formerly they had frequently scolded her for being as they thought a somewhat useless daughter. But now, both of them often waited outside the door, his father and his mother, while his sister tidied his room, and as soon as she came out she had to tell them exactly how things were in the room, what Gregor had eaten, how he had conducted himself this time and whether there was not perhaps some slight improvement in his condition. His mother, moreover, began relatively soon to want to visit him, but his father and sister dissuaded her at first with arguments which Gregor listened to very attentively and altogether approved. Later, however, she had to be held back by main force, and when she cried out: "Do let me in to Gregor, he is my unfortunate son! Can't you understand that I must go to him?" Gregor thought that it might be well to have her come in, not every day, of course, but perhaps once a week; she understood things, after all, much better than his sister, who was only a child despite the efforts she was making and had perhaps taken on so difficult a task merely out of childish thoughtlessness.

Gregor's desire to see his mother was soon fulfilled. During the daytime he did not want to show himself at the window, out of consideration for his parents, but he could not crawl very far around the few square yards of floor space he had, nor could he bear lying quietly at rest all during the night, while he was fast losing any interest he had ever taken in food, so that for mere recreation he had formed the habit of crawling crisscross over the walls and ceiling. He especially enjoyed hanging suspended from the ceiling; it was much better than lying on the floor; one could breathe more freely; one's body swung and rocked lightly; and in the almost blissful absorption induced by this suspension it could happen to his own surprise that he let go and fell plump on the floor. Yet he now had his body much better under control than formerly, and even such a big fall did him no harm. His sister at once remarked the new distraction Gregor had found for himself—he left traces behind him of the sticky stuff on his soles wherever he crawled—and she got the idea in her head of giving him as wide a field as possible to crawl in and of removing the pieces of furniture that hindered him, above all the chest of drawers and the writing desk. But that was more than she could manage all by herself; she did not dare ask her father to help her; and as for the servant girl, a young creature of sixteen who had had the courage to stay on after the cook's departure, she could not be asked to help, for she had begged as an especial favor that she might keep the kitchen door locked and open it only on a definite summons; so there was nothing left but to apply to her mother at an hour when her father was out. And the old lady did come, with exclamations of joyful eagerness, which, however, died away at the door of Gregor's room. Gregor's sister, of course, went in first, to see that everything was in order before letting his mother enter. In great haste Gregor pulled the sheet lower and rucked it more in folds so that it really looked as if it had been thrown accidentally over the sofa. And this time he did not peer out from under it; he renounced the pleasure of seeing his mother on this occasion and was only glad that she had come at all. "Come in, he's out of sight," said his sister, obviously leading her mother in by the hand. Gregor could now hear the two women struggling to shift the heavy old chest from its place, and his sister claiming the greater part of the labor for herself, without listening to the admonitions of her mother who feared she might overstrain herself. It took a long time. After at least a quarter of an hour's tugging his mother objected that the chest had better be left where it was, for in the first place it was too heavy and could never be got out before his father came home; standing in the middle of the room like that it would only hamper Gregor's movements, while in the second place it was not at all certain that removing the furniture would be doing a service to Gregor. She was inclined to think to the contrary; the sight of the naked walls made her own heart heavy, and why shouldn't Gregor have the same feeling, considering that he had been used to his furniture for so long and might feel forlorn without it. "And doesn't it look," she concluded in a low voice—in fact she had been almost whispering all the time as if to avoid letting Gregor, whose exact whereabouts she did not know, hear even the tones of her voice, for she was convinced that he could not understand her words—"doesn't it look as if we were showing him, by taking away his furniture, that we have given up hope of his ever getting better and are just leaving him coldly to himself? I think it would be best to keep his room exactly as it has always been, so that when he comes back to us he will find everything unchanged and be able all the more easily to forget what has happened in between."

On hearing these words from his mother Gregor realized that the lack of all direct human speech for the past two months together with the monotony of family life must have confused his mind, otherwise he could not account for the fact that he had quite earnestly looked forward to having his room emptied of furnishing. Did he really want his warm room, so comfortably fitted with old family furniture, to be turned into a naked den in which he would certainly be able to crawl unhampered in all directions but at the price of shedding simultaneously all recollection of his human background? He had indeed been so near the brink of forgetfulness that only the voice of his mother, which he had not heard for so long, had drawn him back from it. Nothing should be taken out of his room; everything must stay as it was; he could not dispense with the good influence of the furniture on his state of mind; and even if the furniture did hamper him in his senseless crawling round and round, that was no drawback but a great advantage.

Unfortunately his sister was of the contrary opinion; she had grown accustomed, and not without reason, to consider herself an expert in Gregor's affairs as against her parents, and so her mother's advice was now enough to make her determined on the removal not only of the chest and the writing desk, which had been her first intention, but of all the furniture except the indispensable sofa. This determination was not, of course, merely the outcome of childish recalcitrance and of the self-

58 THE METAMORPHOSIS

confidence she had recently developed so unexpectedly
and at such cost; she had in fact perceived that Gregor
needed a lot of space to crawl about in, while on the
other hand he never used the furniture at all, so far as
could be seen. Another factor might have been also the
enthusiastic temperament of an adolescent girl, which
seeks to indulge itself on every opportunity and which
now tempted Grete to exaggerate the horror of her
brother's circumstances in order that she might do all
the more for him. In a room where Gregor lorded it
all alone over empty walls no one save herself was likely
ever to set foot.

And so she was not to be moved from her resolve by
her mother, who seemed moreover to be ill at ease in
Gregor's room and therefore unsure of herself, was soon
reduced to silence and helped her daughter as best she
could to push the chest outside. Now, Gregor could do
without the chest, if need be, but the writing desk he
must retain. As soon as the two women had got the chest
out of his room, groaning as they pushed it, Gregor stuck
his head out from under the sofa to see how he might
intervene as kindly and cautiously as possible. But as
bad luck would have it, his mother was the first to return,
leaving Grete clasping the chest in the room next door
where she was trying to shift it all by herself, without of
course moving it from the spot. His mother however was
not accustomed to the sight of him; it might sicken her
and so in alarm Gregor backed quickly to the other end
of the sofa, yet could not prevent the sheet from swaying
a little in front. That was enough to put her on the alert.

She paused, stood still for a moment and then went back to Grete.

Although Gregor kept reassuring himself that nothing out of the way was happening, but only a few bits of furniture were being changed round, he soon had to admit that all this trotting to and fro of the two women, their little ejaculations and the scraping of furniture along the floor affected him like a vast disturbance coming from all sides at once, and however much he tucked in his head and legs and cowered to the very floor he was bound to confess that he would not be able to stand it for long. They were clearing his room out; taking away everything he loved; the chest in which he kept his fret saw and other tools was already dragged off; they were now loosening the writing desk which had almost sunk into the floor, the desk at which he had done all his homework when he was at the commercial academy, at the grammar school before that, and, yes, even at the primary school—he had no more time to waste in weighing the good intentions of the two women, whose existence he had by now almost forgotten, for they were so exhausted that they were laboring in silence and nothing could be heard but the heavy scuffling of their feet.

And so he rushed out—the women were just leaning against the writing desk in the next room to give themselves a breather—and four times changed his direction, since he really did not know what to rescue first; then on the wall opposite, which was already otherwise cleared, he was struck by the picture of the lady muffled in so much fur and quickly crawled up to it and pressed himself to the glass, which was a good surface to hold on to and comforted his hot belly. This picture at least, which was entirely hidden beneath him, was going to be removed by nobody. He turned his head towards the door of the living room so as to observe the women when they came back.

They had not allowed themselves much of a rest and were already coming; Grete had twined her arm round her mother and was almost supporting her. "Well, what shall we take now?" said Grete, looking round. Her eyes met Gregor's from the wall. She kept her composure, presumably because of her mother, bent her head down to her mother, to keep her from looking up, and said, although in a fluttering, unpremeditated voice: "Come, hadn't we better go back to the living room for a moment?" Her intentions were clear enough to Gregor; she wanted to bestow her mother in safety and then chase him down from the wall. Well, just let her try it! He clung to his picture and would not give it up. He would rather fly in Grete's face.

But Grete's words had succeeded in disquieting her mother, who took a step to one side, caught sight of the huge brown mass on the flowered wallpaper, and before she was really conscious that what she saw was Gregor screamed in a loud, hoarse voice: "Oh God, oh God!" fell with outspread arms over the sofa as if giving up and did not move. "Gregor!" cried his sister, shaking her fist and glaring at him. This was the first time she had directly addressed him since his metamorphosis. She ran into the next room for some aromatic essence with which to rouse her mother from her fainting fit. Gregor wanted to help too—there was still time to rescue the picture—but he was stuck fast to the glass and had to tear himself loose; he then ran after his sister into the next room as if he could advise her, as he used to do; but then had to stand helplessly behind her; she meanwhile searched among various small bottles and when she turned round started in alarm at the sight of him; one bottle fell on the floor and broke; a splinter of glass cut Gregor's face and some kind of corrosive medicine splashed him; without pausing a moment longer Grete gathered up all the bottles she could carry and ran to her mother with them; she banged the door shut with her foot. Gregor was now cut off from his mother, who was perhaps nearly dying because of him; he dared not open the door for fear of frightening away his sister, who had to stay with her mother; there was nothing he could do but wait; and harassed by self-reproach and worry he began now to crawl to and fro, over everything, walls, furniture and ceiling, and finally in his despair, when the whole room seemed to be reeling round him, fell down on to the middle of the big table.

A little while elapsed. Gregor was still lying there feebly and all around was quiet; perhaps that was a good omen. Then the doorbell rang. The servant girl was of course locked in her kitchen, and Grete would have to open the door. It was his father. "What's been happening?" were his first words; Grete's face must have told him everything. Grete answered in a muffled voice, apparently hiding her head on his breast: "Mother has been fainting, but she's better now. Gregor's broken loose." "Just what I expected," said his father, "just what I've been telling you, but you women would never listen." It was clear to Gregor that his father had taken the worst interpretation of Grete's all too brief statement and was assuming that Gregor had been guilty of some violent act. Therefore Gregor must now try to propitiate his father, since he had neither time nor means for an explanation. And so he fled to the door of his own room and crouched against it, to let his father see as soon as he came in from the hall that his son had the good intention of getting back into his room immediately and that it was not necessary to drive him there, but that if only the door were opened he would disappear at once.

Yet his father was not in the mood to perceive such fine distinctions. "Ah!" he cried as soon as he appeared, in a tone which sounded at once angry and exultant. Gregor drew his head back from the door and lifted it to look at his father. Truly, this was not the father he had imagined to himself; admittedly he had been too absorbed of late in his new recreation of crawling over the ceiling to take the same interest as before in what was happening elsewhere in the flat, and he ought really to be prepared for some changes. And yet, and yet, could that be his father? The man who used to lie wearily sunk in bed whenever Gregor set out on a business journey; who welcomed him back of an evening lying in a long chair in a dressing gown; who could not really rise to his feet but only lifted his arms in greeting, and on the rare occasions when he did go out with his family, on one or two Sundays a year and on high holidays, walked between Gregor and his mother, who were slow walkers anyhow, even more slowly than they did, muffled in his old greatcoat, shuffling laboriously forward with the help of his crook-handled stick which he set down most cautiously at every step and, whenever he wanted to say anything, nearly always came to a full stop and gathered his escort around him? Now he was standing there in fine shape; dressed in a smart blue uniform with gold buttons, such as bank messengers wear; his strong double chin bulged over the stiff high collar of his jacket; from under his bushy eyebrows his black eyes darted fresh and penetrating glances; his onetime tangled white hair had been combed flat on either side of a shining and carefully exact parting. He pitched his cap, which bore a gold monogram, probably the badge of some bank, in a wide sweep across the whole room on to a sofa and with the tail-ends of his jacket thrown back, his hands in his trouser pockets, advanced with a grim visage towards Gregor. Likely enough he did not himself know what he meant to do; at any rate he lifted his feet uncommonly high, and Gregor was dumbfounded at the enormous size of his shoe soles. But Gregor could not risk standing up to him, aware as he had been from the very first day of his new life that his father believed only the severest measures suitable for dealing with him. And so he ran before his father, stopping when he stopped and scuttling forward again when his father made any kind of move. In this way they circled the room several times without anything decisive happening; indeed the whole operation did not even look like a pursuit because it was carried out so slowly. And so Gregor did not leave the floor, for he feared that his father might take as a piece of peculiar wickedness any excursion of his over the walls or the ceiling. All the same, he could not stay this course much longer, for while his father took one step he had to carry out a whole series of movements. He was already beginning to feel breathless, just as in his former life his lungs had not been very dependable. As he was staggering along, trying to concentrate his energy on running, hardly keeping his eyes open; in his dazed state never even thinking of any other escape than simply going forward; and having almost forgotten that the walls were free to him, which in this room were well provided with finely carved pieces of furniture full of knobs and crevices—suddenly something lightly flung landed close behind him and rolled before him. It was an apple; a second apple followed immediately; Gregor came to a stop in alarm; there was no point in running on, for his father was determined to bombard him. He had filled his pockets with fruit from the dish on the sideboard and was now shying apple after apple, without taking particularly good aim for the moment. The small red apples rolled about the floor as if magnetized and cannoned into each other. An apple thrown without much force grazed Gregor's back and glanced off harmlessly. But another following immediately landed right on his back and sank in; Gregor wanted to drag himself forward, as if this startling, incredible pain could be left behind him; but he felt as if nailed to the spot and flattened himself out in a complete derangement of all his senses. With his last conscious look he saw the door of his room being torn

open and his mother rushing out ahead of his screaming
sister, in her underbodice, for her daughter had loosened
her clothing to let her breathe more freely and recover
from her swoon, he saw his mother rushing towards his
father, leaving one after another behind her on the floor
her loosened petticoats, stumbling over her petticoats
straight to his father and embracing him, in complete
union with him—but here Gregor's sight began to fail—
with her hands clasped round his father's neck as she
begged for her son's life.

III

THE SERIOUS INJURY done to Gregor, which disabled
him for more than a month—the apple went on sticking
in his body as a visible reminder, since no one ventured
to remove it—seemed to have made even his father rec-
ollect that Gregor was a member of the family, despite
his present unfortunate and repulsive shape, and ought
not to be treated as an enemy, that, on the contrary, family duty required the suppression of disgust and the exercise of patience, nothing but patience.

And although his injury had impaired, probably forever, his powers of movement, and for the time being it
took him long, long minutes to creep across his room
like an old invalid—there was no question now of crawling up the wall—yet in his own opinion he was sufficiently compensated for this worsening of his condition
by the fact that towards evening the living-room door,
which he used to watch intently for an hour or two be-

forehand, was always thrown open, so that lying in the darkness of his room, invisible to the family, he could see them all at the lamp-lit table and listen to their talk, by general consent as it were, very different from his earlier eavesdropping.

True, their intercourse lacked the lively character of former times, which he had always called to mind with a certain wistfulness in the small hotel bedrooms where he had been wont to throw himself down, tired out, on damp bedding. They were now mostly very silent. Soon after supper his father would fall asleep in his arm-chair; his mother and sister would admonish each other to be silent; his mother, bending low over the lamp, stitched at fine sewing for an underwear firm; his sister, who had taken a job as a salesgirl, was learning shorthand and French in the evenings on the chance of bettering herself. Sometimes his father woke up, and as if quite unaware that he had been sleeping said to his mother: "What a lot of sewing you're doing today!" and at once fell asleep again, while the two women exchanged a tired smile.

With a kind of mulishness his father persisted in keeping his uniform on even in the house; his dressing gown hung uselessly on its peg and he slept fully dressed where he sat, as if he were ready for service at any moment and even here only at the beck and call of his superior. As a result, his uniform, which was not brand-new to start with, began to look dirty, despite all the loving care of the mother and sister to keep it clean, and Gregor often spent whole evenings gazing at the many greasy spots on the garment, gleaming with gold but-

tons always in a high state of polish, in which the old
man sat sleeping in extreme discomfort and yet quite
peacefully.

As soon as the clock struck ten his mother tried to
rouse his father with gentle words and to persuade him
after that to get into bed, for sitting there he could not
have a proper sleep and that was what he needed most,
since he had to go on duty at six. But with the mulishness that had obsessed him since he became a bank messenger he always insisted on staying longer at the table,
although he regularly fell asleep again and in the end
only with the greatest trouble could be got out of his
armchair and into his bed. However insistently Greg-
or's mother and sister kept urging him with gentle re-
minders, he would go on slowly shaking his head for a
quarter of an hour, keeping his eyes shut, and refuse to
get to his feet. The mother plucked at his sleeve, whispering endearments in his ear, the sister left her lessons
to come to her mother's help, but Gregor's father was
not to be caught. He would only sink down deeper in
his chair. Not until the two women hoisted him up by
the armpits did he open his eyes and look at them both,
one after the other, usually with the remark: "This is
a life. This is the peace and quiet of my old age." And
leaning on the two of them he would heave himself up,
with difficulty, as if he were a great burden to himself, suffer them to lead him as far as the door and then
wave them off and go on alone, while the mother abandoned her needlework and the sister her pen in order
to run after him and help him farther.

Who could find time, in this overworked and tired

out family, to bother about Gregor more than was absolutely needful? The household was reduced more and more; the servant girl was turned off; a gigantic bony charwoman with white hair flying round her head came in morning and evening to do the rough work; everything else was done by Gregor's mother, as well as great piles of sewing. Even various family ornaments, which his mother and sister used to wear with pride at parties and celebrations, had to be sold, as Gregor discovered of an evening from hearing them all discuss the prices obtained. But what they lamented most was the fact that they could not leave the flat which was much too big for their present circumstances, because they could not think of any way to shift Gregor. Yet Gregor saw well enough that consideration for him was not the main difficulty preventing the removal, for they could have easily shifted him in some suitable box with a few air holes in it; what really kept them from moving into another flat was rather their own complete hopelessness and the belief that they had been singled out for a misfortune such as had never happened to any of their relations or acquaintances. They fulfilled to the uttermost all that the world demands of poor people: the father fetched breakfast for the small clerks in the bank, the mother devoted her energy to making underwear for strangers, the sister trotted to and fro behind the counter at the behest of customers, but more than this they had not the strength to do. And the wound in Gregor's back began to nag at him afresh when his mother and sister, after getting his father into bed, came back again, left their work lying, drew close to each other and sat cheek by cheek; when his mother, pointing towards his room, said: "Shut that door now, Grete," and he was left again in darkness, while next door the women mingled their tears or perhaps sat dry-eyed staring at the table.

Gregor hardly slept at all by night or by day. He was often haunted by the idea that next time the door opened he would take the family's affairs in hand again just as he used to do; once more, after this long interval, there appeared in his thoughts the figures of the chief and the chief clerk, the commercial travelers and the apprentices, the porter who was so dull-witted, two or three friends in other firms, a chambermaid in one of the rural hotels, a sweet and fleeting memory, a cashier in a milliner's shop, whom he had wooed earnestly but too slowly—they all appeared, together with strangers or people he had quite forgotten, but instead of helping him and his family they were one and all unapproachable and he was glad when they vanished. At other times he would not be in the mood to bother about his family, he was only filled with rage at the way they were neglecting him, and although he had no clear idea of what he might care to eat he would make plans for getting into the larder to take the food that was after all his due, even if he were not hungry. His sister no longer took thought to bring him what might especially please him, but in the morning and at noon before she went to business hurriedly pushed into his room with her foot any food that was available, and in the evening cleared it out again with one sweep of the broom, heedless of whether it had been merely tasted, or-—as most frequently happened—left untouched. The cleaning of his room, which she now did always in the evenings, could not have been more hastily done. Streaks of dirt stretched along the walls, here and there lay balls of dust and filth. At first Gregor used to station himself in some particularly filthy corner when his sister arrived, in order to reproach her with it, so to speak. But he could have sat there for weeks without getting her to make any improvement; she could see the dirt as well as he did, but she had simply made up her mind to leave it alone. And yet, with a touchiness that was new to her, which seemed anyhow to have infected the whole family, she jealously guarded her claim to be the sole caretaker of Gregor's room. His mother once subjected his room to a thorough cleaning, which was achieved only by means of several buckets of water—all this dampness of course upset Gregor too and he lay widespread, sulky and motionless on the sofa—but she was well punished for it. Hardly had his sister noticed the changed aspect of his room that evening than she rushed in high dudgeon into the living room and, despite the imploringly raised hands of her mother, burst into a storm of weeping, while her parents—her father had of course been startled out of his chair—looked on at first in helpless amazement; then they too began to go into action; the father reproached the mother on his right for not having left the cleaning of Gregor's room to his sister; shrieked at the sister on his left that never again was she to be allowed to clean Gregor's room; while the mother tried to pull the father into his bedroom, since he was beyond himself

with agitation; the sister, shaken with sobs, then beat
upon the table with her small fists; and Gregor hissed
loudly with rage because not one of them thought of
shutting the door to spare him such a spectacle and so
much noise.

Still, even if the sister, exhausted by her daily work,
had grown tired of looking after Gregor as she did formerly, there was no need for his mother's intervention
or for Gregor's being neglected at all. The charwoman
was there. This old widow, whose strong bony frame
had enabled her to survive the worst a long life could
offer, by no means recoiled from Gregor. Without being in the least curious she had once by chance opened
the door of his room and at the sight of Gregor, who,
taken by surprise, began to rush to and fro although
no one was chasing him, merely stood there with her
arms folded. From that time she never failed to open
his door a little for a moment, morning and evening,
to have a look at him. At first she even used to call him
to her, with words which apparently she took to be
friendly, such as: "Come along, then, you old dung beetle!" or "Look at the old dung beetle, then!" To such
allocutions Gregor made no answer, but stayed motionless where he was, as if the door had never been opened.
Instead of being allowed to disturb him so senselessly
whenever the whim took her, she should rather have
been ordered to clean out his room daily, that charwoman! Once, early in the morning—heavy rain was
lashing on the windowpanes, perhaps a sign that spring
was on the way—Gregor was so exasperated when she
began addressing him again that he ran at her, as if to

attack her, although slowly and feebly enough. But the charwoman instead of showing fright merely lifted high a chair that happened to be beside the door, and as she stood there with her mouth wide open it was clear that she meant to shut it only when she brought the chair down on Gregor's back. "So you're not coming any nearer?" she asked, as Gregor turned away again, and quietly put the chair back into the corner.

Gregor was now eating hardly anything. Only when he happened to pass the food laid out for him did he take a bit of something in his mouth as a pastime, kept it there for an hour at a time and usually spat it out again. At first he thought it was chagrin over the state of his room that prevented him from eating, yet he soon got used to the various changes in his room. It had become a habit in the family to push into his room things there was no room for elsewhere, and there were plenty of these now, since one of the rooms had been let to three lodgers. These serious gentlemen—all three of them with full beards, as Gregor once observed through a crack in the door—had a passion for order, not only in their own room but, since they were now members of the household, in all its arrangements, especially in the kitchen. Superfluous, not to say dirty, objects they could not bear. Besides, they had brought with them most of the furnishings they needed. For this reason many things could be dispensed with that it was no use trying to sell but that should not be thrown away either. All of them found their way into Gregor's room. The ash can likewise and the kitchen garbage can. Anything that was not needed for the moment was simply flung into Gregor's room by the charwoman, who did everything in a hurry; fortunately Gregor usually saw only the object, whatever it was, and the hand that held it. Perhaps she intended to take the things away again as time and opportunity offered, or to collect them until she could throw them all out in a heap, but in fact they just lay wherever she happened to throw them, except when Gregor pushed his way through the junk heap and shifted it somewhat, at first out of necessity, because he had not room enough to crawl, but later with increasing enjoyment, although after such excursions, being sad and weary to death, he would lie motionless for hours. And since the lodgers often ate their supper at home in the common living room, the living-room door stayed shut many an evening, yet Gregor reconciled himself quite easily to the shutting of the door, for often enough on evenings when it was opened he had disregarded it entirely and lain in the darkest corner of his room, quite unnoticed by the family. But on one occasion the charwoman left the door open a little and it stayed ajar even when the lodgers came in for supper and the lamp was lit. They set themselves at the top end of the table where formerly Gregor and his father and mother had eaten their meals, unfolded their napkins and took knife and fork in hand. At once his mother appeared in the other doorway with a dish of meat and close behind her his sister with a dish of potatoes piled high. The food steamed with a thick vapor. The lodgers bent over the food set before them as if to scrutinize it before eating, in fact the man in the niddle, who seemed to pass for an authority with the other two, cut a piece of meat as it lay on the dish, obviously to discover if it were tender or should be sent back to the kitchen. He showed satisfaction, and Gregor's mother and sister, who had been watching anxiously, breathed freely and began to smile.

The family itself took its meals in the kitchen. None the less, Gregor's father came into the living room before going into the kitchen and with one prolonged bow, cap in hand, made a round of the table. The lodgers all stood up and murmured something in their beards. When they were alone again they ate their food in almost complete silence. It seemed remarkable to Gregor that among the various noises coming from the table he could always distinguish the sound of their masticating teeth, as if this were a sign to Gregor that one needed teeth in order to eat, and that with toothless jaws even of the finest make one could do nothing. "I'm hungry enough," said Gregor sadly to himself, "but not for that kind of food. How these lodgers are stuffing themselves, and here am I dying of starvation!"

On that very evening—during the whole of his time there Gregor could not remember ever having heard the violin—the sound of violin-playing came from the kitchen. The lodgers had already finished their supper, the one in the middle had brought out a newspaper and given the other two a page apiece, and now they were leaning back at ease reading and smoking. When the violin began to play they pricked up their ears, got to their feet, and went on tiptoe to the hall door where they stood huddled together. Their movements must have been heard in the kitchen, for Gregor's father called out: "Is the violin-playing disturbing you, gentlemen? It can be stopped at once." "On the contrary," said the middle lodger, "could not Fräulein Samsa come and play in this room, beside us, where it is much more convenient and comfortable?" "Oh, certainly," cried Gregor's father, as if he were the violin-player. The lodgers came back into the living room and waited. Presently Gregor's father arrived with the music stand, his mother carrying the music and his sister with the violin. His sister quietly made everything ready to start playing; his parents, who had never let rooms before and so had an exaggerated idea of the courtesy due to lodgers, did not venture to sit down on their own chairs; his father leaned against the door, the right hand thrust between two buttons of his livery coat, which was formally buttoned up; but his mother was offered a chair by one of the lodgers and, since she left the chair just where he had happened to put it, sat down in a corner to one side.

Gregor's sister began to play; the father and mother, from either side, intently watched the movements of her hands. Gregor, attracted by the playing, ventured to move forward a little until his head was actually inside the living room. He felt hardly any surprise at his growing lack of consideration for the others; there had been a time when he prided himself on being considerate. And yet just on this occasion he had more reason than ever to hide himself, since owing to the amount of dust which lay thick in his room and rose into the air at the slightest movement, he too was covered with dust; fluff and hair and remnants of food trailed with him.

caught on his back and along his sides; his indifference to everything was much too great for him to turn on his back and scrape himself clean on the carpet, as once he had done several times a day. And in spite of his condition, no shame deterred him from advancing a little over the spotless floor of the living room.

To be sure, no one was aware of him. The family was entirely absorbed in the violin-playing; the lodgers, however, who first of all had stationed themselves, hands in pockets, much too close behind the music stand so that they could all have read the music, which must have bothered his sister, had soon retreated to the window, half-whispering with downbent heads, and stayed there while his father turned an anxious eye on them. Indeed, they were making it more than obvious that they had been disappointed in their expectation of hearing good or enjoyable violin-playing, that they had had more than enough of the performance and only out of courtesy suffered a continued disturbance of their peace. From the way they all kept blowing the smoke of their cigars high in the air through nose and mouth one could divine their irritation. And yet Gregor's sister was playing so beautifully. Her face leaned sideways, intently and sadly her eyes followed the notes of music. Gregor crawled a little farther forward and lowered his head to the ground so that it might be possible for his eyes to meet hers. Was he an animal, that music had such an effect upon him? He felt as if the way were opening before him to the unknown nourishment he craved. He was determined to push forward till he reached his sister, to pull at her skirt and so let her know that she was to come into his room with her violin, for no one here appreciated her playing as he would appreciate it. He would never let her out of his room, at least, not so long as he lived; his frightful appearance would become, for the first time, useful to him; he would watch all the doors of his room at once and spit at intruders; but his sister should need no constraint, she should stay with him of her own free will; she should sit beside him on the sofa, bend down her ear to him and hear him confide that he had had the firm intention of sending her to the Conservatorium, and that, but for his mishap, last Christmas—surely Christmas was long past?—he would have announced it to everybody without allowing a single objection. After this confession his sister would be so touched that she would burst into tears, and Gregor would then raise himself to her shoulder and kiss her on the neck, which, now that she went to business, she kept free of any ribbon or collar.

"Mr. Samsa!" cried the middle lodger, to Gregor's father, and pointed, without wasting any more words, at Gregor, now working himself slowly forwards. The violin fell silent, the middle lodger first smiled to his friends with a shake of the head and then looked at Gregor again. Instead of driving Gregor out, his father seemed to think it more needful to begin by soothing down the lodgers, although they were not at all agitated and apparently found Gregor more entertaining than the violin-playing. He hurried towards them and, spreading out his arms, tried to urge them back into their own room and at the same time to block their view of Gregor. They now began to be really a little angry, one could not tell whether because of the old man's behavior or because it had just dawned on them that all unwittingly they had such a neighbor as Gregor next door. They demanded explanations of his father, they waved their arms like him, tugged uneasily at their beards, and only with reluctance backed towards their room. Meanwhile Gregor's sister, who stood there as if lost when her playing was so abruptly broken off, came to life again, pulled herself together all at once after standing for a while holding violin and bow in nerve-lessly hanging hands and staring at her music, pushed her violin into the lap of her mother, who was still sitting in her chair fighting asthmatically for breath, and ran into the lodgers' room to which they were now being shepherded by her father rather more quickly than before. One could see the pillows and blankets on the beds flying under her accustomed fingers and being laid in order. Before the lodgers had actually reached their room she had finished making the beds and slipped out.

The old man seemed once more to be so possessed by his mulish self-assertiveness that he was forgetting all the respect he should show to his lodgers. He kept driving them on and driving them on until in the very door of the bedroom the middle lodger stamped his foot loudly on the floor and so brought him to a halt. "I beg to announce," said the lodger, lifting one hand and looking also at Gregor's mother and sister, "that because of the disgusting conditions prevailing in this house-hold and family"—here he spat on the floor with emphatic brevity—"I give you notice on the spot. Natu-rally I won't pay you a penny for the days I have lived here; on the contrary I shall consider bringing an action for damages against you, based on claims—believe me—that will be easily susceptible of proof." He ceased and stared straight in front of him, as if he expected something. In fact his two friends at once rushed into the breach with these words: "And we too give notice on the spot." On that he seized the door-handle and shut the door with a slam.

Gregor's father, groping with his hands, staggered forward and fell into his chair; it looked as if he were stretching himself there for his ordinary evening nap, but the marked jerkings of his head, which was as if uncontrollable, showed that he was far from asleep. Gregor had simply stayed quietly all the time on the spot where the lodgers had espied him. Disappointment at the failure of his plan, perhaps also the weakness arising from extreme hunger, made it impossible for him to move. He feared, with a fair degree of certainty, that at any moment the general tension would discharge itself in a combined attack upon him, and he lay waiting. He did not react even to the noise made by the violin as it fell off his mother's lap from under her trembling fingers and gave out a resonant note.

"My dear parents," said his sister, slapping her hand on the table by way of introduction, "things can't go on like this. Perhaps you don't realize that, but I do. I won't utter my brother's name in the presence of this creature, and so all I say is: we must try to get rid of it. We've tried to look after it and to put up with it as far as is humanly possible, and I don't think anyone could reproach us in the slightest."

"She is more than right," said Gregor's father to himself. His mother, who was still choking for lack of breath, began to cough hollowly into her hand with a wild look in her eyes.

His sister rushed over to her and held her forehead. His father's thoughts seemed to have lost their vagueness at Grete's words; he sat more upright, fingering his service cap that lay among the plates still lying on the table from the lodgers' supper, and from time to time looked at the still form of Gregor.

"We must try to get rid of it," his sister now said explicitly to her father, since her mother was coughing too much to hear a word. "It will be the death of both of you, I can see that coming. When one has to work as hard as we do, all of us, one can't stand this continual torment at home on top of it. At least I can't stand it any longer." And she burst into such a passion of sobbing that her tears dropped on her mother's face, where she wiped them off mechanically.

"My dear," said the old man sympathetically, and with evident understanding, "but what can we do?"

Gregor's sister merely shrugged her shoulders to indicate the feeling of helplessness that had now overmastered her during her weeping fit, in contrast to her former confidence.

"If he could understand us," said her father, half questioningly; Grete, still sobbing, vehemently waved a hand to show how unthinkable that was.

"If he could understand us," repeated the old man, shutting his eyes to consider his daughter's conviction that understanding was impossible, "then perhaps we might come to some agreement with him. But as it is—"

"He must go," cried Gregor's sister, "that's the only solution, Father. You must just try to get rid of the idea that this is Gregor. The fact that we've believed it for so long is the root of all our trouble. But how can it be Gregor? If this were Gregor, he would have realized long ago that human beings can't live with such a creature, and he'd have gone away on his own accord. Then we wouldn't have any brother, but we'd be able to go on living and keep his memory in honor. As it is, this creature persecutes us, drives away our lodgers, obviously wants the whole apartment to himself and would have us all sleep in the gutter. Just look, Father," she shrieked all at once, "he's at it again!" And in an access of panic that was quite incomprehensible to Gregor she even quitted her mother, literally thrusting the chair from her as if she would rather sacrifice her mother than stay so near to Gregor, and rushed behind her father, who also rose up, being simply upset by her agitation, and half-spread his arms out as if to protect her.

Yet Gregor had not the slightest intention of frightening anyone, far less his sister. He had only begun to turn round in order to crawl back to his room, but it was certainly a startling operation to watch, since because of his disabled condition he could not execute the difficult turning movements except by lifting his head and then bracing it against the floor over and over again. He paused and looked round. His good intentions seemed to have been recognized; the alarm had only been momentary. Now they were all watching him in melancholy silence. His mother lay in her chair, her legs stiffly outstretched and pressed together, her eyes almost closing for sheer weariness; his father and his sister were sitting beside each other, his sister's arm around the old man's neck.

Perhaps I can go on turning round now, thought Gregor, and began his labors again. He could not stop himself from panting with the effort, and had to pause now and then to take breath. Nor did anyone harass him; he was left entirely to himself. When he had completed the turn-round he began at once to crawl straight back. He was amazed at the distance separating him from his room and could not understand how in his weak state he had managed to accomplish the same journey so recently, almost without remarking it. Intent on crawling as fast as possible, he barely noticed that not a single word, not an ejaculation from his family, interfered with his progress. Only when he was already in the doorway did he turn his head round, not completely, for his neck muscles were getting stiff, but enough to see that nothing had changed behind him except that his sister had risen to her feet. His last glance fell on his mother, who was not quite overcome by sleep.

Hardly was he well inside his room when the door was hastily pushed shut, bolted and locked. The sudden noise in his rear startled him so much that his little legs gave beneath him. It was his sister who had shown such haste. She had been standing ready waiting and had made a light spring forward. Gregor had not even heard her coming, and she cried "At last!" to her parents as she turned the key in the lock.

"And what now?" said Gregor to himself, looking

round in the darkness. Soon he made the discovery that he was now unable to stir a limb. This did not surprise him, rather it seemed unnatural that he should ever actually have been able to move on these feeble little legs. Otherwise he felt relatively comfortable. True, his whole body was aching, but it seemed that the pain was gradually growing less and would finally pass away. The rotting apple in his back and the inflamed area around it, all covered with soft dust, already hardly troubled him. He thought of his family with tenderness and love. The decision that he must disappear was one that he held to even more strongly than his sister, if that were possible. In this state of vacant and peaceful meditation he remained until the tower clock struck three in the morning. The first broadening of light in the world outside the window entered his consciousness once more. Then his head sank to the floor of its own accord and from his nostrils came the last faint flicker of his breath.

When the charwoman arrived early in the morning —what between her strength and her impatience she slammed all the doors so loudly, never mind how often she had been begged not to do so, that no one in the whole apartment could enjoy any quiet sleep after her arrival—she noticed nothing unusual as she took her customary peep into Gregor's room. She thought he was lying motionless on purpose, pretending to be in the sulks; she credited him with every kind of intelligence. Since she happened to have the long-handled broom in her hand she tried to tickle him up with it from the doorway. When that too produced no reaction she felt provoked and poked at him a little harder, and only when she had pushed him along the floor without meeting any resistance was her attention aroused. It did not take her long to establish the truth of the matter, and her eyes widened, she let out a whistle, yet did not waste much time over it but tore open the door of the Samsas' bedroom and yelled into the darkness at the top of her voice: "Just look at this, it's dead; it's lying here dead and done for!"

Mr. and Mrs. Samsa started up in their double bed and before they realized the nature of the charwoman's announcement had some difficulty in overcoming the shock of it. But then they got out of bed quickly, one on either side, Mr. Samsa throwing a blanket over his shoulders, Mrs. Samsa in nothing but her nightgown; in this array they entered Gregor's room. Meanwhile the door of the living room opened, too, where Grete had been sleeping since the advent of the lodgers; she was completely dressed as if she had not been to bed, which seemed to be confirmed also by the paleness of her face. "Dead?" said Mrs. Samsa, looking questioningly at the charwoman, although she could have investigated for herself, and the fact was obvious enough without investigation. "I should say so," said the charwoman, proving her words by pushing Gregor's corpse a long way to one side with her broomstick. Mrs. Samsa made a movement as if to stop her, but checked it. "Well," said Mr. Samsa, "now thanks be to God." He crossed himself, and the three women followed his example. Grete, whose eyes never left the corpse, said: "Just see how thin he was. It's such a long time since he's eaten anything. The food came out again just as it went in." Indeed, Gregor's body was completely flat and dry, as could only now be seen when it was no longer supported by the legs and nothing prevented one from looking closely at it.

"Come in beside us, Grete, for a little while," said Mrs. Samsa with a tremulous smile, and Grete, not without looking back at the corpse, followed her parents into their bedroom. The charwoman shut the door and opened the window wide. Although it was so early in the morning a certain softness was perceptible in the fresh air. After all, it was already the end of March.

The three lodgers emerged from their room and were surprised to see no breakfast; they had been forgotten. "Where's our breakfast?" said the middle lodger peevishly to the charwoman. But she put her finger to her lips and hastily, without a word, indicated by gestures that they should go into Gregor's room. They did so and stood, their hands in the pockets of their somewhat shabby coats, around Gregor's corpse in the room where it was now fully light.

At that the door of the Samsas' bedroom opened and Mr. Samsa appeared in his uniform, his wife on one arm, his daughter on the other. They all looked a little as if they had been crying; from time to time Grete hid her face on her father's arm.

"Leave my house at once!" said Mr. Samsa, and pointed to the door without disengaging himself from the women. "What do you mean by that?" said the middle lodger, taken somewhat aback, with a feeble smile. The two others put their hands behind them and kept rubbing them together, as if in gleeful expectation of a

fine set-to in which they were bound to come off the win-
ners. "I mean just what I say," answered Mr. Samsa, and
advanced in a straight line with his two companions towards the lodger. He stood his ground at first quietly,
looking at the floor as if his thoughts were taking a new
pattern in his head. "Then let us go, by all means," he
said, and looked up at Mr. Samsa as if in a sudden access of humility he were expecting some renewed sanc-
tion for this decision Mr. Samsa merely nodded briefly
once or twice with meaningful eyes. Upon that the
lodger really did go with long strides into the hall, his
two friends had been listening and had quite stopped
rubbing their hands for some moments and now went
scuttling after him as if afraid that Mr. Samsa might get
into the hall before them and cut them off from their
leader In the hall they all three took their hats from the
rack, their sticks from the umbrella stand, bowed in silence and quitted the apartment. With a suspiciousness
which proved quite unfounded Mr. Samsa and the two
women followed them out to the landing; leaning over
the banister they watched the three figures slowly but
surely going down the long stairs, vanishing from sight
at a certain turn of the staircase on every floor and coming into view again after a moment or so; the more they
dwindled, the more the Samsa family's interest in them
dwindled, and when a butcher's boy met them and
passed them on the stairs coming up proudly with a tray
on his head, Mr. Samsa and the two women soon left the
landing and as if a burden had been lifted from them
went back into their apartment.

They decided to spend this day in resting and going

for a stroll; they had not only deserved such a respite from work, but absolutely needed it. And so they sat down at the table and wrote three notes of excuse, Mr. Samsa to his board of management, Mrs. Samsa to her employer and Grete to the head of her firm. While they were writing, the charwoman came in to say that she was going now, since her morning's work was finished. At first they only nodded without looking up, but as she kept hovering there they eyed her irritably. "Well?" said Mr. Samsa. The charwoman stood grinning in the doorway as if she had good news to impart to the family but meant not to say a word unless properly questioned. The small ostrich feather standing upright on her hat, which had annoyed Mr. Samsa ever since she was engaged, was waving gaily in all directions. "Well, what is it then?" asked Mrs. Samsa, who obtained more respect from the charwoman than the others. "Oh," said the charwoman, giggling so amiably that she could not at once continue, "just this, you don't need to bother about how to get rid of the thing next door. It's been seen to already." Mrs. Samsa and Grete bent over their letters again, as if preoccupied; Mr. Samsa, who perceived that she was eager to begin describing it all in detail, stopped her with a decisive hand. But since she was not allowed to tell her story, she remembered the great hurry she was in, being obviously deeply huffed: "Bye, everybody," she said, whirling off violently, and departed with a frightful slamming of doors.

"She'll be given notice tonight," said Mr. Samsa, but neither from his wife nor his daughter did he get any answer, for the charwoman seemed to have shattered again the composure they had barely achieved. They rose, went to the window and stayed there, clasping each other tight. Mr. Samsa turned in his chair to look at them and quietly observed them for a little. Then he called out: "Come along, now, do. Let bygones be bygones. And you might have some consideration for me." The two of them complied at once, hastened to him, caressed him and quickly finished their letters.

Then they all three left the apartment together, which was more than they had done for months, and went by tram into the open country outside the town. The tram, in which they were the only passengers, was filled with warm sunshine. Leaning comfortably back in their seats they canvassed their prospects for the future, and it appeared on closer inspection that these were not at all bad, for the jobs they had got, which so far they had never really discussed with each other, were all three admirable and likely to lead to better things later on. The greatest immediate improvement in their condition would of course arise from moving to another house; they wanted to take a smaller and cheaper but also better situated and more easily run apartment than the one they had, which Gregor had selected. While they were thus conversing, it struck both Mr. and Mrs. Samsa, almost at the same moment, as they became aware of their daughter's increasing vivacity, that in spite of all the sorrow of recent times, which had made her cheeks pale, she had bloomed into a pretty girl with a good figure. They grew quieter and half unconsciously exchanged glances of complete agreement, having come to the conclusion that it would soon be time to find a good husband for her. And it was like a confirmation of their new dreams and excellent intentions that at the end of their journey their daughter sprang to her feet first and stretched her young body.

In the Penal Colony

"IT's A REMARKABLE piece of apparatus," said the officer to the explorer and surveyed with a certain air of
admiration the apparatus which was after all quite familiar to him. The explorer seemed to have accepted
merely out of politeness the Commandant's invitation
to witness the execution of a soldier condemned to death
for disobedience and insulting behavior to a superior.
Nor did the colony itself betray much interest in this
execution. At least, in the small sandy valley, a deep hol-
low surrounded on all sides by naked crags, there was
no one present save the officer, the explorer, the condemned man, who was a stupid-looking wide-mouthed
creature with bewildered hair and face, and the soldier
who held the heavy chain controlling the small chains
locked on the prisoner's ankles, wrists and neck, chains
which were themselves attached to each other by communicating links. In any case, the condemned man
looked so like a submissive dog that one might have
thought he could be left to run free on the surrounding
hills and would only need to be whistled for when the
execution was due to begin.

The explorer did not much care about the apparatus

and walked up and down behind the prisoner with almost visible indifference while the officer made the last adjustments, now creeping beneath the structure, which was bedded deep in the earth, now climbing a ladder to inspect its upper parts. These were tasks that might well have been left to a mechanic, but the officer performed them with great zeal, whether because he was a devoted admirer of the apparatus or because of other reasons the work could be entrusted to no one else. "Ready now!" he called at last and climbed down from the ladder. He looked uncommonly limp, breathed with his mouth wide open and had tucked two fine ladies' handkerchiefs under the collar of his uniform. "These uniforms are too heavy for the tropics, surely," said the explorer, instead of making some inquiry about the apparatus, as the officer had expected. "Of course," said the officer, washing his oily and greasy hands in a bucket of water that stood ready, "but they mean home to us; we don't want to forget about home. Now just have a look at this machine," he added at once, simultaneously drying his hands on a towel and indicating the apparatus. "Up till now a few things still had to be set by hand, but from this moment it works all by itself." The explorer nodded and followed him. The officer, anxious to secure himself against all contingencies, said: "Things sometimes go wrong, of course; I hope that nothing goes wrong today, but we have to allow for the possibility. The machinery should go on working continuously for twelve hours. But if anything does go wrong it will only be some small matter that can be set right at once.

"Won't you take a seat?" he asked finally, drawing a

cane chair out from among a heap of them and offering it to the explorer, who could not refuse it. He was now sitting at the edge of a pit, into which he glanced for a fleeting moment. It was not very deep. On one side of the pit the excavated soil had been piled up in a rampart, on the other side of it stood the apparatus. "I don't know," said the officer, "if the Commandant has already explained this apparatus to you." The explorer waved one hand vaguely; the officer asked for nothing better, since now he could explain the apparatus himself. "This apparatus," he said, taking hold of a crank handle and leaning against it, "was invented by our former Commandant. I assisted at the very earliest experiments and had a share in all the work until its completion. But the credit of inventing it belongs to him alone. Have you ever heard of our former Commandant? No? Well, it isn't saying too much if I tell you that the organization of the whole penal colony is his work. We who were his friends knew even before he died that the organization of the colony was so perfect that his successor, even with a thousand new schemes in his head, would find it impossible to alter anything, at least for many years to come. And our prophecy has come true; the new Commandant has had to acknowledge its truth. A pity you never met the old Commandant!—But," the officer interrupted himself, "I am rambling on, and here stands his apparatus before us. It consists, as you see, of three parts. In the course of time each of these parts has acquired a kind of popular nickname. The lower one is called the 'Bed,' the upper one the 'Designer,' and this one here in the middle that moves up and down is called the 'Harrow.'" "The Harrow?" asked the explorer. He had not been listening very attentively, the glare of the sun in the shadeless valley was altogether too strong, it was difficult to collect one's thoughts. All the more did he admire the officer, who in spite of his tight-fitting full-dress uniform coat, amply befrogged and weighed down by epaulettes, was pursuing his subject with such enthusiasm and, besides talking, was still tightening a screw here and there with a spanner. As for the soldier, he seemed to be in much the same condition as the explorer. He had wound the prisoner's chain round both his wrists, propped himself on his rifle, let his head hang and was paying no attention to anything. That did not surprise the explorer, for the officer was speaking French, and certainly neither the soldier nor the prisoner understood a word of French. It was all the more remarkable, therefore, that the prisoner was none the less making an effort to follow the officer's explanations. With a kind of drowsy persistence he directed his gaze wherever the officer pointed a finger, and at the interruption of the explorer's question he, too, as well as the officer, looked round.

"Yes, the Harrow," said the officer, "a good name for it. The needles are set in like the teeth of a harrow and the whole thing works something like a harrow, although its action is limited to one place and contrived with much more artistic skill. Anyhow, you'll soon understand it. On the Bed here the condemned man is laid —I'm going to describe the apparatus first before I set it in motion. Then you'll be able to follow the proceedings better. Besides, one of the cogwheels in the Designer is badly worn; it creaks a lot when it's working, you can hardly hear yourself speak; spare parts, unfortunately, are difficult to get here.—Well, here is the Bed, as I told you. It is completely covered with a layer of cotton wool; you'll find out why later. On this cotton wool the condemned man is laid, face down, quite naked, of course; here are straps for the hands, here for the feet, and here for the neck, to bind him fast. Here at the head of the bed, where the man, as I said, first lays down his face, is this little gag of felt, which can be easily regulated to go straight into his mouth. It is meant to keep him from screaming and biting his tongue. Of course the man is forced to take the felt into his mouth, for otherwise his neck would be broken by the strap." "Is that cotton wool?" asked the explorer, bending forward. "Yes, certainly," said the officer, with a smile. "Feel it for yourself." He took the explorer's hand and guided it over the bed. "It's specially prepared cotton wool; that's why it looks so different; I'll tell you presently what it's for." The explorer already felt a dawning interest in the apparatus; he sheltered his eyes from the sun with one hand and gazed up at the structure. It was a huge affair. The Bed and the Designer were of the same size and looked like two dark wooden chests. The Designer hung about two meters above the Bed; each of them was bound at the corners with four rods of brass that almost flashed out rays in the sunlight. Between the chests shuttled the Harrow on a ribbon of steel.

The officer had scarcely noticed the explorer's previous indifference, but he was now well aware of his dawning interest; so he stopped explaining in order to

leave a space of time for quiet observation. The condemned man imitated the explorer; since he could not
use a hand to shelter his eyes he gazed upwards without
shade.

"Well, the man lies down," said the explorer, leaning
back in his chair and crossing his legs.

"Yes," said the officer, pushing his cap back a little
and passing one hand over his heated face, "now listen!
Both the Bed and the Designer have an electric battery
each; the Bed needs one for itself, the Designer for the
Harrow. As soon as the man is strapped down, the Bed
is set in motion. It quivers in minute, very rapid vibrations, both from side to side and up and down. You will
have seen similar apparatus in hospitals; but in our Bed
the movements are all precisely calculated; you see, they
have to correspond very exactly to the movements of the
Harrow. And the Harrow is the instrument for the
actual execution of the sentence."

"And how does the sentence run?" asked the explorer.

"You don't know that either?" said the officer in
amazement, and bit his lips. "Forgive me if my explanations seem rather incoherent. I do beg your pardon. You
see, the Commandant always used to do the explaining;
but the new Commandant shirks this duty; yet that such
an important visitor"—the explorer tried to deprecate
the honor with both hands; the officer, however, insisted
—"that such an important visitor should not even be
told about the kind of sentence we pass is a new development, which—" He was just on the point of using strong
language but checked himself and said only: "I was not
informed, it is not my fault. In any case, I am certainly

the best person to explain our procedure, since I have here"—he patted his breast pocket—"the relevant drawings made by our former Commandant."

"The Commandant's own drawings?" asked the explorer. "Did he combine everything in himself, then? Was he soldier, judge, mechanic, chemist and draughtsman?"

"Indeed he was," said the officer, nodding assent, with a remote, glassy look. Then he inspected his hands critically; they did not seem clean enough to him for touching the drawings; so he went over to the bucket and washed them again. Then he drew out a small leather wallet and said: "Our sentence does not sound severe. Whatever commandment the prisoner has disobeyed is written upon his body by the Harrow. This prisoner, for instance"—the officer indicated the man—"will have written on his body: HONOR THY SUPERIORS!"

The explorer glanced at the man; he stood, as the officer pointed him out, with bent head, apparently listening with all his ears in an effort to catch what was being said. Yet the movement of his blubber lips, closely pressed together, showed clearly that he could not understand a word. Many questions were troubling the explorer, but at the sight of the prisoner he asked only: "Does he know his sentence?" "No," said the officer, eager to go on with his exposition, but the explorer interrupted him: "He doesn't know the sentence that has been passed on him?" "No," said the officer again, pausing a moment as if to let the explorer elaborate his question, and then said: "There would be no point in telling him. He'll learn it on his body." The explorer intended to make no answer, but he felt the prisoner's gaze turned on him; it seemed to ask if he approved such goings on. So he bent forward again, having already leaned back in his chair, and put another question: "But surely he knows that he has been sentenced?" "Nor that either," said the officer, smiling at the explorer as if expecting him to make further surprising remarks. "No," said the explorer, wiping his forehead, "then he can't know either whether his defense was effective?" "He has had no chance of putting up a defense," said the officer, turning his eyes away as if speaking to himself and so sparing the explorer the shame of hearing self-evident matters explained. "But he must have had some chance of defending himself," said the explorer, and rose from his seat.

The officer realized that he was in danger of having his exposition of the apparatus held up for a long time; so he went up to the explorer, took him by the arm, waved a hand towards the condemned man, who was standing very straight now that he had so obviously become the center of attention—the soldier had also given the chain a jerk—and said: "This is how the matter stands. I have been appointed judge in this penal colony. Despite my youth. For I was the former Commandant's assistant in all penal matters and know more about the apparatus than anyone. My guiding principle is this: Guilt is never to be doubted. Other courts cannot follow that principle, for they consist of several opinions and have higher courts to scrutinize them. That is not the case here, or at least, it was not the case in the former Commandant's time. The new man has certainly shown some inclination to interfere with my judgments, but so far I have succeeded in fending him off and will go on succeeding. You wanted to have the case explained; it is quite simple, like all of them. A captain reported to me this morning that this man, who had been assigned to him as a servant and sleeps before his door, had been asleep on duty. It is his duty, you see, to get up every time the hour strikes and salute the captain's door. Not an exacting duty, and very necessary, since he has to be a sentry as well as a servant, and must be alert in both functions. Last night the captain wanted to see if the man was doing his duty. He opened the door as the clock struck two and there was his man curled up asleep. He took his riding whip and lashed him across the face. Instead of getting up and begging pardon, the man caught hold of his master's legs, shook him and cried: 'Throw that whip away or I'll eat you alive.'—That's the evidence. The captain came to me an hour ago, I wrote down his statement and appended the sentence to it. Then I had the man put in chains. That was all quite simple. If I had first called the man before me and interrogated him, things would have got into a confused tangle. He would have told lies, and had I exposed these lies he would have backed them up with more lies, and so on and so forth. As it is, I've got him and I won't let him go.—Is that quite clear now? But we're wasting time, the execution should be beginning and I haven't finished explaining the apparatus yet." He pressed the explorer back into his chair, went up again to the apparatus and began: "As you see, the shape of the Harrow corresponds to the human form; here is the harrow for the torso, here are the harrows for the legs. For the head there is only this one small spike. Is that quite clear?" He bent amiably forward towards the explorer, eager to provide the most comprehensive explanations.

The explorer considered the Harrow with a frown. The explanation of the judicial procedure had not satisfied him. He had to remind himself that this was in any case a penal colony where extraordinary measures were needed and that military discipline must be enforced to the last. He also felt that some hope might be set on the new Commandant, who was apparently of a mind to bring in, although gradually, a new kind of procedure which the officer's narrow mind was incapable of understanding. This train of thought prompted his next question: "Will the Commandant attend the execution?" "It is not certain," said the officer, wincing at the direct question, and his friendly expression darkened. "That is just why we have to lose no time. Much as I dislike it, I shall have to cut my explanations short. But of course tomorrow, when the apparatus has been cleaned—its one drawback is that it gets so messy—I can recapitulate all the details. For the present, then, only the essentials.—When the man lies down on the Bed and it begins to vibrate, the Harrow is lowered onto his body. It regulates itself automatically so that the needles barely touch his skin; once contact is made the steel ribbon stiffens immediately into a rigid band. And then the performance begins. An ignorant onlooker would see no difference between one punishment and another. The Harrow appears to do its work with uniform regularity. As it quivers, its points pierce the skin of the body

which is itself quivering from the vibration of the
Bed. So that the actual progress of the sentence can be
watched, the Harrow is made of glass. Getting the needles fixed in the glass was a technical problem, but after
many experiments we overcame the difficulty. No trouble was too great for us to take, you see. And now anyone
can look through the glass and watch the inscription
taking form on the body. Wouldn't you care to come a
little nearer and have a look at the needles?"

The explorer got up slowly, walked across and bent
over the Harrow. "You see," said the officer, "there are
two kinds of needles arranged in multiple patterns.
Each long needle has a short one beside it. The long
needle does the writing, and the short needle sprays a
jet of water to wash away the blood and keep the inscription clear. Blood and water together are then conducted here through small runnels into this main runnel
and down a waste pipe into the pit." With his finger the
officer traced the exact course taken by the blood and
water. To make the picture as vivid as possible he held
both hands below the outlet of the waste pipe as if to
catch the outflow, and when he did this the explorer
drew back his head and feeling behind him with one
hand sought to return to his chair. To his horror he
found that the condemned man too had obeyed the officer's invitation to examine the Harrow at close quarters and had followed him. He had pulled forward the
sleepy soldier with the chain and was bending over the
glass. One could see that his uncertain eyes were trying
to perceive what the two gentlemen had been looking
at, but since he had not understood the explanation he

could not make head or tail of it. He was peering this way and that way. He kept running his eyes along the glass. The explorer wanted to drive him away, since what he was doing was probably culpable. But the officer firmly restrained the explorer with one hand and with the other took a clod of earth from the rampart and threw it at the soldier. He opened his eyes with a jerk, saw what the condemned man had dared to do, let his rifle fall, dug his heels into the ground, dragged his prisoner back so that he stumbled and fell immediately, and then stood looking down at him, watching him struggling and rattling in his chains. "Set him on his feet!" yelled the officer, for he noticed that the explorer's attention was being too much distracted by the prisoner. In fact he was even leaning right across the Harrow, without taking any notice of it, intent only on finding out what was happening to the prisoner. "Be careful with him!" cried the officer again. He ran round the apparatus, himself caught the condemned man under the shoulders and with the soldier's help got him up on his feet, which kept slithering from under him.

"Now I know all about it," said the explorer as the officer came back to him. "All except the most important thing," he answered, seizing the explorer's arm and pointing upwards: "In the Designer are all the cogwheels that control the movements of the Harrow, and this machinery is regulated according to the inscription demanded by the sentence. I am still using the guiding plans drawn by the former Commandant. Here they are"—he extracted some sheets from the leather wallet —"but I'm sorry I can't let you handle them; they are my most precious possessions. Just take a seat and I'll hold them in front of you like this, then you'll be able to see everything quite well." He spread out the first sheet of paper. The explorer would have liked to say something appreciative, but all he could see was a labyrinth of lines crossing and re-crossing each other, which covered the paper so thickly that it was difficult to discern the blank spaces between them. "Read it," said the officer. "I can't," said the explorer. "Yet it's clear enough," said the officer. "It's very ingenious," said the explorer evasively, "but I can't make it out." "Yes," said the officer with a laugh, putting the paper away again, "it's no calligraphy for school children. It needs to be studied closely. I'm quite sure that in the end you would understand it too. Of course the script can't be a simple one; it's not supposed to kill a man straight off, but only after an interval of, on an average, twelve hours; the turning point is reckoned to come at the sixth hour. So there have to be lots and lots of flourishes around the actual script; the script itself runs round the body only in a narrow girdle; the rest of the body is reserved for the embellishments. Can you appreciate now the work accomplished by the Harrow and the whole apparatus? —Just watch it!" He ran up the ladder, turned a wheel, called down: "Look out, keep to one side!" and everything started working. If the wheel had not creaked, it would have been marvelous. The officer, as if surprised by the noise of the wheel, shook his fist at it, then spread out his arms in excuse to the explorer and climbed down rapidly to peer at the working of the machine from below. Something perceptible to no one save himself was

still not in order; he clambered up again, did something
with both hands in the interior of the Designer, then
slid down one of the rods, instead of using the ladder,
so as to get down quicker, and with the full force of his
lungs, to make himself heard at all in the noise, yelled
in the explorer's ear: "Can you follow it? The Harrow
is beginning to write; when it finishes the first draft of
the inscription on the man's back, the layer of cotton
wool begins to roll and slowly turns the body over, to
give the Harrow fresh space for writing. Meanwhile
the raw part that has been written on lies on the cotton
wool, which is specially prepared to staunch the bleeding and so makes all ready for a new deepening of the
script. Then these teeth at the edge of the Harrow, as
the body turns further round, tear the cotton wool away
from the wounds, throw it into the pit, and there is more
work for the Harrow. So it keeps on writing deeper and
deeper for the whole twelve hours. The first six hours
the condemned man stays alive almost as before, he suffers only pain. After two hours the felt gag is taken
away, for he has no longer strength to scream. Here, into
this electrically heated basin at the head of the bed,
some warm rice pap is poured, from which the man, if
he feels like it, can take as much as his tongue can lap.
Not one of them ever misses the chance. I can remember none, and my experience is extensive. Only about
the sixth hour does the man lose all desire to eat. I usually kneel down here at that moment and observe what
happens. The man rarely swallows his last mouthful,
he only rolls it round his mouth and spits it out into
the pit. I have to duck just then or he would spit it in

my face. But how quiet he grows at just about the sixth
hour! Enlightenment comes to the most dull-witted. It
begins around the eyes. From there it radiates. A moment that might tempt one to get under the Harrow
oneself. Nothing more happens than that the man begins to understand the inscription, he purses his mouth
as if he were listening. You have seen how difficult it is
to decipher the script with one's eyes; but our man de-
ciphers it with his wounds. To be sure, that is a hard
task; he needs six hours to accomplish it. By that time
the Harrow has pierced him quite through and casts
him into the pit, where he pitches down upon the blood
and water and the cotton wool. Then the judgment has
been fulfilled, and we, the soldier and I, bury him."

The explorer had inclined his ear to the officer and
with his hands in his jacket pockets watched the machine at work. The condemned man watched it too, but
uncomprehendingly. He bent forward a little and was
intent on the moving needles when the soldier, at a
sign from the officer, slashed through his shirt and trousers from behind with a knife, so that they fell off; he
tried to catch at his falling clothes to cover his nakedness, but the soldier lifted him into the air and shook
the last remnants from him. The officer stopped the
machine, and in the sudden silence the condemned man
was laid under the Harrow. The chains were loosened
and the straps fastened on instead; in the first moment
that seemed almost a relief to the prisoner. And now the
Harrow was adjusted a little lower, since he was a thin
man. When the needle points touched him a shudder

ran over his skin; while the soldier was busy strapping
his right hand, he flung out his left hand blindly; but
it happened to be in the direction towards where the
explorer was standing. The officer kept watching the
explorer sideways, as if seeking to read from his face
the impression made on him by the execution, which
had been at least cursorily explained to him.

The wrist strap broke; probably the soldier had
drawn it too tight. The officer had to intervene, the
soldier held up the broken piece of strap to show him.
So the officer went over to him and said, his face still
turned towards the explorer: "This is a very complex
machine, it can't be helped that things are breaking or
giving way here and there; but one must not thereby
allow oneself to be diverted in one's general judgment.
In any case, this strap is easily made good; I shall simply use a chain; the delicacy of the vibrations for the
right arm will of course be a little impaired." And while
he fastened the chains, he added: "The resources for
maintaining the machine are now very much reduced.
Under the former Commandant I had free access to a
sum of money set aside entirely for this purpose. There
was a store, too, in which spare parts were kept for re-
pairs of all kinds. I confess I have been almost prodigal
with them, I mean in the past, not now as the new Commandant pretends, always looking for an excuse to attack our old way of doing things. Now he has taken
charge of the machine money himself, and if I send
for a new strap they ask for the broken old strap as evidence, and the new strap takes ten days to appear and

then is of shoddy material and not much good. But how I am supposed to work the machine without a strap, that's something nobody bothers about."

The explorer thought to himself: It's always a ticklish matter to intervene decisively in other people's affairs. He was neither a member of the penal colony nor a citizen of the state to which it belonged. Were he to denounce this execution or actually try to stop it, they could say to him: You are a foreigner, mind your own business. He could make no answer to that, unless he were to add that he was amazed at himself in this connection, for he traveled only as an observer, with no intention at all of altering other people's methods of administering justice. Yet here he found himself strongly tempted. The injustice of the procedure and the inhumanity of the execution were undeniable. No one could suppose that he had any selfish interest in the matter, for the condemned man was a complete stranger, not a fellow countryman or even at all sympathetic to him. The explorer himself had recommendations from high quarters, had been received here with great courtesy, and the very fact that he had been invited to attend the execution seemed to suggest that his views would be welcome. And this was all the more likely since the Commandant, as he had heard only too plainly, was no upholder of the procedure and maintained an attitude almost of hostility to the officer.

At that moment the explorer heard the officer cry out in rage. He had just, with considerable difficulty, forced the felt gag into the condemned man's mouth when the man in an irresistible access of nausea shut his eyes and vomited. Hastily the officer snatched him away from the gag and tried to hold his head over the pit; but it was too late, the vomit was running all over the machine. "It's all the fault of that Commandant!" cried the officer, senselessly shaking the brass rods in front, "the machine is befouled like a pigsty." With trembling hands he indicated to the explorer what had happened. "Have I not tried for hours at a time to get the Commandant to understand that the prisoner must fast for a whole day before the execution? But our new, mild doctrine thinks otherwise. The Commandant's ladies stuff the man with sugar candy before he's led off. He has lived on stinking fish his whole life long and now he has to eat sugar candy! But it could still be possible, I should have nothing to say against it, but why won't they get me a new felt gag, which I have been begging for the last three months. How should a man not feel sick when he takes a felt gag into his mouth which more than a hundred men have already slobbered and gnawed in their dying moments?"

The condemned man had laid his head down and looked peaceful; the soldier was busy trying to clean the machine with the prisoner's shirt. The officer advanced towards the explorer, who in some vague presentiment fell back a pace, but the officer seized him by the hand, and drew him to one side. "I should like to exchange a few words with you in confidence," he said, "may I?" "Of course," said the explorer, and listened with downcast eyes.

"This procedure and method of execution, which you are now having the opportunity to admire, has at the moment no longer any open adherents in our colony. I am its sole advocate, and at the same time the sole advocate of the old Commandant's tradition. I can no longer reckon on any further extension of the method; it takes all my energy to maintain it as it is. During the old Commandant's lifetime the colony was full of his adherents; his strength of conviction I still have in some measure, but not an atom of his power; consequently the adherents have skulked out of sight, there are still many of them but none of them will admit it. If you were to go into the teahouse today, on execution day, and listen to what is being said, you would perhaps hear only ambiguous remarks. These would all be made by adherents, but under the present Commandant and his present doctrines they are of no use to me. And now I ask you: because of this Commandant and the women who influence him, is such a piece of work, the work of a lifetime"—he pointed to the machine—"to perish? Ought one to let that happen? Even if one has only come as a stranger to our island for a few days? But there's no time to lose, an attack of some kind is impending on my function as judge; conferences are already being held in the Commandant's office from which I am excluded; even your coming here today seems to me a significant move; they are cowards and use you as a screen, you, a stranger.—How different an execution was in the old days! A whole day before the ceremony the valley was packed with people; they all came only to look on; early in the morning the Commandant appeared with his ladies; fanfares roused the whole camp; I reported that everything was in readiness; the assembled company—

no high official dared to absent himself—arranged itself
round the machine; this pile of cane chairs is a miserable survival from that epoch. The machine was freshly
cleaned and glittering, I got new spare parts for almost
every execution. Before hundreds of spectators—all of
them standing on tiptoe as far as the heights there—the
condemned man was laid under the Harrow by the
Commandant himself. What is left today for a common
soldier to do was then my task, the task of the presiding
judge, and was an honor for me. And then the execution
began! No discordant noise spoilt the working of the
machine. Many did not care to watch it but lay with
closed eyes in the sand; they all knew: Now Justice is
being done. In the silence one heard nothing but the
condemned man's sighs, half muffled by the felt gag.
Nowadays the machine can no longer wring from anyone a sigh louder than the felt gag can stifle; but in those
days the writing needles let drop an acid fluid, which
we're no longer permitted to use. Well, and then came
the sixth hour! It was impossible to grant all the re-
quests to be allowed to watch it from near by. The
Commandant in his wisdom ordained that the children
should have the preference; I, of course, because of my
office had the privilege of always being at hand; often
enough I would be squatting there with a small child
in either arm. How we all absorbed the look of trans-
figuration on the face of the sufferer, how we bathed
our cheeks in the radiance of that justice, achieved at
last and fading so quickly! What times these were, my
comrade!" The officer had obviously forgotten whom
he was addressing; he had embraced the explorer and

laid his head on his shoulder. The explorer was deeply embarrassed, impatiently he stared over the officer's head. The soldier had finished his cleaning job and was now pouring rice pap from a pot into the basin. As soon as the condemned man, who seemed to have recovered entirely, noticed this action he began to reach for the rice with his tongue. The soldier kept pushing him away, since the rice pap was certainly meant for a later hour, yet it was just as unfitting that the soldier himself should thrust his dirty hands into the basin and eat out of it before the other's avid face.

The officer quickly pulled himself together. "I didn't want to upset you," he said. "I know it is impossible to make those days credible now. Anyhow, the machine is still working and it is still effective in itself. It is effective in itself even though it stands alone in this valley. And the corpse still falls at the last into the pit with an incomprehensibly gentle wafting motion, even although there are no hundreds of people swarming round like flies as formerly. In those days we had to put a strong fence round the pit; it has long since been torn down."

The explorer wanted to withdraw his face from the officer and looked round him at random. The officer thought he was surveying the valley's desolation; so he seized him by the hands, turned him round to meet his eyes, and asked: "Do you realize the shame of it?"

But the explorer said nothing. The officer left him alone for a little; with legs apart, hands on hips, he stood very still, gazing at the ground. Then he smiled encouragingly at the explorer and said: "I was quite near you yesterday when the Commandant gave you the invitation. I heard him giving it. I know the Commandant. I divined at once what he was after. Although he is powerful enough to take measures against me, he doesn't dare to do it yet, but he certainly means to use your verdict against me, the verdict of an illustrious foreigner. He has calculated it carefully: this is your second day on the island, you did not know the old Commandant and his ways, you are conditioned by European ways of thought, perhaps you object on principle to capital punishment in general and to such mechanical instruments of death in particular, besides you will see that the execution has no support from the public, a shabby ceremony—carried out with a machine already somewhat old and worn—now, taking all that into consideration, would it not be likely (so thinks the Commandant) that you might disapprove of my methods? And if you disapprove, you wouldn't conceal the fact (I'm still speaking from the Commandant's point of view), for you are a man to feel confidence in your own well-tried conclusions. True, you have seen and learned to appreciate the peculiarities of many peoples, and so you would not be likely to take a strong line against our proceedings, as you might do in your own country. But the Commandant has no need of that. A casual, even an unguarded remark will be enough. It doesn't even need to represent what you really think, so long as it can be used speciously to serve his purpose. He will try to prompt you with sly questions, of that I am certain. And his ladies will sit around you and prick up their ears; you might be saying something like this: 'In our country we have a different criminal procedure,' or 'In our country the prisoner is interrogated before he is sentenced,' or 'We haven't used torture since the Middle Ages.' All these statements are as true as they seem natural to you, harmless remarks that pass no judgment on my methods. But how would the Commandant react to them? I can see him, our good Commandant, pushing his chair away immediately and rushing onto the balcony, I can see his ladies streaming out after him, I can hear his voice —the ladies call it a voice of thunder—well, and this is what he says: 'A famous Western investigator, sent out to study criminal procedure in all the countries of the world, has just said that our old tradition of administering justice is inhumane. Such a verdict from such a personality makes it impossible for me to countenance these methods any longer. Therefore from this very day I ordain . . .' and so on. You may want to interpose that you never said any such thing, that you never called my methods inhumane; on the contrary your profound experience leads you to believe they are most humane and most in consonance with human dignity, and you admire the machine greatly—but it will be too late; you won't even get onto the balcony, crowded as it will be with ladies; you may try to draw attention to yourself; you may want to scream out; but a lady's hand will close your lips—and I and the work of the old Commandant will be done for."

The explorer had to suppress a smile; so easy, then, was the task he had felt to be so difficult. He said evasively: "You overestimate my influence; the Commandant has read my letters of recommendation, he knows that I am no expert in criminal procedure. If I were to give an opinion, it would be as a private individual, an opinion no more influential than that of any ordinary person, and in any case much less influential than that of the Commandant, who, I am given to understand, has very extensive powers in this penal colony. If his attitude to your procedure is as definitely hostile as you believe, then I fear the end of your tradition is at hand even without any humble assistance from me."

Had it dawned on the officer at last? No, he still did not understand. He shook his head emphatically, glanced briefly round at the condemned man and the soldier, who both flinched away from the rice, came close up to the explorer and without looking at his face but fixing his eye on some spot on his coat said in a lower voice than before: "You don't know the Commandant; you feel yourself—forgive the expression—a kind of out-sider so far as all of us are concerned; yet, believe me, your influence cannot be rated too highly. I was simply delighted when I heard that you were to attend the execution all by yourself. The Commandant arranged it to aim a blow at me, but I shall turn it to my advantage. Without being distracted by lying whispers and con-temptuous glances—which could not have been avoided had a crowd of people attended the execution—you have heard my explanations, seen the machine and are now in course of watching the execution. You have doubtless already formed your own judgment; if you still have some small uncertainties the sight of the execution will resolve them. And now I make this request to you: help me against the Commandant!"

The explorer would not let him go on. "How could

I do that?" he cried. "It's quite impossible. I can neither help nor hinder you."

"Yes, you can," the officer said. The explorer saw with a certain apprehension that the officer had clenched his fists. "Yes, you can," repeated the officer, still more insistently. "I have a plan that is bound to succeed. You believe your influence is insufficient. I know that it is sufficient. But even granted that you are right, is it not necessary, for the sake of preserving this tradition, to try even what might prove insufficient? Listen to my plan, then. The first thing necessary for you to carry it out is to be as reticent as possible today regarding your verdict on these proceedings. Unless you are asked a direct question you must say nothing at all; but what you do say must be brief and general; let it be remarked that you would prefer not to discuss the matter, that you are out of patience with it, that if you are to let yourself go you would use strong language. I don't ask you to tell any lies; by no means; you should only give curt answers, such as: 'Yes, I saw the execution,' or 'Yes, I had it explained to me.' Just that, nothing more. There are grounds enough for any impatience you betray, although not such as will occur to the Commandant. Of course, he will mistake your meaning and interpret it to please himself. That's what my plan depends on. Tomorrow in the Commandant's office there is to be a large conference of all the high administrative officials, the Commandant presiding. Of course the Commandant is the kind of man to have turned these conferences into public spectacles. He has had a gallery built that is always packed with spectators. I am compelled to take part in the conferences, but they make me sick with disgust. Now, whatever happens, you will certainly be invited to this conference; if you behave today as I suggest the invitation will become an urgent request. But if for some mysterious reason you're not invited, you'll have to ask for an invitation; there's no doubt of your getting it then. So tomorrow you're sitting in the Commandant's box with the ladies. He keeps looking up to make sure you're there. After various trivial and ridiculous matters, brought in merely to impress the audience—mostly harbor works, nothing but harbor works!—our judicial procedure comes up for discussion too. If the Commandant doesn't introduce it, or not soon enough, I'll see that it's mentioned. I'll stand up and report that today's execution has taken place. Quite briefly, only a statement. Such a statement is not usual, but I shall make it. The Commandant thanks me, as always, with an amiable smile, and then he can't restrain himself, he seizes the excellent opportunity. 'It has just been reported,' he will say, or words to that effect, 'that an execution has taken place. I should like merely to add that this execution was witnessed by the famous explorer who has, as you all know, honored our colony so greatly by his visit to us. His presence at today's session of our conference also contributes to the importance of this occasion. Should we not now ask the famous explorer to give us his verdict on our traditional mode of execution and the procedure that leads up to it?' Of course there is loud applause, general agreement, I am more insistent than anyone. The Commandant bows to you and says: 'Then in the name of the assembled company, I put the question to you.' And now you advance to the front of the box. Lay your hands where everyone can see them, or the ladies will catch them and press your fingers.—And then at last you can speak out. I don't know how I'm going to endure the tension of waiting for that moment. Don't put any restraint on yourself when you make your speech, publish the truth aloud, lean over the front of the box, shout, yes, indeed, shout your verdict, your unshakable conviction, at the Commandant. Yet perhaps you wouldn't care to do that, it's not in keeping with your character, in your country perhaps people do these things differently, well, that's all right too, that will be quite as effective, don't even stand up, just say a few words, even in a whisper, so that only the officials beneath you will hear them, that will quite enough, you don't even need to mention the lack of public support for the execution, the creaking wheel, the broken strap, the filthy gag of felt, no, I'll take all that upon me, and, believe me, if my indictment doesn't drive him out of the conference hall, it will force him to his knees to make the acknowledgment: Old Commandant, I humble myself before you.—That is my plan; will you help me to carry it out? But of course you are willing, what is more, you must." And the officer seized the explorer by both arms and gazed, breathing heavily, into his face. He had shouted the last sentence so loudly that even the soldier and the condemned man were startled into attending; they had not understood a word but they stopped eating and looked over at the explorer, chewing their previous mouthfuls.

From the very beginning the explorer had no doubt about what answer he must give; in his lifetime he had experienced too much to have any uncertainty here; he was fundamentally honorable and unafraid. And yet now, facing the soldier and the condemned man, he did hesitate, for as long as it took to draw one breath. At last, however, he said, as he had to: "No." The officer blinked several times but did not turn his eyes away. "Would you like me to explain?" asked the explorer. The officer nodded wordlessly. "I do not approve of your procedure," said the explorer then, "even before you took me into your confidence—of course I shall never in any circumstances betray your confidence—I was already wondering whether it would be my duty to intervene and whether my intervention would have the slightest chance of success. I realized to whom I ought to turn: to the Commandant, of course. You have made that fact even clearer, but without having strengthened my resolution; on the contrary, your sincere conviction has touched me, even though it cannot influence my judgment."

The officer remained mute, turned to the machine, caught hold of a brass rod, and then, leaning back a little, gazed at the Designer as if to assure himself that all was in order. The soldier and the condemned man seemed to have come to some understanding; the condemned man was making signs to the soldier, difficult though his movements were because of the tight straps; the soldier was bending down to him; the condemned man whispered something and the soldier nodded.

The explorer followed the officer and said: "You don't

know yet what I mean to do. I shall tell the Commandant what I think of the procedure, certainly, but
not at a public conference, only in private; nor shall I
stay here long enough to attend any conference; I am
going away early tomorrow morning, or at least em-
barking on my ship."

It did not look as if the officer had been listening. "So
you did not find the procedure convincing," he said to
himself and smiled, as an old man smiles at childish
nonsense and yet pursues his own meditations behind
the smile.

"Then the time has come," he said at last, and suddenly looked at the explorer with bright eyes that held
some challenge, some appeal for co-operation. "The
time for what?" asked the explorer uneasily, but got no
answer.

"You are free," said the officer to the condemned man
in the native tongue. The man did not believe it at first.
"Yes, you are set free," said the officer. For the first time
the condemned man's face woke to real animation. Was
it true? Was it only a caprice of the officer's that might
change again? Had the foreign explorer begged him
off? What was it? One could read these questions on his
face. But not for long. Whatever it might be, he wanted
to be really free if he might, and he began to struggle so
far as the Harrow permitted him.

"You'll burst my straps," cried the officer. "Lie still!
We'll soon loosen them." And signing the soldier to
help him, he set about doing so. The condemned man
laughed wordlessly to himself, now he turned his face

left towards the officer, now right towards the soldier, nor did he forget the explorer.

"Draw him out," ordered the officer. Because of the Harrow this had to be done with some care. The condemned man had already torn himself a little in the back through his impatience.

From now on, however, the officer paid hardly any attention to him. He went up to the explorer, pulled out the small leather wallet again, turned over the papers in it, found the one he wanted and showed it to the explorer. "Read it," he said. "I can't," said the explorer, "I told you before that I can't make out these scripts." "Try taking a close look at it," said the officer and came quite near to the explorer so that they might read it together. But when even that proved useless, he outlined the script with his little finger, holding it high above the paper as if the surface dared not be sullied by touch, in order to help the explorer to follow the script in that way. The explorer did make an effort, meaning to please the officer in this respect at least, but he was quite unable to follow. Now the officer began to spell it, letter by letter, and then read out the words. "'BE JUST!' is what is written there," he said. "Surely you can read it now." The explorer bent so close to the paper that the officer feared he might touch it and drew it farther away; the explorer made no remark, yet it was clear that he still could not decipher it. "'BE JUST!' is what is written there," said the officer once more. "Maybe," said the explorer, "I am prepared to believe you." "Well, then," said the officer, at least partly satisfied,

and climbed up the ladder with the paper; very carefully he laid it inside the Designer and seemed to be
changing the disposition of all the cogwheels; it was a
troublesome piece of work and must have involved
wheels that were extremely small, for sometimes the
officer's head vanished altogether from sight inside the
Designer, so precisely did he have to regulate the machinery.

The explorer, down below, watched the labor unin-
terruptedly, his neck grew stiff and his eyes smarted
from the glare of sunshine over the sky. The soldier and
the condemned man were now busy together. The
man's shirt and trousers, which were already lying in
the pit, were fished out by the point of the soldier's
bayonet. The shirt was abominably dirty and its owner
washed it in the bucket of water. When he put on the
shirt and trousers both he and the soldier could not
help guffawing, for the garments were of course slit up
behind. Perhaps the condemned man felt it incumbent
on him to amuse the soldier, he turned round and
round in his slashed garments before the soldier, who
squatted on the ground beating his knees with mirth.
All the same, they presently controlled their mirth out
of respect for the gentlemen.

When the officer had at length finished his task aloft,
he surveyed the machinery in all its details once more,
with a smile, but this time shut the lid of the Designer,
which had stayed open till now, climbed down, looked
into the pit and then at the condemned man, noting
with satisfaction that the clothing had been taken out,
then went over to wash his hands in the water bucket,

perceived too late that it was disgustingly dirty, was unhappy because he could not wash his hands, in the end thrust them into the sand—this alternative did not please him, but he had to put up with it—then stood upright and began to unbutton his uniform jacket. As he did this, the two ladies' handkerchiefs he had tucked under his collar fell into his hands. "Here are your handkerchiefs," he said, and threw them to the condemned man. And to the explorer he said in explanation: "A gift from the ladies."

In spite of the obvious haste with which he was discarding first his uniform jacket and then all his clothing, he handled each garment with loving care, he even ran his fingers caressingly over the silver lace on the jacket and shook a tassel into place. This loving care was certainly out of keeping with the fact that as soon as he had a garment off he flung it at once with a kind of unwilling jerk into the pit. The last thing left to him was his short sword with the sword belt. He drew it out of the scabbard, broke it, then gathered all together, the bits of the sword, the scabbard and the belt, and flung them so violently down that they clattered into the pit.

Now he stood naked there. The explorer bit his lips and said nothing. He knew very well what was going to happen, but he had no right to obstruct the officer in anything. If the judicial procedure which the officer cherished were really so near its end—possibly as a result of his own intervention, as to which he felt himself pledged—then the officer was doing the right thing; in his place the explorer would not have acted otherwise.

The soldier and the condemned man did not understand at first what was happening; at first they were not even looking on. The condemned man was gleeful at having got the handkerchiefs back, but he was not allowed to enjoy them for long, since the soldier snatched them with a sudden, unexpected grab. Now the condemned man in turn was trying to twitch them from under the belt where the soldier had tucked them, but the soldier was on his guard. So they were wrestling, half in jest. Only when the officer stood quite naked was their attention caught. The condemned man especially seemed struck with the notion that some great change was impending. What had happened to him was now going to happen to the officer. Perhaps even to the very end. Apparently the foreign explorer had given the order for it. So this was revenge. Although he himself had not suffered to the end, he was to be revenged to the end. A broad, silent grin now appeared on his face and stayed there all the rest of the time.

The officer, however, had turned to the machine. It had been clear enough previously that he understood the machine well, but now it was almost staggering to see how he managed it and how it obeyed him. His hand had only to approach the Harrow for it to rise and sink several times till it was adjusted to the right position for receiving him; he touched only the edge of the Bed and already it was vibrating; the felt gag came to meet his mouth, one could see that the officer was really reluctant to take it but he shrank from it only a moment, soon he submitted and received it. Everything was ready, only the straps hung down at the sides, yet they were obviously unnecessary, the officer did not need to be fastened down. Then the condemned man noticed the loose straps, in his opinion the execution was incomplete unless the straps were buckled, he gestured eagerly to the soldier and they ran together to strap the officer down. The latter had already stretched out one foot to push the lever that started the Designer; he saw the two men coming up; so he drew his foot back and let himself be buckled in. But now he could not reach the lever; neither the soldier nor the condemned man would be able to find it, and the explorer was determined not to lift a finger. It was not necessary; as soon as the straps were fastened the machine began to work; the Bed vibrated, the needles flickered above the skin, the Harrow rose and fell. The explorer had been staring at it quite a while before he remembered that a wheel in the Designer should have been creaking; but everything was quiet, not even the slightest hum could be heard.

Because it was working so silently the machine simply escaped one's attention. The explorer observed the soldier and the condemned man. The latter was the more animated of the two, everything in the machine interested him, now he was bending down and now stretching up on tiptoe, his forefinger was extended all the time pointing out details to the soldier. This annoyed the explorer. He was resolved to stay till the end, but he could not bear the sight of these two. "Go back home," he said. The soldier would have been willing enough, but the condemned man took the order as a punishment. With clasped hands he implored to be allowed to stay, and when the explorer shook his head

and would not relent, he even went down on his knees.
The explorer saw that it was no use merely giving orders; he was on the point of going over and driving them
away. At that moment he heard a noise above him in the
Designer. He looked up. Was that cogwheel going to
make trouble after all? But it was something quite different. Slowly the lid of the Designer rose up and then
clicked wide open. The teeth of a cogwheel showed
themselves and rose higher, soon the whole wheel was
visible; it was as if some enormous force were squeezing
the Designer so that there was no longer room for the
wheel; the wheel moved up till it came to the very edge
of the Designer, fell down, rolled along the sand a little
on its rim and then lay flat. But a second wheel was
already rising after it, followed by many others, large
and small and indistinguishably minute, the same thing
happened to all of them, at every moment one imagined
the Designer must now really be empty, but another
complex of numerous wheels was already rising into
sight, falling down, trundling along the sand and lying
flat. This phenomenon made the condemned man completely forget the explorer's command, the cogwheels
fascinated him, he was always trying to catch one and
at the same time urging the soldier to help, but always
drew back his hand in alarm, for another wheel always
came hopping along which, at least on its first advance,
scared him off.

The explorer, on the other hand, felt greatly troubled; the machine was obviously going to pieces; its
silent working was a delusion; he had a feeling that
he must now stand by the officer, since the officer was

no longer able to look after himself. But while the tumbling cogwheels absorbed his whole attention he had forgotten to keep an eye on the rest of the machine; now that the last cogwheel had left the Designer, however, he bent over the Harrow and had a new and still more unpleasant surprise. The Harrow was not writing, it was only jabbing, and the bed was not turning the body over but only bringing it up quivering against the needles. The explorer wanted to do something, if possible, to bring the whole machine to a standstill, for this was no exquisite torture such as the officer desired, this was plain murder. He stretched out his hands. But at that moment the Harrow rose with the body spitted on it and moved to the side, as it usually did only when the twelfth hour had come. Blood was flowing in a hundred streams, not mingled with water, the water jets too had failed to function. And now the last action failed to fulfil itself, the body did not drop off the long needles, streaming with blood it went on hanging over the pit without falling into it. The Harrow tried to move back to its old position, but as if it had itself noticed that it had not yet got rid of its burden it stuck after all where it was, over the pit. "Come and help!" cried the explorer to the other two, and himself seized the officer's feet. He wanted to push against the feet while the others seized the head from the opposite side and so the officer might be slowly eased off the needles. But the other two could not make up their minds to come; the condemned man actually turned away; the explorer had to go over to them and force them into position at the officer's head. And here, almost against

his will, he had to look at the face of the corpse. It was
as it had been in life; no sign was visible of the promised
redemption; what the others had found in the machine
the officer had not found; the lips were firmly pressed
together, the eyes were open, with the same expression
as in life, the look was calm and convinced, through the
forehead went the point of the great iron spike.

As the explorer, with the soldier and the condemned
man behind him, reached the first houses of the colony,
the soldier pointed to one of them and said: "There is
the teahouse."

In the ground floor of the house was a deep, low,
cavernous space, its walls and ceiling blackened with
smoke. It was open to the road all along its length. Although this teahouse was very little different from the
other houses of the colony, which were all very dilapidated, even up to the Commandant's palatial headquar-
ters, it made on the explorer the impression of a historic
tradition of some kind, and he felt the power of past
days. He went near to it, followed by his companions,
right up between the empty tables which stood in the
street before it, and breathed the cool, heavy air that
came from the interior. "The old man's buried here,"
said the soldier. "The priest wouldn't let him lie in the
churchyard. Nobody knew where to bury him for a
while, but in the end they buried him here. The officer
never told you about that, for sure, because of course
that's what he was most ashamed of. He even tried several times to dig the old man up by night, but he was
always chased away." "Where is the grave?" asked the

explorer, who found it impossible to believe the soldier. At once both of them, the soldier and the condemned man, ran before him pointing with outstretched hands in the direction where the grave should be. They led the explorer right up to the back wall, where guests were sitting at a few tables. They were apparently dock laborers, strong men with short, glistening, full black beards. None had a jacket, their shirts were torn, they were poor, humble creatures. As the explorer drew near, some of them got up, pressed close to the wall, and stared at him. "It's a foreigner," ran the whisper around him. "He wants to see the grave." They pushed one of the tables aside, and under it there was really a grave-stone. It was a simple stone, low enough to be covered by a table. There was an inscription on it in very small letters, the explorer had to kneel down to read it. This was what it said: "Here rests the old Commandant. His adherents, who now must be nameless, have dug this grave and set up this stone. There is a prophecy that after a certain number of years the Commandant will rise again and lead his adherents from this house to recover the colony. Have faith and wait!" When the explorer had read this and risen to his feet he saw all the bystanders around him smiling, as if they too had read the inscription, had found it ridiculous and were expecting him to agree with them. The explorer ignored this, distributed a few coins among them, waiting till the table was pushed over the grave again, quitted the teahouse and made for the harbor.

The soldier and the condemned man had found some acquaintances in the teahouse, who detained them. But they must have soon shaken them off, for the explorer was only halfway down the long flight of steps leading to the boats when they came rushing after him. Probably they wanted to force him at the last minute to take them with him. While he was bargaining below with a ferryman to row him to the steamer, the two of them came headlong down the steps, in silence, for they did not dare to shout. But by the time they reached the foot of the steps the explorer was already in the boat, and the ferryman was just casting off from the shore. They could have jumped into the boat, but the explorer lifted a heavy knotted rope from the floor boards, threatened them with it and so kept them from attempting the leap.

The Great Wall of China

THE GREAT WALL of China was finished off at its north ernmost corner. From the south-east and the south-west it came up in two sections that finally converged there. This principle of piecemeal construction was also applied on a smaller scale by both of the two great armies of labor, the eastern and the western. It was done in this way: gangs of some twenty workers were formed who had to accomplish a length, say, of five hundred yards of wall, while a similar gang built another stretch of the same length to meet the first. But after the junction had been made the construction of the wall was not carried on from the point, let us say, where this thousand yards ended; instead the two groups of workers were transferred to begin building again in quite different neighborhoods. Naturally in this way many great gaps were left, which were only filled in gradually and bit by bit, some, indeed, not till after the official announcement that the wall was finished. In fact it is said that there are gaps which have never been filled in at all, an assertion, however, which is probably merely one of the many legends to which the building of the wall gave rise, and which cannot be verified, at least by any single man with his own eyes and judgment, on account of the extent of the structure.

Now on first thoughts one might conceive that it would have been more advantageous in every way to build the wall continuously, or at least continuously within the two main divisions. After all the wall was intended, as was universally proclaimed and known, to be a protection against the peoples of the north. But how can a wall protect if it is not a continuous structure? Not only cannot such a wall protect, but what there is of it is in perpetual danger. These blocks of wall left standing in deserted regions could be easily pulled down again and again by the nomads, especially as these tribes, rendered apprehensive by the building operations, kept changing their encampments with incredible rapidity, like locusts, and so perhaps had a better general view of the progress of the wall than we, the builders. Nevertheless the task of construction probably could not have been carried out in any other way. To understand this we must take into account the following: The wall was to be a protection for centuries: accordingly the most scrupulous care in the building, the application of the architectural wisdom of all known ages and peoples, an unremitting sense of personal responsibility in the builders, were indispensable prerequisites for the work. True, for the more purely manual tasks ignorant day laborers from the populace, men, women and children who offered their services for good money, could be employed; but for the supervision even of every four day laborers an expert versed in the art of building was required, a man who was capable of entering into and feeling with all his heart what was involved. And the higher the task, the greater the responsibility. And such men were actually to be had, if not indeed so abundantly as the work of construction could have absorbed, yet in great numbers.

For the work had not been undertaken without thought. Fifty years before the first stone was laid the art of architecture, and especially that of masonry, had been proclaimed as the most important branch of knowledge throughout the whole area of a China that was to be walled round, and all other arts gained recognition only in so far as they had reference to it. I can still remember quite well us standing as small children, scarcely sure on our feet, in our teacher's garden, and being ordered to build a sort of wall out of pebbles; and then the teacher, girding up his robe, ran full tilt against the wall, of course knocking it down, and scolded us so terribly for the shoddiness of our work that we ran weeping in all directions to our parents. A trivial incident, but significant of the spirit of the time.

I was lucky inasmuch as the building of the wall was just beginning when, at twenty, I had passed the last examination of the lowest grade school. I say lucky, for many who before my time had achieved the highest degree of culture available to them could find nothing year after year to do with their knowledge, and drifted uselessly about with the most splendid architectural plans in their heads, and sank by thousands into hopelessness. But those who finally came to be employed in the work as supervisors, even though it might be of the lowest rank, were truly worthy of their task. They were

masons who had reflected much, and did not cease to
reflect, on the building of the wall, men who with the
first stone which they sank in the ground felt themselves a part of the wall. Masons of that kind, of course,
had not only a desire to perform their work in the most
thorough manner, but were also impatient to see the
wall finished in its complete perfection. Day laborers
have not this impatience, for they look only to their
wages, and the higher supervisors, indeed even the
supervisors of middle rank, could see enough of the manifold growth of the construction to keep their spirits
confident and high. But to encourage the subordinate
supervisors, intellectually so vastly superior to their apparently petty tasks, other measures must be taken. One
could not, for instance, expect them to lay one stone
on another for months or even years on end, in an
uninhabited mountainous region, hundreds of miles
from their homes; the hopelessness of such hard toil,
which yet could not reach completion even in the longest lifetime, would have cast them into despair and
above all made them less capable for the work. It was
for this reason that the system of piecemeal building
was decided on. Five hundred yards could be accomplished in about five years; by that time, however, the
supervisors were as a rule quite exhausted and had lost
all faith in themselves, in the wall, in the world. Accordingly, while they were still exalted by the jubilant
celebrations marking the completion of the thousand
yards of wall, they were sent far, far away, saw on their
journey finished sections of the wall rising here and
there, came past the quarters of the high command and

were presented with badges of honor, heard the re-
joicings of new armies of labor streaming past from
the depths of the land, saw forests being cut down to
become supports for the wall, saw mountains being
hewn into stones for the wall, heard at the holy shrines
hymns rising in which the pious prayed for the completion of the wall. All this assuaged their impatience. The
quiet life of their homes, where they rested some time,
strengthened them; the humble credulity with which
their reports were listened to, the confidence with which
the simple and peaceful burgher believed in the even-
tual completion of the wall, all this tightened up again
the cords of the soul. Like eternally hopeful children
they then said farewell to their homes; the desire once
more to labor on the wall of the nation became irresistible. They set off earlier than they needed; half
the village accompanied them for long distances. Groups
of people with banners and scarfs waving were on all
the roads; never before had they seen how great and
rich and beautiful and worthy of love their country was.
Every fellow-countryman was a brother for whom one
was building a wall of protection, and who would return lifelong thanks for it with all he had and did.
Unity! Unity! Shoulder to shoulder, a ring of brothers,
a current of blood no longer confined within the narrow
circulation of one body, but sweetly rolling and yet
ever returning throughout the endless leagues of China.

Thus, then, the system of piecemeal construction
becomes comprehensible; but there were still other
reasons for it as well. Nor is there anything odd in my
pausing over this question for so long; it is one of the

crucial problems in the whole building of the wall, unimportant as it may appear at first glance. If I am to con-
vey and make understandable the ideas and feelings of
that time I cannot go deeply enough into this very question.

First, then, it must be said that in those days things
were achieved scarcely inferior to the construction of
the Tower of Babel, although as regards divine approval, at least according to human reckoning, strongly
at variance with that work. I say this because during
the early days of building a scholar wrote a book in
which he drew the comparison in the most exhaustive
way. In it he tried to prove that the Tower of Babel
failed to reach its goal, not because of the reasons universally advanced, or at least that among those recognized reasons the most important of all was not to be
found. His proofs were drawn not merely from written
documents and reports; he also claimed to have made
enquiries on the spot, and to have discovered that the
tower failed and was bound to fail because of the weakness of the foundation. In this respect at any rate our
age was vastly superior to that ancient one. Almost every
educated man of our time was a mason by profession
and infallible in the matter of laying foundations. That,
however, was not what our scholar was concerned to
prove; for he maintained that the Great Wall alone
would provide for the first time in the history of mankind a secure foundation for a new Tower of Babel.
First the wall, therefore, and then the tower. His book
was in everybody's hands at that time, but I admit that
even today I cannot quite make out how he conceived

this tower. How could the wall, which did not form even a circle, but only a sort of quarter or half-circle, provide the foundation for a tower? That could obviously be meant only in a spiritual sense. But in that case why build the actual wall, which after all was something con-crete, the results of the lifelong labor of multitudes of people? And why were there in the book plans, some-what nebulous plans, it must be admitted, of the tower, and proposals worked out in detail for mobilizing the people's energies for the stupendous new work?

There were many wild ideas in people's heads at that time—this scholar's book is only one example—perhaps simply because so many were trying to join forces as far as they could for the achievement of a single aim. Human nature, essentially changeable, unstable as the dust, can endure no restraint; if it binds itself it soon begins to tear madly at its bonds, until it rends every-thing asunder, the wall, the bonds and its very self.

It is possible that these very considerations, which militated against the building of the wall at all, were not left out of account by the high command when the system of piecemeal construction was decided on. We—and here I speak in the name of many people—did not really know ourselves until we had carefully scruti-nized the decrees of the high command, when we dis-covered that without the high command neither our book learning nor our human understanding would have sufficed for the humble tasks which we performed in the great whole. In the office of the command—where it was and who sat there no one whom I have asked knew then or knows now—in that office one may be certain that all human thoughts and desires were revolved, and counter to them all human aims and fulfilments. And through the window the reflected splendors of divine worlds fell on the hands of the leaders as they traced their plans.

And for that reason the incorruptible observer must hold that the command, if it had seriously desired it, could also have overcome those difficulties which prevented a system of continuous construction. There remains, therefore, nothing but the conclusion that the command deliberately chose the system of piecemeal construction. But the piecemeal construction was only a makeshift and therefore inexpedient. Remains the conclusion that the command willed something inexpedient.—Strange conclusion!—True, and yet in one respect it has much to be said for it. One can perhaps safely discuss it now. In those days many people, and among them the best, had a secret maxim which ran: Try with all your might to comprehend the decrees of the high command, but only up to a certain point; then avoid further meditation. A very wise maxim, which moreover was elaborated in a parable that was later often quoted: Avoid further meditation, but not because it might be harmful; it is not at all certain that it would be harmful. What is harmful or not harmful has nothing to do with the question. Consider rather the river in spring. It rises until it grows mightier and nourishes more richly the soil on the long stretch of its banks, still maintaining its own course until it reaches the sea, where it is all the more welcome because it is a worthier ally.—Thus far may you urge your meditations on the decrees of the high command.—But after that the river overflows its banks, loses outline and shape, slows down the speed of its current, tries to ignore its destiny by forming little seas in the interior of the land, damages the fields, and yet cannot maintain itself for long in its new expanse, but must run back between its banks again, must even dry up wretchedly in the hot season that presently follows.—Thus far may you not urge your meditations on the decrees of the high command.

Now though this parable may have had extraordinary point and force during the building of the wall, it has at most only a restricted relevance for my present essay. My enquiry is purely historical; no lightning flashes any longer from the long since vanished thunderclouds, and so I may venture to seek for an explanation of the system of piecemeal construction which goes farther than the one that contented people then. The limits which my capacity for thought imposes upon me are narrow enough, but the province to be traversed here is infinite. Against whom was the Great Wall to serve as a protection? Against the people of the north. Now, I come from the south-east of China. No northern people can menace us there. We read of them in the books of the ancients; the cruelties which they commit in accordance with their nature make us sigh beneath our peaceful trees. The faithful representations of the artist show us these faces of the damned, their gaping mouths, their jaws furnished with great pointed teeth, their half-shut eyes that already seem to be seeking out the victim which their jaws will rend and devour. When our children are unruly we show them these pictures, and at once they fly weeping into our arms. But nothing more than that do we know about these northerners. We have not seen them, and if we remain in our villages we shall never see them, even if on their wild horses they should ride as hard as they can straight towards us—the land is too vast and would not let them reach us, they would end their course in the empty air.

Why, then, since that is so, did we leave our homes, the stream with its bridges, our mothers and fathers, our weeping wives, our children who needed our care, and depart for the distant city to be trained there, while our thoughts journeyed still farther away to the wall in the north? Why? A question for the high command. Our leaders know us. They, absorbed in gigantic anxieties, know of us, know our petty pursuits, see us sitting together in our humble huts, and approve or disapprove the evening prayer which the father of the house recites in the midst of his family. And if I may be allowed to express such ideas about the high command, then I must say that in my opinion the high command has existed from old time, and was not assembled, say, like a gathering of mandarins summoned hastily to discuss somebody's fine dream in a conference as hastily terminated, so that that very evening the people are drummed out of their beds to carry out what has been decided, even if it should be nothing but an illumination in honor of a god who may have shown great favor to their masters the day before, only to drive them into some dark corner with cudgel blows tomorrow, almost before the illuminations have died down. Far rather do I believe that the high command has existed from all eternity, and the decision to build the wall likewise. Unwitting peoples of the north, who imagined they were the cause of it! Honest, unwitting Emperor, who imagined he decreed it! We builders of the wall know that it was not so and hold our tongues.

* * *

During the building of the wall and ever since to this very day I have occupied myself almost exclusively with the comparative history of races—there are certain questions which one can probe to the marrow, as it were, only by this method—and I have discovered that we Chinese possess certain folk and political institutions that are unique in their clarity, others again unique in their obscurity. The desire to trace the causes of these phenomena, especially the latter, has always teased me and teases me still, and the building of the wall is itself essentially involved with these problems.

Now one of the most obscure of our institutions is that of the empire itself. In Pekin, naturally, at the imperial court, there is some clarity to be found on this subject, though even that is more illusive than real. Also the teachers of political law and history in the high schools claim to be exactly informed on these matters, and to be capable of passing on their knowledge to their students. The further one descends among the lower schools the more, naturally enough, does one find teachers' and pupils' doubts of their own knowledge vanishing, and superficial culture mounting sky-high round a few precepts that have been drilled into people's minds for centuries, precepts which, though they have lost nothing of their eternal truth, remain eternally invisible in this fog of confusion.

But it is precisely this question of the empire which in my opinion the common people should be asked to answer, since after all they are the empire's final support. Here, I must confess, I can only speak once more for my native place. Except for the nature gods and their ritual, which fills the whole year in such beautiful and rich alternation, we think only about the Emperor. But not about the present one; or rather we would think about the present one if we knew who he was or knew anything definite about him. True—and it is the sole curiosity that fills us—we are always trying to get information on this subject, but, strange as it may sound, it is almost impossible to discover anything, either from pilgrims, though they have wandered through many lands, or from near or distant villages, or from sailors, though they have navigated not only our little stream, but also the sacred rivers. One hears a great many things, true, but can gather nothing definite.

So vast is our land that no fable could do justice to its vastness, the heavens can scarcely span it—and Pekin is only a dot in it, and the imperial palace less than a dot. The Emperor as such, on the other hand, is mighty throughout all the hierarchies of the world: admitted. But the existent Emperor, a man like us, lies much like us on a couch which is of generous proportions, perhaps, and yet very possibly may be quite narrow and short. Like us he sometimes stretches himself and when he is very tired yawns with his delicately cut mouth. But

how should we know anything about that—thousands
of miles away in the South—almost on the borders of the
Tibetan Highlands? And besides, any tidings, even if
they did reach us, would arrive far too late, would
have become obsolete long before they reached us. The
Emperor is always surrounded by a brilliant and yet
ambiguous throng of nobles and courtiers—malice and
enmity in the guise of servants and friends—who form
a counter-weight to the Imperial power and perpetually
labor to unseat the ruler from his place with poisoned
arrows. The Empire is immortal, but the Emperor himself totters and falls from his throne, yes, whole dynasties
sink in the end and breathe their last in one death-rattle.
Of these struggles and sufferings the people will never
know; like tardy arrivals, like strangers in a city, they
stand at the end of some densely thronged side street
peacefully munching the food they have brought with
them, while far away in front, in the market square at
the heart of the city, the execution of their ruler is
proceeding.

There is a parable that describes this situation very
well: The Emperor, so it runs, has sent a message to
you, the humble subject, the insignificant shadow cow-
ering in the remotest distance before the imperial sun;
the Emperor from his death-bed has sent a message to
you alone. He has commanded the messenger to kneel
down by the bed, and has whispered the message to him;
so much store did he lay on it that he ordered the messenger to whisper it back into his ear again. Then by
a nod of the head he has confirmed that it is right. Yes,
before the assembled spectators of his death—all the

obstructing walls have been broken down, and on the spacious and loftily mounting open staircases stand in a ring the great princes of the Empire—before all these he has delivered his message. The messenger immediately sets out on his journey; a powerful, an indefatigable man, now pushing with his right arm, now with his left, he cleaves a way for himself through the throng; if he encounters resistance he points to his breast, where the symbol of the sun glitters; the way, too, is made easier for him than it would be for any other man. But the multitudes are so vast; their numbers have no end. If he could reach the open fields, how fast he would fly, and soon doubtless you would hear the welcome hammering of his fists on your door. But instead how vainly does he wear out his strength; still he is only making his way through the chambers of the innermost palace; never will he get to the end of them; and if he succeeded in that nothing would be gained; he must fight his way next down the stair; and if he succeeded in that nothing would be gained; the courts would still have to be crossed; and after the courts the second outer palace; and once more stairs and courts; and once more another palace; and so on for thousands of years; and if at last he should burst through the outermost gate—but never, never can that happen—the imperial capital would lie before him, the center of the world, crammed to bursting with its own refuse. Nobody could fight his way through here even with a message from a dead man.—But you sit at your window when evening falls and dream it to yourself.

Just so, as hopelessly and as hopefully, do our people

regard the Emperor. They do not know what emperor is reigning, and there exist doubts regarding even the name of the dynasty. In school a great deal is taught about the dynasties with the dates of succession, but the universal uncertainty in this matter is so great that even the best scholars are drawn into it. Long-dead emperors are set on the throne in our villages, and one that only lives in song recently had a proclamation of his read out by the priest before the altar. Battles that are old history are new to us, and one's neighbor rushes in with a jubilant face to tell the news. The wives of the emperors, pampered and overweening, seduced from noble custom by wily courtiers, swelling with ambition, vehement in their greed, uncontrollable in their lust, practise their abominations ever anew. The more deeply they are buried in time the more glaring are the colors in which their deeds are painted, and with a loud cry of woe our village eventually hears how an Empress drank her husband's blood in long draughts thousands of years ago.

Thus, then, do our people deal with departed emperors, but the living ruler they confuse among the dead. If once, only once in a man's lifetime, an imperial official on his tour of the provinces should arrive by chance at our village, make certain announcements in the name of the government, scrutinize the tax lists, examine the school children, enquire of the priest regarding our doings and affairs, and then, before he steps into his litter, should sum up his impressions in verbose admonitions to the assembled commune—then a smile flits over every face, each man throws a stolen glance at his neighbor, and bends over his children so as not to be observed by the official. Why, they think to themselves, he's speaking of a dead man as if he were alive, this Emperor of his died long ago, the dynasty is blotted out, the good official is having his joke with us, but we will behave as if we did not notice it, so as not to offend him. But we shall obey in earnest no one but our present ruler, for not to do so would be a crime. And behind the departing litter of the official there rises in might as ruler of the village some figure fortuitously exalted from an urn already crumbled to dust.

Similarly our people are but little affected by revolutions in the state or contemporary wars. I recall an incident in my youth. A revolt had broken out in a neighboring, but yet quite distant, province. What caused it I can no longer remember, nor is it of any importance now; occasions for revolt can be found there any day; the people are an excitable people. Well, one day a leaflet published by the rebels was brought to my father's house by a beggar who had crossed that province. It happened to be a feast day, our rooms were filled with guests, the priest sat in the chief place and studied the sheet. Suddenly everybody started to laugh; in the confusion the sheet was torn; the beggar, who however had already received abundant alms, was driven out of the room with blows, the guests dispersed to enjoy the beautiful day. Why? The dialect of this neighboring province differs in some essential respects from ours, and this difference occurs also in certain turns of the written speech, which for us have an archaic character. Hardly had the priest read out two lines before we had already come to our decision. Ancient history told long ago, old sorrows long since healed. And though —so it seems to me in recollection—the gruesomeness of the living present was irrefutably conveyed by the beggar's words, we laughed and shook our heads and refused to listen any longer. So eager are our people to obliterate the present.

If from such appearances any one should draw the conclusion that in reality we have no Emperor, he would not be far from the truth. Over and over again it must be repeated: There is perhaps no people more faithful to the Emperor than ours in the south, but the Emperor derives no advantage from our fidelity. True, the sacred dragon stands on the little column at the end of our village, and ever since the beginning of human memory it has breathed out its fiery breath in the direction of Pekin in token of homage—but Pekin itself is far stranger to the people in our village than the next world. Can there really be a village where the houses stand side by side, covering all the fields for a greater distance than one can see from our hills, and can there be dense crowds of people packed between these houses day and night? We find it more difficult to picture such a city than to believe that Pekin and its Emperor are one, a cloud, say, peacefully voyaging beneath the sun in the course of the ages.

Now the result of holding such opinions is a life on the whole free and unconstrained. By no means immoral, however; hardly ever have I found in my travels such pure morals as in my native village. But yet a life that is subject to no contemporary law, and attends only to the exhortations and warnings which come to us from olden times.

I guard against large generalizations, and do not assert that in all the countless villages in my province it is so, far less in all the five hundred provinces of China. Yet perhaps I may venture to assert on the basis of the many writings on this subject which I have read, as well as from my own observation—the building of the wall in particular, with its abundance of human material, provided a man of sensibility with the opportunity of traversing the souls of almost all the provinces—on the basis of all this, then, perhaps I may venture to assert that the prevailing attitude to the Emperor shows persistently and universally something fundamentally in common with that of our village. Now I have no wish whatever to represent this attitude as a virtue; on the contrary. True, the essential responsibility for it lies with the government, which in the most ancient empire in the world has not yet succeeded in developing, or has neglected to develop, the institution of the empire to such precision that its workings extend directly and unceasingly to the farthest frontiers of the land. On the other hand, however, there is also involved a certain feebleness of faith and imaginative power on the part of the people that prevents them from raising the empire out of its stagnation in Pekin and clasping it in all its palpable living reality to their own breasts, which yet desire nothing better than but once to feel that touch and then to die.

This attitude then is certainly no virtue. All the more remarkable is it that this very weakness should seem to be one of the greatest unifying influences among our people; indeed, if one may dare to use the expression, the very ground on which we live. To set about establishing a fundamental defect here would mean undermining not only our consciences, but, what is far worse, our feet. And for that reason I shall not proceed any further at this stage with my enquiry into these questions.

A Country Doctor

I was in great perplexity; I had to start on an urgent journey; a seriously ill patient was waiting for me in a village ten miles off; a thick blizzard of snow filled all the wide spaces between him and me; I had a gig, a light gig with big wheels, exactly right for our country roads; muffled in furs, my bag of instruments in my hand, I was in the courtyard all ready for the journey; but there was no horse to be had, no horse. My own horse had died in the night, worn out by the fatigues of this icy winter; my servant girl was now running round the village trying to borrow a horse; but it was hopeless, I knew it, and I stood there forlornly, with the snow gathering more and more thickly upon me, more and more unable to move. In the gateway the girl appeared, alone, and waved the lantern; of course, who would lend a horse at this time for such a journey? I strode through the courtyard once more; I could see no way out; in my confused distress I kicked at the dilapidated door of the year-long uninhabited pigsty. It flew open and flapped to and fro on its hinges. A steam and smell as of horses came out from it. A dim stable lantern was swinging inside from a rope. A man, crouching on his

hams in that low space, showed an open blue-eyed face.
"Shall I yoke up?" he asked, crawling out on all fours. I
did not know what to say and merely stooped down to
see what else was in the sty. The servant girl was standing beside me. "You never know what you're going to
find in your own house," she said, and we both laughed.
"Hey there, Brother, hey there, Sister!" called the
groom, and two horses, enormous creatures with powerful flanks, one after the other, their legs tucked close
to their bodies, each well-shaped head lowered like a
camel's, by sheer strength of buttocking squeezed out
through the door hole which they filled entirely. But
at once they were standing up, their legs long and their
bodies steaming thickly. "Give him a hand," I said, and
the willing girl hurried to help the groom with the
harnessing. Yet hardly was she beside him when the
groom clipped hold of her and pushed his face against
hers. She screamed and fled back to me; on her cheek
stood out in red the marks of two rows of teeth. "You
brute," I yelled in fury, "do you want a whipping?" but
in the same moment reflected that the man was a
stranger; that I did not know where he came from,
and that of his own free will he was helping me out
when everyone else had failed me. As if he knew my
thoughts he took no offense at my threat but, still busied
with the horses, only turned round once towards me.
"Get in," he said then, and indeed everything was
ready. A magnificent pair of horses, I observed, such as
I had never sat behind, and I climbed in happily. "But
I'll drive, you don't know the way," I said. "Of course,"
said he, "I'm not coming with you anyway, I'm staying

with Rose." "No," shrieked Rose, fleeing into the house
with a justified presentiment that her fate was inescapa-
ble; I heard the door chain rattle as she put it up; I
heard the key turn in the lock; I could see, moreover,
how she put out the lights in the entrance hall and in
further flight all through the rooms to keep herself from
being discovered. "You're coming with me," I said to
the groom, "or I won't go, urgent as my journey is. I'm
not thinking of paying for it by handing the girl over to
you." "Gee up!" he said; clapped his hands; the gig
whirled off like a log in a freshet; I could just hear the
door of my house splitting and bursting as the groom
charged at it and then I was deafened and blinded by
a storming rush that steadily buffeted all my senses. But
this only for a moment, since, as if my patient's farm-
yard had opened out just before my courtyard gate,
I was already there; the horses had come quietly to
a standstill; the blizzard had stopped; moonlight all
around; my patient's parents hurried out of the house,
his sister behind them; I was almost lifted out of the
gig; from their confused ejaculations I gathered not a
word; in the sickroom the air was almost unbreathable;
the neglected stove was smoking; I wanted to push
open a window; but first I had to look at my patient.
Gaunt, without any fever, not cold, not warm, with
vacant eyes, without a shirt, the youngster heaved himself up from under the feather bedding, threw his arms
round my neck, and whispered in my ear: "Doctor,
let me die." I glanced round the room; no one had
heard it; the parents were leaning forward in silence
waiting for my verdict; the sister had set a chair for my

handbag; I opened the bag and hunted among my instruments; the boy kept clutching at me from his bed
to remind me of his entreaty; I picked up a pair of
tweezers, examined them in the candlelight and laid
them down again. "Yes," I thought blasphemously, "in
cases like this the gods are helpful, send the missing
horse, add to it a second because of the urgency, and to
crown everything bestow even a groom—" And only now
did I remember Rose again; what was I to do, how could
I rescue her, how could I pull her away from under that
groom at ten miles' distance, with a team of horses I
couldn't control. These horses, now, they had somehow slipped the reins loose, pushed the windows open
from outside, I did not know how; each of them had
stuck a head in at a window and, quite unmoved by the
startled cries of the family, stood eyeing the patient.
"Better go back at once," I thought, as if the horses
were summoning me to the return journey, yet I permitted the patient's sister, who fancied that I was dazed
by the heat, to take my fur coat from me. A glass of rum
was poured out for me, the old man clapped me on the
shoulder, a familiarity justified by this offer of his treas-
ure. I shook my head; in the narrow confines of the old
man's thoughts I felt ill; that was my only reason for
refusing the drink. The mother stood by the bedside
and cajoled me towards it; I yielded, and, while one of
the horses whinnied loudly to the ceiling, laid my head
to the boy's breast, which shivered under my wet beard.
I confirmed what I already knew; the boy was quite
sound, something a little wrong with his circulation,
saturated with coffee by his solicitous mother, but sound

and best turned out of bed with one shove. I am no
world reformer and so I let him lie. I was the district
doctor and did my duty to the uttermost, to the point
where it became almost too much. I was badly paid and
yet generous and helpful to the poor. I had still to see
that Rose was all right, and then the boy might have
his way and I wanted to die too. What was I doing there
in that endless winter! My horse was dead, and not a
single person in the village would lend me another. I
had to get my team out of the pigsty; if they hadn't
chanced to be horses I should have had to travel with
swine. That was how it was. And I nodded to the family.
They knew nothing about it, and, had they known,
would not have believed it. To write prescriptions is
easy, but to come to an understanding with people is
hard. Well, this should be the end of my visit, I had
once more been called out needlessly, I was used to that,
the whole district made my life a torment with my night
bell, but that I should have to sacrifice Rose this time as
well, the pretty girl who had lived in my house for years
almost without my noticing her—that sacrifice was too
much to ask, and I had somehow to get it reasoned out
in my head with the help of what craft I could muster,
in order not to let fly at this family, which with the best
will in the world could not restore Rose to me. But as
I shut my bag and put an arm out for my fur coat, the
family meanwhile standing together, the father sniffing
at the glass of rum in his hand, the mother, apparently
disappointed in me—why, what do people expect?—
biting her lips with tears in her eyes, the sister fluttering
a blood-soaked towel, I was somehow ready to admit

conditionally that the boy might be ill after all. I went
towards him, he welcomed me smiling as if I were bringing him the most nourishing invalid broth—ah, now
both horses were whinnying together; the noise, I suppose, was ordained by heaven to assist my examination
of the patient—and this time I discovered that the boy
was indeed ill. In his right side, near the hip, was an
open wound as big as the palm of my hand. Rose-red, in
many variations of shade, dark in the hollows, lighter
at the edges, softly granulated, with irregular clots of
blood, open as a surface mine to the daylight. That
was how it looked from a distance. But on a closer inspection there was another complication. I could not
help a low whistle of surprise. Worms, as thick and as
long as my little finger, themselves rose-red and blood-
spotted as well, were wriggling from their fastness in
the interior of the wound towards the light, with small
white heads and many little legs. Poor boy, you were
past helping. I had discovered your great wound; this
blossom in your side was destroying you. The family
was pleased; they saw me busying myself; the sister told
the mother, the mother the father, the father told several guests who were coming in, through the moonlight at the open door, walking on tiptoe, keeping their
balance with outstretched arms. "Will you save me?"
whispered the boy with a sob, quite blinded by the
life within his wound. That is what people are like in
my district. Always expecting the impossible from the
doctor. They have lost their ancient beliefs; the parson
sits at home and unravels his vestments, one after another; but the doctor is supposed to be omnipotent

with his merciful surgeon's hand. Well, as it pleases them; I have not thrust my services on them; if they misuse me for sacred ends, I let that happen to me too; what better do I want, old country doctor that I am, bereft of my servant girl! And so they came, the family and the village elders, and stripped my clothes off me; a school choir with the teacher at the head of it stood before the house and sang these words to an utterly simple tune:

> Strip his clothes off, then he'll heal us,
> If he doesn't, kill him dead!
> Only a doctor, only a doctor.

Then my clothes were off and I looked at the people quietly, my fingers in my beard and my head cocked to one side. I was altogether composed and equal to the situation and remained so, although it was no help to me, since they now took me by the head and feet and carried me to the bed. They laid me down in it next to the wall, on the side of the wound. Then they all left the room; the door was shut; the singing stopped; clouds covered the moon; the bedding was warm around me; the horses' heads in the open windows wavered like shadows. "Do you know," said a voice in my ear, "I have very little confidence in you. Why, you were only blown in here, you didn't come on your own feet. Instead of helping me, you're cramping me on my deathbed. What I'd like best is to scratch your eyes out." "Right," I said, "it is a shame. And yet I am a doctor. What am I to do? Believe me, it is not

too easy for me either." "Am I supposed to be content
with this apology? Oh, I must be, I can't help it. I always have to put up with things. A fine wound is all I
brought into the world; that was my sole endowment."
"My young friend," said I, "your mistake is: you have
not a wide enough view. I have been in all the sick-
rooms, far and wide, and I tell you: your wound is not
so bad. Done in a tight corner with two strokes of the
ax. Many a one proffers his side and can hardly hear
the ax in the forest, far less that it is coming nearer to
him." "Is that really so, or are you deluding me in my
fever?" "It is really so, take the word of honor of an official doctor." And he took it and lay still. But now it
was time for me to think of escaping. The horses were
still standing faithfully in their places. My clothes, my
fur coat, my bag were quickly collected; I didn't want
to waste time dressing; if the horses raced home as they
had come, I should only be springing, as it were, out of
this bed into my own. Obediently a horse backed away
from the window; I threw my bundle into the gig; the
fur coat missed its mark and was caught on a hook only
by the sleeve. Good enough. I swung myself onto the
horse. With the reins loosely trailing, one horse barely
fastened to the other, the gig swaying behind, my fur
coat last of all in the snow. "Gee up!" I said, but there
was no galloping; slowly, like old men, we crawled
through the snowy wastes; a long time echoed behind
us the new but faulty song of the children:

> O be joyful, all you patients,
> The doctor's laid in bed beside you!

Never shall I reach home at this rate; my flourishing practice is done for; my successor is robbing me, but in vain, for he cannot take my place; in my house the disgusting groom is raging; Rose is his victim; I do not want to think about it any more. Naked, exposed to the frost of this most unhappy of ages, with an earthly vehicle, unearthly horses, old man that I am, I wander astray. My fur coat is hanging from the back of the gig, but I cannot reach it, and none of my limber pack of patients lifts a finger. Betrayed! Betrayed! A false alarm on the night bell once answered—it cannot be made good, not ever.

A Common Confusion

A COMMON EXPERIENCE, resulting in a common confusion. A has to transact important business with B in H. He goes to H for a preliminary interview, accomplishes the journey there in ten minutes, and the journey back in the same time, and on returning boasts to his family of his expedition. Next day he goes again to H, this time to settle his business finally. As that by all appearances will require several hours, A leaves very early in the morning. But although all the accessory circumstances, at least in A's estimation, are exactly the same as the day before, it takes him ten hours this time to reach H. When he arrives there quite exhausted in the evening he is informed that B, annoyed at his absence, had left half an hour before to go to A's village, and that they must have passed each other on the road. A is advised to wait. But in his anxiety about his business he sets off at once and hurries home.

This time he achieves the journey, without paying any particular attention to the fact, exactly in a second. At home he learns that B had arrived quite early, immediately after A's departure, indeed that he had met A on the threshold and reminded him of his business;

but A had replied that he had no time to spare, he must go at once.

In spite of this incomprehensible behavior of A, however, B had stayed on to wait for A's return. It is true, he had asked several times whether A was not back yet, but he was still sitting up in A's room. Overjoyed at the opportunity of seeing B at once and explaining everything to him, A rushes upstairs. He is almost at the top, when he stumbles, twists a sinew, and almost fainting with the pain, incapable even of uttering a cry, only able to moan faintly in the darkness, he hears B—impossible to tell whether at a great distance or quite near him—stamping down the stairs in a violent rage and vanishing for good.

The New Advocate

WE HAVE a new advocate, Dr. Bucephalus. There is lit.
tle in his appearance to remind you that he was once
Alexander of Macedon's battle charger. Of course, if
you know his story, you are aware of something. But
even a simple usher whom I saw the other day on the
front steps of the Law Courts, a man with the professional appraisal of the regular small punter in a race-
course, was running an admiring eye over the advocate
as he mounted the marble steps with a high action that
made them ring beneath his feet.

In general the Bar approves the admission of
Bucephalus. With astonishing insight people tell themselves that, modern society being what it is, Bucephalus is in a difficult position, and therefore, considering
also his importance in the history of the world, he deserves at least a friendly reception. Nowadays—it can
not be denied—there is no Alexander the Great. There
are plenty of men who know how to murder people;
the skill needed to reach over a banqueting table and
pink a friend with a lance is not lacking; and for many
Macedonia is too confining, so that they curse Philip,
the father—but no one, no one at all, can blaze a trail

to India. Even in his day the gates of India were beyond reach, yet the King's sword pointed the way to them. Today the gates have receded to remoter and loftier places; no one points the way; many carry swords, but only to brandish them, and the eye that tries to follow them is confused.

So perhaps it is really best to do as Bucephalus has done and absorb oneself in law books. In the quiet lamplight, his flanks unhampered by the thighs of a rider, free and far from the clamor of battle, he reads and turns the pages of our ancient tomes.

An Old Manuscript

It looks as if much had been neglected in our country's system of defense. We have not concerned ourselves with it until now and have gone about our daily work; but things that have been happening recently begin to trouble us.

I have a cobbler's workshop in the square that lies before the Emperor's palace. Scarcely have I taken my shutters down, at the first glimmer of dawn, when I see armed soldiers already posted in the mouth of every street opening on the square. But these soldiers are not ours, they are obviously nomads from the North. In some way that is incomprehensible to me they have pushed right into the capital, although it is a long way from the frontier. At any rate, here they are; it seems that every morning there are more of them.

As is their nature, they camp under the open sky, for they abominate dwelling houses. They busy themselves sharpening swords, whittling arrows and practicing horsemanship. This peaceful square, which was always kept so scrupulously clean, they have made literally into a stable. We do try every now and then to run out of our shops and clear away at least the worst of the filth, but this happens less and less often, for the labor is in vain and brings us besides into danger of falling under the hoofs of the wild horses or of being crippled with lashes from the whips.

Speech with the nomads is impossible. They do not know our language, indeed they hardly have a language of their own. They communicate with each other much as jackdaws do. A screeching as of jackdaws is always in our ears. Our way of living and our institutions they neither understand nor care to understand. And so they are unwilling to make sense even out of our sign language. You can gesture at them till you dislocate your jaws and your wrists and still they will not have understood you and will never understand. They often make grimaces; then the whites of their eyes turn up and foam gathers on their lips, but they do not mean anything by that, not even a threat; they do it because it is their nature to do it. Whatever they need, they take. You cannot call it taking by force. They grab at something and you simply stand aside and leave them to it.

From my stock, too, they have taken many good articles. But I cannot complain when I see how the butcher, for instance, suffers across the street. As soon as he brings in any meat the nomads snatch it all from him and gobble it up. Even their horses devour flesh; often enough a horseman and his horse are lying side by side, both of them gnawing at the same joint, one at either end. The butcher is nervous and does not care to stop his deliveries of meat. We understand that, however, and subscribe money to keep him going. If the nomads got no meat, who knows what they might think of doing; who knows anyhow what they may think of, even though they get meat every day.

Not long ago the butcher thought he might at least spare himself the trouble of slaughtering, and so one morning he brought along a live ox. But he will never dare to do that again. I lay for a whole hour flat on the floor at the back of my workshop with my head muffled in all the clothes and rugs and pillows I had, simply to keep from hearing the bellowing of that ox, which the nomads were leaping on from all sides, tearing morsels out of its living flesh with their teeth. It had been quiet for a long time before I risked coming out; they were lying overcome round the remains of the carcass like drunkards round a wine cask.

This was the occasion when I fancied I actually saw the Emperor himself at a window of the palace; usually he never enters these outer rooms but spends all his time in the innermost garden; yet on this occasion he was standing, or so at least it seemed to me, at one of the windows, watching with bent head the goings on before his residence.

"What is going to happen?" we all ask ourselves. "How long can we endure this burden and torment? The Emperor's palace has drawn the nomads here but does not know how to drive them away again. The gate stays shut; the guards, who used to be always marching out and in with ceremony, keep close behind barred windows. It is left to us artisans and tradesmen to save our country; but we are not equal to such a task; nor have we ever claimed to be capable of it. This is a misunderstanding of some kind; and it will be the ruin of us."

A Fratricide

The evidence shows that this is how the murder was committed:

Schmar, the murderer, took up his post about nine o'clock one night in clear moonlight by the corner where Wese, his victim, had to turn from the street where his office was into the street he lived in.

The night air was shivering cold. Yet Schmar was wearing only a thin blue suit; the jacket was unbuttoned, too. He felt no cold; besides, he was moving about all the time. His weapon, half a bayonet and half a kitchen knife, he kept firmly in his grasp, quite naked. He looked at the knife against the light of the moon; the blade glittered; not enough for Schmar; he struck it against the bricks of the pavement till the sparks flew; regretted that, perhaps; and to repair the damage drew it like a violin bow across his boot sole while he bent forward, standing on one leg, and listened both to the whetting of the knife on his boot and for any sound out of the fateful side street.

Why did Pallas, the private citizen who was watching it all from his window near by in the second story, permit it to happen? Unriddle the mysteries of human nature! With his collar turned up, his dressing gown girt round his portly body, he stood looking down, shaking his head.

And five houses farther along, on the opposite side of the street, Mrs. Wese, with a fox-fur coat over her nightgown, peered out to look for her husband who was lingering unusually late tonight.

At last there rang out the sound of the doorbell before Wese's office, too loud for a doorbell, right over the town and up to heaven, and Wese, the industrious nightworker, issued from the building, still invisible in that street, only heralded by the sound of the bell; at once the pavement registered his quiet footsteps.

Pallas bent far forward; he dared not miss anything. Mrs. Wese, reassured by the bell, shut her window with a clatter. But Schmar knelt down; since he had no other parts of his body bare, he pressed only his face and his hands against the pavement; where everything else was freezing, Schmar was glowing hot.

At the very corner dividing the two streets Wese paused; only his walking stick came round into the other street to support him. A sudden whim. The night sky invited him, with its dark blue and its gold. Unknowing, he gazed up at it, unknowing he lifted his hat and stroked his hair; nothing up there drew together in a pattern to interpret the immediate future for him; everything stayed in its senseless, inscrutable place. In itself it was a highly reasonable action that Wese should walk on, but he walked on to Schmar's knife.

"Wese!" shrieked Schmar, standing on tiptoe, his arm outstretched, the knife sharply lowered, "Wese!

You will never see Julia again!" And right into the throat and left into the throat and a third time deep into the belly stabbed Schmar's knife. Water rats, slit open, give out such a sound as came from Wese.

"Done," said Schmar, and pitched the knife, now superfluous blood-stained ballast, against the nearest house front. "The bliss of murder! The relief, the soaring ecstasy from the shedding of another's blood! Wese, old nightbird, friend, alehouse crony, you are oozing away into the dark earth below the street. Why aren't you simply a bladder of blood so that I could stamp on you and make you vanish into nothingness? Not all we want comes true, not all the dreams that blossomed have borne fruit; your solid remains lie here, already indifferent to every kick. What's the good of the dumb question you are asking?"

Pallas, choking on the poison in his body, stood at the double-leafed door of his house as it flew open. "Schmar! Schmar! I saw it all, I missed nothing." Pallas and Schmar scrutinized each other. The result of the scrutiny satisfied Pallas; Schmar came to no conclusion.

Mrs. Wese, with a crowd of people on either side, came rushing up, her face grown quite old with the shock. Her fur coat swung open, she collapsed on top of Wese; the nightgowned body belonged to Wese, the fur coat spreading over the couple like the smooth turf of a grave belonged to the crowd.

Schmar, fighting down with difficulty the last of his nausea, pressed his mouth against the shoulder of the policeman who, stepping lightly, led him away.

A Report to an Academy

Honored Members of the Academy!

You have done me the honor of inviting me to give your Academy an account of the life I formerly led as an ape.

I regret that I cannot comply with your request to the extent you desire. It is now nearly five years since I was an ape, a short space of time, perhaps, according to the calendar, but an infinitely long time to gallop through at full speed, as I have done, more or less accompanied by excellent mentors, good advice, applause and orchestral music, and yet essentially alone, since all my escorters, to keep the image, kept well off the course. I could never have achieved what I have done had I been stubbornly set on clinging to my origins, to the remembrances of my youth. In fact, to give up being stubborn was the supreme commandment I laid upon myself; free ape as I was, I submitted myself to that yoke. In revenge, however, my memory of the past has closed the door against me more and more. I could have returned at first, had human beings allowed it, through an archway as wide as the span of heaven over the earth, but as I spurred myself on in my forced ca-

reer, the opening narrowed and shrank behind me; I
felt more comfortable in the world of men and fitted it
better; the strong wind that blew after me out of my
past began to slacken; today it is only a gentle puff of
air that plays around my heels; and the opening in the
distance, through which it comes and through which I
once came myself, has grown so small that, even if my
strength and my will power sufficed to get me back to
it, I should have to scrape the very skin from my body
to crawl through. To put it plainly, much as I like expressing myself in images, to put it plainly: your life
as apes, gentlemen, insofar as something of that kind
lies behind you, cannot be farther removed from you
than mine is from me. Yet everyone on earth feels a
tickling at the heels; the small chimpanzee and the great
Achilles alike.

But to a lesser extent I can perhaps meet your demand, and indeed I do so with the greatest pleasure.
The first thing I learned was to give a handshake; a
handshake betokens frankness; well, today, now that I
stand at the very peak of my career, I hope to add frankness in words to the frankness of that first handshake.
What I have to tell the Academy will contribute nothing essentially new, and will fall far behind what you
have asked of me and what with the best will in the
world I cannot communicate—none the less, it should
indicate the line an erstwhile ape has had to follow in
entering and establishing himself in the world of men.
Yet I could not risk putting into words even such insignificant information as I am going to give you if I were
not quite sure of myself and if my position on all the

great variety stages of the civilized world had not become quite unassailable.

I belong to the Gold Coast. For the story of my capture I must depend on the evidence of others. A hunting expedition sent out by the firm of Hagenbeck—by the way, I have drunk many a bottle of good red wine since then with the leader of that expedition—had taken up its position in the bushes by the shore when I came down for a drink at evening among a troop of apes. They shot at us; I was the only one that was hit; I was hit in two places.

Once in the cheek; a slight wound; but it left a large, naked, red scar which earned me the name of Red Peter, a horrible name, utterly inappropriate, which only some ape could have thought of, as if the only difference between me and the performing ape Peter, who died not so long ago and had some small local reputation, were the red mark on my cheek. This by the way.

The second shot hit me below the hip. It was a severe wound; it is the cause of my limping a little to this day. I read an article recently by one of the ten thousand windbags who vent themselves concerning me in the newspapers, saying: my ape nature is not yet quite under control; the proof being that when visitors come to see me, I have a predilection for taking down my trousers to show them where the shot went in. The hand which wrote that should have its fingers shot away one by one. As for me, I can take my trousers down before anyone if I like; you would find nothing but a well-groomed fur and the scar made—let me be particular in the choice of a word for this particular purpose, to avoid misunderstanding—the scar made by a wanton shot. Everything is open and aboveboard; there is nothing to conceal; when the plain truth is in question, great minds discard the niceties of refinement. But if the writer of the article were to take down his trousers before a visitor that would be quite another story, and I will let it stand to his credit that he does not do it. In return, let him leave me alone with his delicacy!

After these two shots I came to myself—and this is where my own memories gradually begin—between decks in the Hagenbeck steamer, inside a cage. It was not a four-sided barred cage; it was only a three-sided cage nailed to a locker; the locker made the fourth side of it. The whole construction was too low for me to stand up in and too narrow to sit down in. So I had to squat with my knees bent and trembling all the time, and also, since probably for a time I wished to see no one, and to stay in the dark, my face was turned towards the locker while the bars of the cage cut into my flesh behind. Such a method of confining wild beasts is supposed to have its advantages during the first days of captivity, and out of my own experiences I cannot deny that from the human point of view this is really the case.

But that did not occur to me then. For the first time in my life I could see no way out; at least no direct way out; directly in front of me was the locker, board fitted close to board. True, there was a gap running right through the boards which I greeted with the blissful howl of ignorance when I first discovered it, but the hole was not even wide enough to stick one's tail through and not all the strength of an ape could enlarge it.

I am supposed to have made uncommonly little noise, as I was later informed, from which the conclusion was drawn that I would either soon die or if I managed to survive the first critical period would be very amenable to training. I did survive this period. Hopelessly sobbing, painfully hunting for fleas, apathetically licking a cocoanut, beating my skull against the locker, sticking out my tongue at anyone who came near me—that was how I filled in time at first in my new life. But over and above it all only the one feeling: no way out. Of course what I felt then as an ape I can represent now only in human terms, and therefore I misrepresent it, but although I cannot reach back to the truth of the old ape life, there is no doubt that it lies somewhere in the direction I have indicated.

Until then I had had so many ways out of everything, and now I had none. I was pinned down. Had I been nailed down, my right to free movement would not have been lessened. Why so? Scratch your flesh raw between your toes, but you won't find the answer. Press yourself against the bar behind you till it nearly cuts you in two, you won't find the answer. I had no way out but I had to devise one, for without it I could not live. All the time facing that locker—I should certainly have perished. Yet as far as Hagenbeck was concerned, the place for apes was in front of a locker—well, then, I had to stop being an ape. A fine, clear train of thought, which I must have constructed somehow with my belly, since apes think with their bellies.

I fear that perhaps you do not quite understand what I mean by "way out." I use the expression in its fullest and most popular sense. I deliberately do not use the word "freedom." I do not mean the spacious feeling of freedom on all sides. As an ape, perhaps, I knew that, and I have met men who yearn for it. But for my part I desired such freedom neither then nor now. In passing: may I say that all too often men are betrayed by the word freedom? And as freedom is counted among the most sublime feelings, so the corresponding disillusionment can be also sublime. In variety theaters I have often watched, before my turn came on, a couple of acrobats performing on trapezes high in the roof. They swung themselves, they rocked to and fro, they sprang into the air, they floated into each other's arms, one hung by the hair from the teeth of the other. "And that too is human freedom," I thought, "self-controlled movement." What a mockery of holy Mother Nature! Were the apes to see such a spectacle, no theater walls could stand the shock of their laughter.

No, freedom was not what I wanted. Only a way out; right or left, or in any direction; I made no other demand; even should the way out prove to be an illusion; the demand was a small one, the disappointment could be no bigger. To get out somewhere, to get out! Only not to stay motionless with raised arms, crushed against a wooden wall.

Today I can see it clearly; without the most profound inward calm I could never have found my way out. And indeed perhaps I owe all that I have become to the calm that settled within me after my first few days in

the ship. And again for that calmness it was the ship's
crew I had to thank.

They were good creatures, in spite of everything. I
find it still pleasant to remember the sound of their
heavy footfalls which used to echo through my half-
dreaming head. They had a habit of doing everything
as slowly as possible. If one of them wanted to rub his
eyes, he lifted a hand as if it were a drooping weight.
Their jests were coarse, but hearty. Their laughter had
always a gruff bark in it that sounded dangerous but
meant nothing. They always had something in their
mouths to spit out and did not care where they spat it.
They always grumbled that they got fleas from me; yet
they were not seriously angry about it; they knew that
my fur fostered fleas, and that fleas jump; it was a simple matter of fact to them. When they were off duty
some of them often used to sit down in a semicircle
round me; they hardly spoke but only grunted to each
other; smoked their pipes, stretched out on lockers;
smacked their knees as soon as I made the slightest
movement; and now and then one of them would take
a stick and tickle me where I liked being tickled. If I
were to be invited today to take a cruise on that ship
I should certainly refuse the invitation, but just as certainly the memories I could recall between its decks
would not all be hateful.

The calmness I acquired among these people kept
me above all from trying to escape. As I look back now,
it seems to me I must have had at least an inkling that
I had to find a way out or die, but that my way out
could not be reached through flight. I cannot tell now

whether escape was possible, but I believe it must have been; for an ape it must always be possible. With my teeth as they are today I have to be careful even in simply cracking nuts, but at that time I could certainly have managed by degrees to bite through the lock of my cage. I did not do it. What good would it have done me? As soon as I had poked out my head I should have been caught again and put in a worse cage; or I might have slipped among the other animals without being noticed, among the pythons, say, who were opposite me, and so breathed out my life in their embrace; or supposing I had actually succeeded in sneaking out as far as the deck and leaping overboard, I should have rocked for a little on the deep sea and then been drowned. Desperate remedies. I did not think it out in this human way, but under the influence of my surroundings I acted as if I had thought it out.

I did not think things out; but I observed everything quietly. I watched these men go to and fro, always the same faces, the same movements, often it seemed to me there was only the same man. So this man or these men walked about unimpeded. A lofty goal faintly dawned before me. No one promised me that if I became like them the bars of my cage would be taken away. Such promises for apparently impossible contingencies are not given. But if one achieves the impossible, the promises appear later retrospectively precisely where one had looked in vain for them before. Now, these men in themselves had no great attraction for me. Had I been devoted to the aforementioned idea of freedom, I should certainly have preferred the deep sea to the way out that suggested itself in the heavy faces of these men. At any rate, I watched them for a long time before I even thought of such things; indeed, it was only the mass weight of my observations that impelled me in the right direction.

It was so easy to imitate these people. I learned to spit in the very first days. We used to spit in each other's faces; the only difference was that I licked my face clean afterwards and they did not. I could soon smoke a pipe like an old hand; and if I also pressed my thumb into the bowl of the pipe, a roar of appreciation went up between-decks; only it took me a very long time to understand the difference between a full pipe and an empty one.

My worst trouble came from the schnapps bottle. The smell of it revolted me; I forced myself to it as best I could; but it took weeks for me to master my repulsion. This inward conflict, strangely enough, was taken more seriously by the crew than anything else about me. I cannot distinguish the men from each other in my recollection, but there was one of them who came again and again, alone or with friends, by day, by night, at all kinds of hours; he would post himself before me with the bottle and give me instructions. He could not understand me, he wanted to solve the enigma of my being. He would slowly uncork the bottle and then look at me to see if I had followed him; I admit that I always watched him with wildly eager, too eager attention; such a student of humankind no human teacher ever found on earth. After the bottle was uncorked he lifted it to his mouth; I followed it with my eyes right up to his jaws; he would nod, pleased with me, and set the bottle to his lips; I, enchanted with my gradual enlightenment, squealed and scratched myself comprehensively wherever scratching was called for; he rejoiced, tilted the bottle and took a drink; I, impatient and desperate to emulate him, befouled myself in my cage, which again gave him great satisfaction; and then, holding the bottle at arm's length and bringing it up with a swing, he would empty it at one draught, leaning back at an exaggerated angle for my better instruction. I, exhausted by too much effort, could follow him no farther and hung limply to the bars, while he ended his theoretical exposition by rubbing his belly and grinning.

After theory came practice. Was I not already quite exhausted by my theoretical instruction? Indeed I was; utterly exhausted. That was part of my destiny. And yet I would take hold of the proffered bottle as well as I was able; uncork it, trembling; this successful action would gradually inspire me with new energy; I would lift the bottle, already following my original model almost exactly; put it to my lips and—and then throw it down in disgust, utter disgust, although it was empty and filled only with the smell of the spirit, throw it down on the floor in disgust. To the sorrow of my teacher, to the greater sorrow of myself; neither of us being really comforted by the fact that I did not forget even though I had thrown away the bottle, to rub my belly most admirably and to grin.

Far too often my lesson ended in that way. And to the credit of my teacher, he was not angry; sometimes indeed he would hold his burning pipe against my fur,

until it began to smolder in some place I could not easily reach, but then he would himself extinguish it with
his own kind, enormous hand; he was not angry with
me, he perceived that we were both fighting on the
same side against the nature of apes and that I had the
more difficult task.

What a triumph it was then both for him and for me,
when one evening before a large circle of spectators—
perhaps there was a celebration of some kind, a gramo-
phone was playing, an officer was circulating among the
crew—when on this evening, just as no one was looking,
I took hold of a schnapps bottle that had been carelessly
left standing before my cage, uncorked it in the best
style, while the company began to watch me with
mounting attention, set it to my lips without hesitation,
with no grimace, like a professional drinker, with rolling eyes and full throat, actually and truly drank it
empty; then threw the bottle away, not this time in despair but as an artistic performer; forgot, indeed, to rub
my belly; but instead of that, because I could not help
it, because my senses were reeling, called a brief and
unmistakable "Hallo!" breaking into human speech,
and with this outburst broke into the human community, and felt its echo: "Listen, he's talking!" like a caress over the whole of my sweat-drenched body.

I repeat: there was no attraction for me in imitating
human beings; I imitated them because I needed a way
out, and for no other reason. And even that triumph of
mine did not achieve much. I lost my human voice again
at once; it did not come back for months; my aver-
sion for the schnapps bottle returned again with even

greater force. But the line I was to follow had in any case been decided, once for all.

When I was handed over to my first trainer in Hamburg I soon realized that there were two alternatives before me: the Zoological Gardens or the variety stage. I did not hesitate. I said to myself: do your utmost to get on to the variety stage; the Zoological Gardens means only a new cage; once there, you are done for.

And so I learned things, gentlemen. Ah, one learns when one has to; one learns when one needs a way out; one learns at all costs. One stands over oneself with a whip; one flays oneself at the slightest opposition. My ape nature fled out of me, head over heels and away, so that my first teacher was almost himself turned into an ape by it, had soon to give up teaching and was taken away to a mental hospital. Fortunately he was soon let out again.

But I used up many teachers, indeed, several teachers at once. As I became more confident of my abilities, as the public took an interest in my progress and my future began to look bright, I engaged teachers for myself, established them in five communicating rooms and took lessons from them all at once by dint of leaping from one room to the other.

That progress of mine! How the rays of knowledge penetrated from all sides into my awakening brain! I do not deny it: I found it exhilarating. But I must also confess: I did not overestimate it, not even then, much less now. With an effort which up till now has never been repeated I managed to reach the cultural level of an average European. In itself that might be nothing to

speak of, but it is something insofar as it has helped me
out of my cage and opened a special way out for me,
the way of humanity. There is an excellent idiom: to
fight one's way through the thick of things; that is what
I have done, I have fought through the thick of things.
There was nothing else for me to do, provided always
that freedom was not to be my choice.

As I look back over my development and survey what
I have achieved so far, I do not complain, but I am not
complacent either. With my hands in my trousers pockets, my bottle of wine on the table, I half lie and half
sit in my rocking chair and gaze out of the window: if a
visitor arrives, I receive him with propriety. My man-
ager sits in the anteroom; when I ring, he comes and
listens to what I have to say. Nearly every evening I
give a performance, and I have a success which could
hardly be increased. When I come home late at night
from banquets, from scientific receptions, from social
gatherings, there sits waiting for me a half-trained little chimpanzee and I take comfort from her as apes do.
By day I cannot bear to see her; for she has the insane
look of the bewildered half-broken animal in her eye;
no one else sees it, but I do, and I cannot bear it. On
the whole, at any rate, I have achieved what I set out
to achieve. But do not tell me that it was not worth the
trouble. In any case, I am not appealing for any man's
verdict, I am only imparting knowledge, I am only
making a report. To you also, honored Members of the
Academy, I have only made a report.

The Hunter Gracchus

Two BOYS were sitting on the harbor wall playing with dice. A man was reading a newspaper on the steps of the monument, resting in the shadow of a hero who was flourishing his sword on high. A girl was filling her bucket at the fountain. A fruitseller was lying beside his scales, staring out to sea. Through the vacant window and door openings of a café one could see two men quite at the back drinking their wine. The proprietor was sitting at a table in front and dozing. A bark was silently making for the little harbor, as if borne by invisible means over the water. A man in a blue blouse climbed ashore and drew the rope through a ring. Behind the boatman two other men in dark coats with silver buttons carried a bier, on which, beneath a great flower-patterned tasselled silk cloth, a man was apparently lying.

Nobody on the quay troubled about the newcomers; even when they lowered the bier to wait for the boatman, who was still occupied with his rope, nobody went nearer, nobody asked them a question, nobody accorded them an inquisitive glance.

The pilot was still further detained by a woman who,

a child at her breast, now appeared with loosened hair
on the deck of the boat. Then he advanced and indicated a yellowish two-storeyed house that rose abruptly
on the left beside the sea; the bearers took up their burden and bore it to the low but gracefully pillared door.
A little boy opened a window just in time to see the
party vanishing into the house, then hastily shut the
window again. The door too was now shut; it was of
black oak, and very strongly made. A flock of doves
which had been flying round the belfry alighted in the
street before the house. As if their food were stored
within, they assembled in front of the door. One of
them flew up to the first storey and pecked at the win-
dow-pane. They were bright-hued, well-tended, beautiful birds. The woman on the boat flung grain to them
in a wide sweep; they ate it up and flew across to the
woman.

A man in a top hat tied with a band of crêpe now descended one of the narrow and very steep lanes that led
to the harbor. He glanced round vigilantly, everything
seemed to displease him, his mouth twisted at the sight
of some offal in a corner. Fruit skins were lying on the
steps of the monument; he swept them off in passing
with his stick. He rapped at the house door, at the same
time taking his top hat from his head with his black-
gloved hand. The door was opened at once, and some
fifty little boys appeared in two rows in the long entry-
hall, and bowed to him.

The boatman descended the stairs, greeted the gentleman in black, conducted him up to the first storey,
'ed him round the bright and elegant loggia which en-

circled the courtyard, and both of them entered, while
the boys pressed after them at a respectful distance, a
cool spacious room looking towards the back, from
whose window no habitation, but only a bare, blackish
grey rocky wall was to be seen. The bearers were busied
in setting up and lighting several long candles at the
head of the bier, yet these did not give light, but only
scared away the shadows which had been immobile till
then, and made them flicker over the walls. The cloth
covering the bier had been thrown back. Lying on it
was a man with wildly matted hair, who looked somewhat like a hunter. He lay without motion and, it
seemed, without breathing, his eyes closed; yet only his
trappings indicated that this man was probably dead.

The gentleman stepped up to the bier, laid his hand
on the brow of the man lying upon it, then kneeled
down and prayed. The boatman made a sign to the
bearers to leave the room; they went out, drove away
the boys who had gathered outside, and shut the door.
But even that did not seem to satisfy the gentleman; he
glanced at the boatman; the boatman understood, and
vanished through a side door into the next room. At
once the man on the bier opened his eyes, turned his
face painfully towards the gentleman, and said: "Who
are you?" Without any mark of surprise the gentleman
rose from his kneeling posture and answered: "The
Burgomaster of Riva."

The man on the bier nodded, indicated a chair with
a feeble movement of his arm, and said, after the Burgomaster had accepted his invitation: "I knew that, of
course, Burgomaster, but in the first moments of re-

turning consciousness I always forget, everything goes round before my eyes, and it is best to ask about anything even if I know. You too probably know that I am the hunter Gracchus."

"Certainly," said the Burgomaster. "Your arrival was announced to me during the night. We had been asleep for a good while. Then towards midnight my wife cried: 'Salvatore'—that's my name—'look at that dove at the window.' It was really a dove, but as big as a cock. It flew over me and said in my ear: 'Tomorrow the dead hunter Gracchus is coming; receive him in the name of the city.' "

The hunter nodded and licked his lips with the tip of his tongue: "Yes, the doves flew here before me. But do you believe, Burgomaster, that I shall remain in Riva?"

"I cannot say that yet," replied the Burgomaster. "Are you dead?"

"Yes," said the hunter, "as you see. Many years ago, yes, it must be a great many years ago, I fell from a precipice in the Black Forest—that is in Germany—when I was hunting a chamois. Since then I have been dead."

"But you are alive too," said the Burgomaster.

"In a certain sense," said the hunter, "in a certain sense I am alive too. My death ship lost its way; a wrong turn of the wheel, a moment's absence of mind on the pilot's part, a longing to turn aside towards my lovely native country, I cannot tell what it was; I only know this, that I remained on earth and that ever since my ship has sailed earthly waters. So I, who asked for nothing better than to live among my mountains, travel after my death through all the lands of the earth."

"And you have no part in the other world?" asked the Burgomaster, knitting his brow.

"I am forever," replied the hunter, "on the great stair that leads up to it. On that infinitely wide and spacious stair I clamber about, sometimes up, some-times down, sometimes on the right, sometimes on the left, always in motion. The hunter has been turned into a butterfly. Do not laugh."

"I am not laughing," said the Burgomaster in self-defense.

"That is very good of you," said the hunter. "I am always in motion. But when I make a supreme flight and see the gate actually shining before me I awaken presently on my old ship, still stranded forlornly in some earthly sea or other. The fundamental error of my one-time death grins at me as I lie in my cabin. Julia, the wife of the pilot, knocks at the door and brings me on my bier the morning drink of the land whose coasts we chance to be passing. I lie on a wooden pallet, I wear—it cannot be a pleasure to look at me—a filthy winding sheet, my hair and beard, black tinged with grey, have grown together inextricably, my limbs are covered with a great flower-patterned woman's shawl with long fringes. A sacramental candle stands at my head and lights me. On the wall opposite me is a little picture, evidently of a Bushman who is aiming his spear at me and taking cover as best he can behind a beautifully painted shield. On shipboard one is often a prey to stupid imaginations, but that is the stupidest of them all. Otherwise my wooden case is quite empty. Through a hole in the side wall come in the warm airs of the southern night, and I hear the water slapping against the old boat.

"I have lain here ever since the time when, as the hunter Gracchus living in the Black Forest, I followed a chamois and fell from a precipice. Everything happened in good order. I pursued, I fell, bled to death in a ravine, died, and this ship should have conveyed me to the next world. I can still remember how gladly I stretched myself out on this pallet for the first time. Never did the mountains listen to such songs from me as these shadowy walls did then.

"I had been glad to live and I was glad to die. Before I stepped aboard, I joyfully flung away my wretched load of ammunition, my knapsack, my hunting rifle that I had always been proud to carry, and I slipped into my winding sheet like a girl into her marriage dress. I lay and waited. Then came the mishap."

"A terrible fate," said the Burgomaster, raising his hand defensively. "And you bear no blame for it?"

"None," said the hunter. "I was a hunter; was there any sin in that? I followed my calling as a hunter in the Black Forest, where there were still wolves in those days. I lay in ambush, shot, hit my mark, flayed the skins from my victims: was there any sin in that? My labors were blessed. 'The great hunter of the Black Forest' was the name I was given. Was there any sin in that?"

"I am not called upon to decide that," said the Burgomaster, "but to me also there seems to be no sin in such things. But, then, whose is the guilt?"

"The boatman's," said the hunter. "Nobody will read what I say here, no one will come to help me; even if all the people were commanded to help me, every door and window would remain shut, everybody would take to bed and draw the bedclothes over his head, the whole earth would become an inn for the night. And there is sense in that, for nobody knows of me, and if anyone knew he would not know where I could be found, and if he knew where I could be found, he would not know how to deal with me, he would not know how to help me. The thought of helping me is an illness that has to be cured by taking to one's bed.

"I know that, and so I do not shout to summon help, even though at moments—when I lose control over myself, as I have done just now, for instance—I think seriously of it. But to drive out such thoughts I need only look round me and verify where I am, and—I can safely assert—have been for hundreds of years."

"Extraordinary," said the Burgomaster, "extraordinary.—And now do you think of staying here in Riva with us?"

"I think not," said the hunter with a smile, and, to excuse himself, he laid his hand on the Burgomaster's knee. "I am here, more than that I do not know, further than that I cannot go. My ship has no rudder, and it is driven by the wind that blows in the undermost regions of death."

A Hunger Artist

DURING THESE last decades the interest in professional fasting has markedly diminished. It used to pay very well to stage such great performances under one's own management, but today that is quite impossible. We live in a different world now. At one time the whole town took a lively interest in the hunger artist; from day to day of his fast the excitement mounted; everybody wanted to see him at least once a day; there were people who bought season tickets for the last few days and sat from morning till night in front of his small barred cage; even in the nighttime there were visiting hours, when the whole effect was heightened by torch flares; on fine days the cage was set out in the open air, and then it was the children's special treat to see the hunger artist; for their elders he was often just a joke that happened to be in fashion, but the children stood open-mouthed, holding each other's hands for greater security, marveling at him as he sat there pallid in black tights, with his ribs sticking out so prominently, not even on a seat but down among straw on the ground, sometimes giving a courteous nod, answering questions with a constrained smile, or perhaps stretching an arm through the bars so that one might feel how thin it was, and then again withdrawing deep into himself, paying no attention to anyone or anything, not even to the all-important striking of the clock that was the only piece of furniture in his cage, but merely staring into vacancy with half-shut eyes, now and then taking a sip from a tiny glass of water to moisten his lips.

Besides casual onlookers there were also relays of permanent watchers selected by the public, usually butchers, strangely enough, and it was their task to watch the hunger artist day and night, three of them at a time, in case he should have some secret recourse to nourishment. This was nothing but a formality, instituted to reassure the masses, for the initiates knew well enough that during his fast the artist would never in any circumstances, not even under forcible compulsion, swallow the smallest morsel of food; the honor of his profession forbade it. Not every watcher, of course, was capable of understanding this, there were often groups of night watchers who were very lax in carrying out their duties and deliberately huddled together in a retired corner to play cards with great absorption, obviously intending to give the hunger artist the chance of a little refreshment, which they supposed he could draw from some private hoard. Nothing annoyed the artist more than such watchers; they made him miserable; they made his fast seem unendurable; sometimes he mastered his feebleness sufficiently to sing during their watch for as long as he could keep going, to show them how unjust their suspicions were. But that was of little use; they only wondered at his cleverness in being able to fill his mouth even while singing. Much more to his taste were the watchers who sat close up to the bars, who were not content with the dim night lighting of the hall but focused him in the full glare of the electric pocket torch given them by the impresario. The harsh light did not trouble him at all. In any case he could never sleep properly, and he could always drowse a little, whatever the light, at any hour, even when the hall was thronged with noisy onlookers. He was quite happy at the prospect of spending a sleepless night with such watchers; he was ready to exchange jokes with them, to tell them stories out of his nomadic life, anything at all to keep them awake and demonstrate to them again that he had no eatables in his cage and that he was fasting as not one of them could fast. But his happiest moment was when the morning came and an enormous breakfast was brought them, at his expense, on which they flung themselves with the keen appetite of healthy men after a weary night of wakefulness. Of course there were people who argued that this breakfast was an unfair attempt to bribe the watchers, but that was going rather too far, and when they were invited to take on a night's vigil without a breakfast, merely for the sake of the cause, they made themselves scarce, although they stuck stubbornly to their suspicions.

Such suspicions, anyhow, were a necessary accompaniment to the profession of fasting. No one could possibly watch the hunger artist continuously, day and night, and so no one could produce first-hand evidence that the fast had really been rigorous and continuous; only the artist himself could know that; he was therefore

bound to be the sole completely satisfied spectator of
his own fast. Yet for other reasons he was never satisfied; it was not perhaps mere fasting that had brought
him to such skeleton thinness that many people had re-
gretfully to keep away from his exhibitions, because the
sight of him was too much for them, perhaps it was dissatisfaction with himself that had worn him down. For
he alone knew, what no other initiate knew, how easy
it was to fast. It was the easiest thing in the world. He
made no secret of this, yet people did not believe him;
at the best they set him down as modest, most of them,
however, thought he was out for publicity or else was
some kind of cheat who found it easy to fast because he
had discovered a way of making it easy, and then had
the impudence to admit the fact, more or less. He
had to put up with all that, and in the course of time had
got used to it, but his inner dissatisfaction always ran-
kled, and never yet, after any term of fasting—this must
be granted to his credit—had he left the cage of his own
free will. The longest period of fasting was fixed by his
impresario at forty days, beyond that term he was not
allowed to go, not even in great cities, and there was
good reason for it, too. Experience had proved that for
about forty days the interest of the public could be stimulated by a steadily increasing pressure of advertise-
ment, but after that the town began to lose interest,
sympathetic support began notably to fall off; there
were of course local variations as between one town and
another or one country and another, but as a general
rule forty days marked the limit. So on the fortieth day
the flower-bedecked cage was opened, enthusiastic spec-

tators filled the hall, a military band played, two doc-
tors entered the cage to measure the results of the
fast, which were announced through a megaphone, and
finally two young ladies appeared, blissful at having
been selected for the honor, to help the hunger artist
down the few steps leading to a small table on which
was spread a carefully chosen invalid repast. And at
this very moment the artist always turned stubborn.
True, he would entrust his bony arms to the outstretched helping hands of the ladies bending over him,
but stand up he would not. Why stop fasting at this
particular moment, after forty days of it? He had held
out for a long time, an illimitably long time; why stop
now, when he was in his best fasting form, or rather,
not yet quite in his best fasting form? Why should he
be cheated of the fame he would get for fasting longer,
for being not only the record hunger artist of all time,
which presumably he was already, but for beating his
own record by a performance beyond human imagination, since he felt that there were no limits to his capacity for fasting? His public pretended to admire him so
much, why should it have so little patience with him;
if he could endure fasting longer, why shouldn't the
public endure it? Besides, he was tired, he was comfortable sitting in the straw, and now he was supposed to
lift himself to his full height and go down to a meal the
very thought of which gave him a nausea that only the
presence of the ladies kept him from betraying, and
even that with an effort. And he looked up into the eyes
of the ladies who were apparently so friendly and in
reality so cruel, and shook his head, which felt too heavy

on its strengthless neck. But then there happened yet
again what always happened. The impresario came forward, without a word—for the band made speech impossible—lifted his arms in the air above the artist, as if
inviting Heaven to look down upon its creature here
in the straw, this suffering martyr, which indeed he was,
although in quite another sense; grasped him round
the emaciated waist, with exaggerated caution, so that
the frail condition he was in might be appreciated; and
committed him to the care of the blenching ladies, not
without secretly giving him a shaking so that his legs
and body tottered and swayed. The artist now submitted completely; his head lolled on his breast as if it had
landed there by chance; his body was hollowed out; his
legs in a spasm of self-preservation clung close to each
other at the knees, yet scraped on the ground as if it
were not really solid ground, as if they were only trying to find solid ground; and the whole weight of his
body, a featherweight after all, relapsed onto one of the
ladies, who, looking round for help and panting a little
—this post of honor was not at all what she had expected
it to be—first stretched her neck as far as she could to
keep her face at least free from contact with the artist,
then finding this impossible, and her more fortunate
companion not coming to her aid but merely holding
extended on her own trembling hand the little bunch
of knucklebones that was the artist's, to the great delight
of the spectators burst into tears and had to be replaced
by an attendant who had long been stationed in readiness. Then came the food, a little of which the impresario managed to get between the artist's lips, while he

sat in a kind of half-fainting trance, to the accompaniment of cheerful patter designed to distract the public's attention from the artist's condition; after that, a toast was drunk to the public, supposedly prompted by a whisper from the artist in the impresario's ear; the band confirmed it with a mighty flourish, the spectators melted away, and no one had any cause to be dissatisfied with the proceedings, no one except the hunger artist himself, he only, as always.

So he lived for many years, with small regular intervals of recuperation, in visible glory, honored by the world, yet in spite of that troubled in spirit, and all the more troubled because no one would take his trouble seriously. What comfort could he possibly need? What more could he possibly wish for? And if some good-natured person, feeling sorry for him, tried to console him by pointing out that his melancholy was probably caused by fasting, it could happen, especially when he had been fasting for some time, that he reacted with an outburst of fury and to the general alarm began to shake the bars of his cage like a wild animal. Yet the impresario had a way of punishing these outbreaks which he rather enjoyed putting into operation. He would apologize publicly for the artist's behavior, which was only to be excused, he admitted, because of the irritability caused by fasting; a condition hardly to be understood by well-fed people; then by natural transition he went on to mention the artist's equally incomprehensible boast that he could fast for much longer than he was doing; he praised the high ambition, the good will, the great self-denial undoubtedly implicit in such a statement; and then quite simply countered it by bringing out photographs, which were also on sale to the public, showing the artist on the fortieth day of a fast lying in bed almost dead from exhaustion. This perversion of the truth, familiar to the artist though it was, always unnerved him afresh and proved too much for him. What was a consequence of the premature ending of his fast was here presented as the cause of it! To fight against this lack of understanding, against a whole world of non-understanding, was impossible. Time and again in good faith he stood by the bars listening to the impresario, but as soon as the photographs appeared he always let go and sank with a groan back on to his straw, and the reassured public could once more come close and gaze at him.

A few years later when the witnesses of such scenes called them to mind, they often failed to understand themselves at all. For meanwhile the aforementioned change in public interest had set in; it seemed to happen almost overnight; there may have been profound causes for it, but who was going to bother about that; at any rate the pampered hunger artist suddenly found himself deserted one fine day by the amusement seekers, who went streaming past him to other more favored attractions. For the last time the impresario hurried him over half Europe to discover whether the old interest might still survive here and there; all in vain; everywhere, as if by secret agreement, a positive revulsion from professional fasting was in evidence. Of course it could not really have sprung up so suddenly as all that, and many premonitory symptoms which had not been sufficiently remarked or suppressed during the rush and glitter of success now came retrospectively to mind, but it was now too late to take any countermeasures. Fasting would surely come into fashion again at some future date, yet that was no comfort for those living in the present. What, then, was the hunger artist to do? He had been applauded by thousands in his time and could hardly come down to showing himself in a street booth at village fairs, and as for adopting another profession, he was not only too old for that but too fanatically devoted to fasting. So he took leave of the impresario, his partner in an unparalleled career, and hired himself to a large circus; in order to spare his own feelings he avoided reading the conditions of his contract.

A large circus with its enormous traffic in replacing and recruiting men, animals and apparatus can always find a use for people at any time, even for a hunger artist, provided of course that he does not ask too much, and in this particular case anyhow it was not only the artist who was taken on but his famous and long-known name as well; indeed considering the peculiar nature of his performance, which was not impaired by advancing age, it could not be objected that here was an artist past his prime, no longer at the height of his professional skill, seeking a refuge in some quiet corner of a circus; on the contrary, the hunger artist averred that he could fast as well as ever, which was entirely credible; he even alleged that if he were allowed to fast as he liked, and this was at once promised him without more ado, he could astound the world by establishing a record never yet achieved, a statement which certainly provoked a smile among the other professionals, since it left out of account the change in public opinion, which the hun‹ ger artist in his zeal conveniently forgot.

He had not, however, actually lost his sense of the real situation and took it as a matter of course that he and his cage should be stationed, not in the middle of the ring as a main attraction, but outside, near the ani‐ mal cages, on a site that was after all easily accessible. Large and gaily painted placards made a frame for the cage and announced what was to be seen inside it. When the public came thronging out in the intervals to see the animals, they could hardly avoid passing the hunger artist's cage and stopping there for a moment, perhaps they might even have stayed longer had not those press‐ ing behind them in the narrow gangway, who did not understand why they should be held up on their way towards the excitements of the menagerie, made it impossible for anyone to stand gazing quietly for any length of time. And that was the reason why the hunger artist, who had of course been looking forward to these visiting hours as the main achievement of his life, be‐ gan instead to shrink from them. At first he could hardly wait for the intervals; it was exhilarating to watch the crowds come streaming his way, until only too soon— not even the most obstinate self-deception, clung to al‐ most consciously, could hold out against the fact—the conviction was borne in upon him that these people, most of them, to judge from their actions, again and again, without exception, were all on their way to the menagerie. And the first sight of them from the dis‹ tance remained the best. For when they reached his cage he was at once deafened by the storm of shouting and abuse that arose from the two contending factions, which renewed themselves continuously, of those who wanted to stop and stare at him—he soon began to dislike them more than the others—not out of real interest but only out of obstinate self-assertiveness, and those who wanted to go straight on to the animals. When the first great rush was past, the stragglers came along, and these, whom nothing could have prevented from stopping to look at him as long as they had breath, raced past with long strides, hardly even glancing at him, in their haste to get to the menagerie in time. And all too rarely did it happen that he had a stroke of luck, when some father of a family fetched up before him with his children, pointed a finger at the hunger artist and explained at length what the phenomenon meant, telling stories of earlier years when he himself had watched similar but much more thrilling performances, and the children, still rather uncomprehending, since neither inside nor outside school had they been sufficiently prepared for this lesson—what did they care about fasting? —yet showed by the brightness of their intent eyes that new and better times might be coming. Perhaps, said the hunger artist to himself many a time, things would be a little better if his cage were set not quite so near the menagerie. That made it too easy for people to make their choice, to say nothing of what he suffered from the stench of the menagerie, the animals' restlessness by night, the carrying past of raw lumps of flesh for the beasts of prey, the roaring at feeding times, which depressed him continually. But he did not dare to lodge a complaint with the management; after all, he had the animals to thank for the troops of people who passed his cage, among whom there might always be one here and there to take an interest in him, and who could tell where they might seclude him if he called attention to his existence and thereby to the fact that, strictly speaking, he was only an impediment on the way to the menagerie.

A small impediment, to be sure, one that grew steadily less. People grew familiar with the strange idea that they could be expected, in times like these, to take an interest in a hunger artist, and with this familiarity the verdict went out against him. He might fast as much as he could, and he did so; but nothing could save him now, people passed him by. Just try to explain to anyone the art of fasting! Anyone who has no feeling for it cannot be made to understand it. The fine placards grew dirty and illegible, they were torn down; the little notice board telling the number of fast days achieved, which at first was changed carefully every day, had long stayed at the same figure, for after the first few weeks even this small task seemed pointless to the staff; and so the artist simply fasted on and on, as he had once dreamed of doing, and it was no trouble to him, just as he had always foretold, but no one counted the days, no one, not even the artist himself, knew what records he was already breaking, and his heart grew heavy. And when once in a time some leisurely passer-by stopped, made merry over the old figure on the board and spoke of swindling, that was in its way the stupidest lie ever invented by indifference and inborn malice, since it was not the hunger artist who was cheating; he was working honestly, but the world was cheating him of his reward.

Many more days went by, however, and that too came to an end. An overseer's eye fell on the cage one day and he asked the attendants why this perfectly good stage should be left standing there unused with dirty straw inside it; nobody knew, until one man, helped out by the notice board, remembered about the hunger artist. They poked into the straw with sticks and found him in it. "Are you still fasting?" asked the overseer. "When on earth do you mean to stop?" "Forgive me, everybody," whispered the hunger artist; only the overseer, who had his ear to the bars, understood him. "Of course," said the overseer, and tapped his forehead with a finger to let the attendants know what state the man was in, "we forgive you." "I always wanted you to admire my fasting," said the hunger artist. "We do admire it," said the overseer, affably. "But you shouldn't admire it," said the hunger artist. "Well, then we don't admire it," said the overseer, "but why shouldn't we admire it?" "Because I have to fast, I can't help it," said the hunger artist. "What a fellow you are," said the overseer, "and why can't you help it?" "Because," said the hunger artist, lifting his head a little and speaking, with his lips pursed, as if for a kiss, right into the overseer's ear, so that no syllable might be lost, "because I couldn't find the food I liked. If I had found it, believe me, I should have made no fuss and stuffed myself like you or anyone else." These were his last words, but in his dimming eyes remained the firm though no longer proud persuasion that he was still continuing to fast.

"Well, clear this out now!" said the overseer, and they buried the hunger artist, straw and all. Into the cage they put a young panther. Even the most insensitive felt it refreshing to see this wild creature leaping around the cage that had so long been dreary. The panther was all right. The food he liked was brought him without hesitation by the attendants; he seemed not even to miss his freedom; his noble body, furnished almost to the bursting point with all that it needed, seemed to carry freedom around with it too; somewhere in his jaws it seemed to lurk; and the joy of life streamed with such ardent passion from his throat that for the onlookers it was not easy to stand the shock of it. But they braced themselves, crowded round the cage, and did not want ever to move away.

Investigations of a Dog

How MUCH my life has changed, and yet how unchanged it has remained at bottom! When I think back
and recall the time when I was still a member of the
canine community, sharing in all its preoccupations, a
dog among dogs I find on closer examination that from
the very beginning I sensed some discrepancy, some little
maladjustment, causing a slight feeling of discomfort
which not even the most decorous public functions could
eliminate; more, that sometimes, no, not sometimes, but
very often, the mere look of some fellow-dog of my own
circle that I was fond of, the mere look of him, as if I
had just caught it for the first time, would fill me with
helpless embarrassment and fear, even with despair. I
tried to quiet my apprehensions as best I could; friends,
to whom I divulged them, helped me; more peaceful
times came—times, it is true, in which these sudden surprises were not lacking, but in which they were accepted
with more philosophy, fitted into my life with more
philosophy, inducing a certain melancholy and lethargy,
it may be, but nevertheless allowing me to carry on as a
somewhat cold, reserved, shy and calculating, but all
things considered normal enough dog. How, indeed,

without these intervals of convalescence, could I have reached the age that I enjoy at present; how could I have fought my way through to the serenity with which I contemplate the terrors of youth and endure the terrors of age; how could I have come to the point where I am able to draw the consequences of my admittedly unhappy, or, to put it more moderately, not very happy position, and live almost entirely in accordance with them? Solitary and withdrawn, with nothing to occupy me save my hopeless but, as far as I am concerned, indispensable little investigations, that is how I live; yet in my distant isolation I have not lost sight of my people, news often penetrates to me, and now and then I even let news of myself reach them. The others treat me with respect but do not understand my way of life; yet they bear me no grudge, and even young dogs whom I sometimes see passing in the distance, a new generation of whose childhood I have only a vague memory, do not deny me a reverential greeting.

For it must not be assumed that, for all my peculiarities, which lie open to the day, I am in the least exempt from the laws of my species. Indeed when I reflect on it—and I have time and disposition and capacity enough for that—I see that dogdom is in every way a marvelous institution. Apart from us dogs there are all sorts of creatures in the world, wretched, limited, dumb creatures who have no language but mechanical cries; many of us dogs study them, have given them names, try to help them, educate them, uplift them, and so on. For my part I am quite indifferent to them except when they try to disturb me, I confuse them with one another.

I ignore them. But one thing is too obvious to have escaped me; namely how little inclined they are, compared with us dogs, to stick together, how silently and unfamiliarly and with what a curious hostility they pass each other by, how mean are the interests that suffice to bind them together for a little in ostensible union, and how often these very interests give rise to hatred and conflict. Consider us dogs, on the other hand! One can safely say that we all live together in a literal heap, all of us, different as we are from one another on account of numberless and profound modifications which have arisen in the course of time. All in one heap! We are drawn to each other and nothing can prevent us from satisfying that communal impulse; all our laws and institutions, the few that I still know and the many that I have forgotten, go back to this longing for the greatest bliss we are capable of, the warm comfort of being together. But now consider the other side of the picture. No creatures to my knowledge live in such wide dispersion as we dogs, none have so many distinctions of class, of kind, of occupation, distinctions too numerous to review at a glance; we, whose one desire is to stick together—and again and again we succeed at transcendent moments in spite of everything—we above all others are compelled to live separated from one another by strange vocations that are often incomprehensible even to our canine neighbors, holding firmly to laws that are not those of the dog world, but are actually directed against it. How baffling these questions are, questions on which one would prefer not to touch—I understand that standpoint too, even better than my own—and yet questions to which I have completely capitulated. Why do I not do as the others: live in harmony with my people and accept in silence whatever disturbs the harmony, ignoring it as a small error in the great account, always keeping in mind the things that bind us happily together, not those that drive us again and again, as though by sheer force, out of our social circle?

I can recall an incident in my youth; I was at the time in one of those inexplicable blissful states of exaltation which every one must have experienced as a child; I was still quite a puppy, everything pleased me, everything was my concern. I believed that great things were going on around me of which I was the leader and to which I must lend my voice, things which must be wretchedly thrown aside if I did not run for them and wag my tail for them—childish fantasies that fled with riper years. But at the time their power was very great. I was completely under their spell, and presently something actually did happen, something so extraordinary that it seemed to justify my wild expectations. In itself it was nothing very extraordinary, for I have seen many such things, and more remarkable things too, often enough since, but at the time it struck me with all the force of a first impression, one of those impressions which can never be erased and influence much of one's later conduct. I encountered, in short, a little company of dogs, or rather I did not encounter them, they appeared before me. Before that I had been running along in darkness for some time, filled with a premonition of great things—a premonition that may well have been delusive, for I always had it. I had run in darkness for a long time,

up and down, blind and deaf to everything, led on by
nothing but a vague desire, and now I suddenly came to
a stop with the feeling that I was in the right place, and
looking up saw that it was bright day, only a little hazy,
and everywhere a blending and confusion of the most
intoxicating smells; I greeted the morning with an uncertain barking, when—as if I had conjured them up—
out of some place of darkness, to the accompaniment of
terrible sounds such as I had never heard before, seven
dogs stepped into the light. Had I not distinctly seen
that they were dogs and that they themselves brought
the sound of them—though I could not recognize how
they produced it—I would have run away at once; but
as it was I stayed. At that time I still knew hardly anything of the creative gift for music with which the canine race alone is endowed, it had naturally enough escaped my but slowly developing powers of observation;
for though music had surrounded me as a perfectly natural and indispensable element of existence ever since
I was a suckling, an element which nothing impelled
me to distinguish from the rest of existence, my elders
had drawn my attention to it only by such hints as were
suitable for a childish understanding; all the more
astonishing, then, indeed devastating, were these seven
great musical artists to me. They did not speak, they did
not sing, they remained, all of them, silent, almost de-
terminedly silent; but from the empty air they conjured
music. Everything was music, the lifting and setting
down of their feet, certain turns of the head, their running and their standing still, the positions they took up
in relation to one another, the symmetrical patterns

which they produced by one dog setting his front paws
on the back of another and the rest following suit until
the first bore the weight of the other six, or by all lying
flat on the ground and going through complicated con-
certed evolutions; and none made a false move, not even
the last dog, though he was a little unsure, did not always establish contact at once with the others, sometimes hesitated, as it were, on the stroke of the beat, but
yet was unsure only by comparison with the superb
sureness of the others, and even if he had been much
more unsure, indeed quite unsure, would not have been
able to do any harm, the others, great masters all of
them, keeping the rhythm so unshakably. But it is too
much to say that I even saw them, that I actually even
saw them. They appeared from somewhere, I inwardly
greeted them as dogs, and although I was profoundly
confused by the sounds that accompanied them, yet they
were dogs nevertheless, dogs like you and me; I regarded
them by force of habit simply as dogs I had happened to
meet on my road, and felt a wish to approach them and
exchange greetings; they were quite near too, dogs much
older than I, certainly, and not of my woolly, long-
haired kind, but yet not so very alien in size and shape,
indeed quite familiar to me, for I had already seen many
such or similar dogs; but while I was still involved in
these reflections the music gradually got the upper hand,
literally knocked the breath out of me and swept me far
away from those actual little dogs, and quite against my
will, while I howled as if some pain were being inflicted
upon me, my mind could attend to nothing but this
blast of music which seemed to come from all sides, from

the heights, from the deeps, from everywhere, seizing
the listener by the middle, overwhelming him, crushing
him, and over his swooning body still blowing fanfares
so near that they seemed far away and almost inaudible.
And then a respite came, for one was already too exhausted, too annulled, too feeble to listen any longer; a
respite came and I beheld again the seven little dogs
carrying out their evolutions, making their leaps; I
longed to shout to them in spite of their aloofness, to
beg them to enlighten me, to ask them what they were
doing—I was a child and believed I could ask anybody
about anything—but hardly had I begun, hardly did I
feel on good and familiar doggish terms with the seven,
when the music started again, robbed me of my wits,
whirled me round in its circles as if I myself were one
of the musicians instead of being only their victim, cast
me hither and thither, no matter how much I begged
for mercy, and rescued me finally from its own violence
by driving me into a labyrinth of wooden bars which
rose round that place, though I had not noticed it before,
but which now firmly caught me, kept my head pressed
to the ground, and though the music still resounded in
the open space behind me, gave me a little time to get
my breath back. I must admit that I was less surprised
by the artistry of the seven dogs—it was incomprehensible to me, and also quite definitely beyond my capacities
—than by their courage in facing so openly the music of
their own making, and their power to endure it calmly
without collapsing. But now from my hiding hole I
saw, on looking more closely, that it was not so much
coolness as the most extreme tension that characterized

their performance; these limbs apparently so sure in
their movements quivered at every step with a perpetual
apprehensive twitching; as if rigid with despair the
dogs kept their eyes fixed on one another, and their
tongues, whenever the tension weakened for a moment,
hung wearily from their jowls. It could not be fear of
failure that agitated them so deeply; dogs that could
dare and achieve such things had no need to fear that.
Then why were they afraid? Who then forced them to
do what they were doing? And I could no longer restrain myself, particularly as they now seemed in some
incomprehensible way in need of help, and so through
all the din of the music I shouted out my questions
loudly and challengingly. But they—incredible! incredible!—they never replied, behaved as if I were not
there. Dogs who make no reply to the greeting of other
dogs are guilty of an offence against good manners
which the humblest dog would never pardon any more
than the greatest. Perhaps they were not dogs at all?
But how should they not be dogs? Could I not actually
hear on listening more closely the subdued cries with
which they encouraged each other, drew each other's
attention to difficulties, warned each other against er-
rors; could I not see the last and youngest dog, to whom
most of those cries were addressed, often stealing a
glance at me as if he would have dearly wished to
reply, but refrained because it was not allowed? But
why should it not be allowed, why should the very thing
which our laws unconditionally command not be allowed in this one case? I became indignant at the
thought and almost forgot the music. Those dogs were

violating the law. Great magicians they might be, but the law was valid for them too, I knew that quite well though I was a child. And having recognized that I now noticed something else. They had good grounds for remaining silent, that is, assuming that they remained silent from a sense of shame. For how were they conducting themselves? Because of all the music I had not noticed it before, but they had flung away all shame, the wretched creatures were doing the very thing which is both most ridiculous and indecent in our eyes; they were walking on their hind legs. Fie on them! They were uncovering their nakedness, blatantly making a show of their nakedness: they were doing that as though it were a meritorious act, and when, obeying their better instincts for a moment, they happened to let their front paws fall, they were literally appalled as if at an error, as if Nature were an error, hastily raised their legs again, and their eyes seemed to be begging for forgiveness for having been forced to cease momentarily from their abomination. Was the world standing on its head? Where could I be? What could have happened? If only for my own sake I dared not hesitate any longer now, I dislodged myself from the tangle of bars, took one leap into the open and made towards the dogs—I, the younger scholar, must be the teacher now, must make them understand what they were doing, must keep them from committing further sin. "And old dogs too! And old dogs too!" I kept on saying to myself. But scarcely was I free and only a leap or two away from the dogs, when the music again had me in its power. Perhaps in my ardor I might even have managed to withstand it, for

I knew it better now, if in the midst of all its majestic
amplitude, which was terrifying, but still not incon-
querable, a clear, piercing, continuous note which came
without variation literally from the remotest distance
—perhaps the real melody in the midst of the music—
had not now rung out, forcing me to my knees. Oh, the
music these dogs made almost drove me out of my
senses! I could not move a step farther, I no longer
wanted to instruct them; they could go on raising their
front legs, committing sin and seducing others to the sin
of silently regarding them; I was such a young dog—
who could demand such a difficult task from me? I made
myself still more insignificant than I was, I whimpered,
and if the dogs had asked me now what I thought of
their performance, probably I would have had not a
word to say against it. Besides it was not long before
the dogs vanished with all their music and their radiance into the darkness from which they had emerged.

As I have already said, this whole episode contains
nothing of much note; in the course of a long life one
encounters all sorts of things which, taken from their
context and seen through the eyes of a child, might well
seem far more astonishing. Besides, one may, of course
—in the pungent popular phrase—have "got it all
wrong," as well as everything connected with it; then it
could be demonstrated that this was simply a case where
seven musicians had assembled to practise their art in
the morning stillness, that a very young dog had strayed
to the place, a burdensome intruder whom they had
tried to drive away by particularly terrifying or lofty
music, unfortunately with success. He pestered them

with his questions: were they, already disturbed enough by the mere presence of the stranger, to be expected to attend to his distracting interruptions as well and make them worse by responding to them? Even if the law commands us to reply to everybody, was such a tiny stray dog in truth a somebody worthy of the name? And perhaps they did not even understand him, for he likely enough barked his questions very indistinctly. Or perhaps they did understand him and with great self-control answered his questions, but he, a mere puppy unaccustomed to music, could not distinguish the answer from the music. And as for walking on their hind legs, perhaps, unlike other dogs, they actually used only these for walking; if it was a sin, well it was a sin. But they were alone, seven friends together, an intimate gathering within their own four walls so to speak, quite private so to speak; for one's friends, after all, are not the public, and where the public is not present an inquisitive little street dog is certainly not capable of constituting it; but, granting this, is it not as if nothing at all had happened? It's not quite so, but very nearly so, and parents should not let their children run about so freely, and had much better teach them to hold their tongues and respect the aged.

If all this is admitted, then it disposes of the whole case. But many things that are disposed of in the minds of grown-ups are not yet settled in the minds of the young. I rushed about, told my story, asked questions, made accusations and investigations, tried to drag others to the place where all this had happened, and burned to show everybody where I had stood and where the seven had stood, and where and how they had danced and made their music; and if any one had come with me, instead of shaking me off and laughing at me, I would probably have sacrificed my innocence and tried myself to stand on my hind legs so as to reconstruct the scene clearly. Now children are blamed for all they do, but also in the last resort forgiven for all they do. And I have preserved my childish qualities, and in spite of that have grown to be an old dog. Well, just as at that time I kept on unceasingly discussing the foregoing incident —which today I must confess I lay far less importance upon—analyzing it into its constituent parts, arguing it with my listeners without regard to the company I found myself in, devoting my whole time to the problem, which I found as wearisome as everybody else, but which—that was the difference—for that very reason I was resolved to pursue indefatigably until I solved it, so that I might be left free again to regard the ordinary, calm, happy life of every day: just so have I, though with less childish means—yet the difference is not so very great—labored in the years since and go on laboring today.

But it began with that concert. I do not blame the concert; it is my innate disposition that has driven me on, and it would certainly have found some other opportunity of coming into action had the concert never taken place. Yet the fact that it happened so soon used to make me feel sorry for myself; it robbed me of a great part of my childhood; the blissful life of the young dog, which many can spin out for years, in my case lasted for only a few short months. So be it. There are more important things than childhood. And perhaps I have the prospect of far more childish happiness, earned by a life of hard work, in my old age than any actual child would have the strength to bear, but which then I shall possess.

I began my enquiries with the simplest things; there was no lack of material; it is the actual superabundance, unfortunately, that casts me into despair in my darker hours. I began to enquire into the question: What the canine race nourished itself upon. Now that is, if you like, by no means a simple question, of course; it has occupied us since the dawn of time, it is the chief object of all our medication, countless observations and essays and views on this subject have been published, it has grown into a province of knowledge which in its prodigious compass is not only beyond the comprehension of any single scholar, but of all our scholars collectively, a burden which cannot be borne except by the whole of the dog community, and even then with difficulty and not quite in its totality; for it ever and again crumbles away like a neglected ancestral inheritance and must laboriously be rehabilitated anew—not to speak at all of the difficulties and almost unfulfillable conditions of my investigation. No one need point all this out to me, I know it all as well as any average sensual dog can do; I have no ambition to meddle with real scientific matters, I have all the respect for knowledge that it deserves, but to increase knowledge I lack the equipment, the diligence, the leisure, and—not least, and particularly during the past few years—the desire as well. I swallow down my food, but the slightest preliminary methodical politico-economical observation of it does not seem to me worth while. In this connection the essence of all knowledge is enough for me, the simple rule with which the mother weans her young ones from her teats and sends them out into the world: "Water the ground as much as you can." And in this sentence is not almost everything contained? What has scientific enquiry, ever since our first fathers inaugurated it, of decisive importance to add to this? Mere details, mere details, and how uncertain they are: but this rule will remain as long as we are dogs. It concerns our main staple of food: true, we have also other resources, but only at a pinch, and if the year is not too bad we could live on this main staple of our food; this food we find on the earth, but the earth needs our water to nourish it and only at that price provides us with our food, the emergence of which, however, and this should not be forgotten, can also be hastened by certain spells, songs, and ritual movements. But in my opinion that is all; there is nothing else that is fundamental to be said on the question. In this opinion, moreover, I am at one with the vast majority of the dog community, and must firmly dissociate myself from all heretical views on this point. Quite honestly I have no ambition to be peculiar, or to pose as being in the right against the majority; I am only too happy when I can agree with my comrades, as I do in this case. My own enquiries, however, are in another direction. My personal observation tells me that the earth, when it is watered and scratched according to the rules of science, extrudes nourishment, and moreover in such quality, in such abundance, in such ways, in such places, at such hours, as the laws partially or completely established by science demand. I accept all this; my question, however, is the following: "Whence does the earth procure this food?" A question which people in general pretend not to understand, and to which the best answer they can give is: "If you haven't enough to eat, we'll give you some of ours." Now consider this answer. I know that it is not one of the virtues of dogdom to share with others food that one has once gained possession of. Life is hard, the earth stubborn, science rich in knowledge but poor in practical results: any one who has food keeps it to himself; that is not selfishness, but the opposite, dog law, the unanimous decision of the people, the outcome of their victory over egoism, for the possessors are always in a minority. And for that reason this answer: "If you haven't enough to eat, we'll give you some of ours" is merely a way of speaking, a jest, a form of raillery. I have not forgotten that. But all the more significant did it seem to me, when I was rushing about everywhere with my questions during those days, that they put the jest aside as far as I was concerned; true, they did not actually give me anything to eat—where could they have found it at a moment's notice?—and even if any one chanced to have some food, naturally he forgot everything else in the fury of his hunger; yet they all seriously meant what they said when they made the offer, and here and there, right enough, I was presently allowed some slight trifle if I was only smart enough to snatch it quickly. How came it that people treated me so strangely, pampered me, favored me? Because I was a lean dog, badly fed and neglectful

of my needs? But there were countless badly fed dogs
running about, and the others snatched even the wretch-
edest scrap from under their noses whenever they could,
and not often from greed, but generally on principle.
No, they treated me with special favor; I cannot give
much detailed proof of this, but I have a firm conviction
that it was so. Was it my questions, then, that pleased
them, and that they regarded as so clever? No, my questions did not please them and were generally looked on
as stupid. And yet it could only have been my questions
that won me their attention. It was as if they would
rather do the impossible, that is stop my mouth with
food—they did not do it, but they would have liked to do
it—than endure my questions. But in that case they
would have done better to drive me away and refuse to
listen to my questions. No, they did not want to do that;
they did not indeed want to listen to my questions, but
it was because I asked questions that they did not want
to drive me away. That was the time—much as I was
ridiculed and treated as a silly puppy, and pushed here
and pushed there—the time when I actually enjoyed
most public esteem; never again was I to enjoy anything
like it; I had free entry everywhere, no obstacle was put
in my way, I was actually flattered, though the flattery
was disguised as rudeness. And all really because of my
questions, my impatience, my thirst for knowledge. Did
they want to lull me to sleep, to divert me, without violence, almost lovingly, from a false path, yet a path
whose falseness was not so completely beyond all doubt
that violence was permissible?—Also a certain respect
and fear kept them from employing violence. I divined

even in those days something of this; today I know it quite well, far better than those who actually practised it at the time: what they wanted to do was really to divert me from my path. They did not succeed; they achieved the opposite; my vigilance was sharpened. More, it became clear to me that it was I who was trying to seduce the others, and that I was actually successful up to a certain point. Only with the assistance of the whole dog world could I begin to understand my own questions. For instance when I asked: "Whence does the earth procure this food?" was I troubled, as appearances might quite well indicate, about the earth; was I troubled about the labors of the earth? Not in the least; that, as I very soon recognized, was far from my mind; all that I cared for was the race of dogs, that and nothing else. For what is there actually except our own species? To whom but it can one appeal in the wide and empty world? All knowledge, the totality of all questions and all answers, is contained in the dog. If one could but realize this knowledge, if one could but bring it into the light of day, if we dogs would but own that we know infinitely more than we admit to ourselves! Even the most loquacious dog is more secretive of his knowledge than the places where good food can be found. Trembling with desire, whipping yourself with your own tail, you steal cautiously upon your fellow-dog, you ask, you beg, you howl, you bite, and achieve—and achieve what you could have achieved just as well without any effort; amiable attention, friendly contiguity, honest acceptance, ardent embraces, barks that mingle as one: everything is directed towards achieving an

ecstasy, a forgetting and finding again; but the one thing
that you long to win above all, the admission of knowledge, remains denied to you. To such prayers, whether
silent or loud, the only answer you get, even after
you have employed your powers of seduction to the utmost, are vacant stares, averted glances, troubled and
veiled eyes. It is much the same as it was when, a mere
puppy, I shouted to the dog musicians and they remained silent.

Now one might say: "You torment yourself because
of your fellow-dogs, because of their silence on crucial
questions; you assert that they know more than they
admit, more than they will allow to be valid, and that
this silence, the mysterious reason for which is also, of
course, tacitly concealed, poisons existence and makes it
unendurable for you, so that you must either alter it or
have done with it; that may be; but you are yourself a
dog, you have also the dog knowledge; well, bring it
out, not merely in the form of a question, but as an answer. If you utter it, who will think of opposing you?
The great choir of dogdom will join in as if it had been
waiting for you. Then you will have clarity, truth,
avowal, as much of them as you desire. The roof of this
wretched life, of which you say so many hard things, will
burst open, and all of us, shoulder to shoulder, will as-
cend into the lofty realm of freedom. And if we should
not achieve that final consummation, if things should
become worse than before, if the whole truth should be
more insupportable than the half, if it should be proved
that the silent are in the right as the guardians of existence, if the faint hope that we still possess should give

way to complete hopelessness, the attempt is still worth the trial, since you do not desire to live as you are compelled to live. Well, then, why do you make it a reproach against the others that they are silent, and remain silent yourself?" Easy to answer: Because I am a dog; in essentials just as locked in silence as the others, stubbornly resisting my own questions, dour out of fear. To be precise, is it in the hope that they might answer me that I have questioned my fellow-dogs, at least since my adult years? Have I any such foolish hope? Can I contemplate the foundations of our existence, divine their profundity, watch the labor of their construction, that dark labor, and expect all this to be forsaken, neglected, undone, simply because I ask a question? No, that I truly expect no longer. I understand my fellow-dogs, am flesh of their flesh, of their miserable, ever-renewed, ever-desirous flesh. But it is not merely flesh and blood that we have in common, but knowledge also, and not only knowledge, but the key to it as well. I do not possess that key except in common with all the others; I cannot grasp it without their help. The hardest bones, containing the richest marrow, can be conquered only by a united crunching of all the teeth of all dogs. That of course is only a figure of speech and exaggerated; if all teeth were but ready they would not need even to bite, the bones would crack themselves and the marrow would be freely accessible to the feeblest of dogs. If I remain faithful to this metaphor, then the goal of my aims, my ques-tions, my enquiries, appears monstrous, it is true. For I want to compel all dogs thus to assemble together, I want the bones to crack open under the pressure of their collective preparedness, and then I want to dismiss them to the ordinary life that they love, while all by myself, quite alone, I lap up the marrow. That sounds monstrous, almost as if I wanted to feed on the marrow, not merely of a bone, but of the whole canine race itself. But it is only a metaphor. The marrow that I am discussing here is no food; on the contrary it is a poison.

My questions only serve as a goad to myself; I only want to be stimulated by the silence which rises up around me as the ultimate answer. "How long will you be able to endure the fact that the world of dogs, as your researches make more and more evident, is pledged to silence and always will be? How long will you be able to endure it?" That is the real great question of my life, before which all smaller ones sink into insignificance; it is put to myself alone and concerns no one else. Unfortunately I can answer it more easily than the smaller, specific questions: I shall probably hold out till my natural end; the calm of old age will put up a greater and greater resistance to all disturbing questions. I shall very likely die in silence and surrounded by silence, indeed almost peacefully, and I look forward to that with composure. An admirably strong heart, lungs that it is impossible to use up before their time, have been given to us dogs as if in malice; we survive all questions, even our own, bulwarks of silence that we are.

Recently I have taken more and more to casting up my life, looking for the decisive, the fundamental, error that I must surely have made; and I cannot find it. And yet I must have made it, for if I had not made it and yet were unable by the diligent labor of a long life to achieve my desire, that would prove that my desire is impossible, and complete hopelessness must follow. Behold, then, the work of a lifetime. First of all my enquiries into the question: Whence does the earth procure the food it gives us? A young dog, at bottom naturally greedy for life, I renounced all enjoyments, apprehensively avoided all pleasures, buried my head between my front paws when I was confronted by temptation, and addressed myself to my task. I was no scholar, neither in the information I acquired, nor in method, nor in intention. That was probably a defect, but it could not have been a decisive one. I had had little schooling, for I left my mother's care at an early age, soon got used to independence, led a free life; and premature independence is inimical to systematic learning. But I have seen much, listened to much, spoken with dogs of all sorts and conditions, understood everything, I believe, fairly intelligently, and correlated my particular observations fairly intelligently: that has compensated somewhat for my lack of scholarship, not to mention that independence, if it is a disadvantage in learning things, is an actual advantage when one is making one's own enquiries. In my case it was all the more necessary as I was not able to employ the real method of science, to avail myself, that is, of the labors of my predecessors, and establish contact with contemporary investigators. I was entirely cast on my own resources, began at the very beginning, and with the consciousness, inspiriting to youth, but utterly crushing to age, that the fortuitous point to which I carried my labors must also be the final one. Was I really so alone in my enquiries, at

the beginning and up to now? Yes and no. It is incon-
ceivable that there must not always have been and that
there are not today individual dogs in the same case as
myself. I cannot be so accursed as that. I do not deviate from the dog nature by a hairbreadth. Every dog
has like me the impulse to question, and I have like
every dog the impulse not to answer. Every one has the
impulse to question. How otherwise could my questions
have affected my hearers in the slightest—and they were
often affected, to my ecstatic delight, an exaggerated
delight, I must confess—and how otherwise could I have
been prevented from achieving much more than I have
done? And that I have the compulsion to remain silent
needs unfortunately no particular proof. I am at bottom,
then, no different from any other dog; everybody, no
matter how he may differ in opinion from me and reject
my views, will gladly admit that, and I in turn will admit
as much of any other dog. Only the mixture of the elements is different, a difference very important for the
individual, insignificant for the race. And now can one
credit that the composition of these available elements
has never chanced through all the past and present to
result in a mixture similar to mine, one, moreover, if
mine be regarded as unfortunate, more unfortunate
still? To think so would be contrary to all experience.
We dogs are all engaged in the strangest occupations,
occupations in which one would refuse to believe if one
had not the most reliable information concerning them.
The best example that I can quote is that of the soaring
dog. The first time I heard of one I laughed and simply
refused to believe it. What? One was asked to believe

that there was a very tiny species of dog, not much bigger than my head even when it was full grown, and this
dog, who must of course be a feeble creature, an artifi-
cial, weedy, brushed and curled fop by all accounts, incapable of making an honest jump, this dog was supposed, according to people's stories, to remain for the
most part high up in the air, apparently doing nothing
at all but simply resting there? No, to try to make me
swallow such things was exploiting the simplicity of a
young dog too outrageously, I told myself. But shortly
afterwards I heard from another source an account of
another soaring dog. Could there be a conspiracy to
fool me? But after that I saw the dog musicians with my
own eyes, and from that day I considered everything
possible, no prejudices fettered my powers of apprehension, I investigated the most senseless rumors, following them as far as they could take me, and the most senseless seemed to me in this senseless world more probable
than the sensible, and moreover particularly fertile for
investigation. So it was too with the soaring dogs. I discovered a great many things about them; true, I have
succeeded to this day in seeing none of them, but of their
existence I have been firmly convinced for a long time,
and they occupy an important place in my picture of the
world. As usual it is not, of course, their technique that
chiefly gives me to think. It is wonderful—who can gain-
say it?—that these dogs should be able to float in the air:
in my amazed admiration for that I am at one with my
fellow-dogs. But far more strange to my mind is the
senselessness, the dumb senselessness of these existences.
They have no relation whatever to the general life of

the community, they hover in the air, and that is all, and life goes on its usual way; someone now and then refers to art and artists, but there it ends. But why, my good dogs, why on earth do these dogs float in the air? What sense is there in their occupation? Why can one get no word of explanation regarding them? Why do they hover up there, letting their legs, the pride of dogs, fall into desuetude, preserving a detachment from the nour-ishing earth, reaping without having sowed, being par-ticularly well provided for, as I hear, and at the cost of the dog community too? I can flatter myself that my enquiries into these matters made some stir. People began to investigate after a fashion, to collect data; they made a beginning, at least, although they are never likely to go farther. But after all that is something. And though the truth will not be discovered by such means —never can that stage be reached—yet they throw light on some of the profounder ramifications of falsehood. For all the senseless phenomena of our existence, and the most senseless by far of all, are susceptible of in-vestigation. Not completely, of course—that is the dia-bolical jest—but sufficiently to spare one painful ques-tions. Take the soaring dogs once more as an example; they are not haughty as one might imagine at first, but rather particularly dependent upon their fellow-dog; if one tries to put oneself in their place one will see that. For they must do what they can to obtain pardon, and not openly—that would be a violation of the obligation to keep silence—they must do what they can to obtain pardon for their way of life, or else divert attention from it so that it may be forgotten—and they do this, I have been told, by means of an almost unendurable volubility. They are perpetually talking, partly of their philosophical reflections, with which, seeing that they have completely renounced bodily exertion, they can continuously occupy themselves, partly of the observations which they have made from their exalted stations; and although, as is very understandable considering their lazy existence, they are not much distinguished for intellectual power, and their philosophy is as worthless as their observations, and science can make hardly any use of their utterances, and besides is not reduced to draw assistance from such wretched sources, nevertheless if one asks what the soaring dogs are really doing one will invariably receive the reply that they contribute a great deal to knowledge. "That is true," remarks someone, "but their contributions are worthless and wearisome." The reply to that is a shrug, or a change of the subject, or annoyance, or laughter, and in a little while, when you ask again, you learn once more that they contribute to knowledge, and finally when you are asked the question you yourself will reply—if you are not careful—to the same effect. And perhaps indeed it is well not to be too obstinate, but to yield to public sentiment, to accept the extant soaring dogs, and without recognizing their right to existence, which cannot be done, yet to tolerate them. But more than this must not be required; that would be going too far, and yet the demand is made. We are perpetually being asked to put up with new soaring dogs who are always appearing. One does not even know where they come from. Do these dogs multiply by propagation? Have they actually the strength for that?—for they are nothing much more than a beautiful coat of hair, and what is there in that to propagate? But even if that improbable contingency were possible, when could it take place? For they are invariably seen alone, self-complacently floating high up in the air, and if for once in a while they descend to take a run, it lasts only for a minute or two, a few mincing struts and once more they are back in strict solitude, absorbed in what is supposed to be profound thought, from which, even when they exert themselves to the utmost, they cannot tear themselves free, or at least so they say. But if they do not propagate their kind, is it credible that there can be dogs who voluntarily give up life on the solid ground, voluntarily become soaring dogs, and merely for the sake of the comfort and a certain technical accomplishment choose that empty life on cushions up there? It is unthinkable; neither propagation nor voluntary transition is thinkable. The facts, however, show that there are always new soaring dogs in evidence; from which one must conclude that, in spite of obstacles which appear insurmountable to our understanding, no dog species, however curious, ever dies out, once it exists, or, at least, not without a tough struggle, not without being capable of putting up a successful defense for a long time.

But if that is valid for such an out-of-the-way, externally odd, inefficient species as the soaring dog, must I not also accept it as valid for mine? Besides, I am not in the least queer outwardly; an ordinary middle-class dog such as is very prevalent, in this neighborhood, at least, I am neither particularly exceptional in any way, nor particularly repellent in any way; and in my youth and to some extent also in maturity, so long as I attended to my appearance and had lots of exercise, I was actually considered a very handsome dog. My front view was particularly admired, my slim legs, the fine set of my head; but my silvery white and yellow coat, which curled only at the hair tips, was very pleasing too; in all that there was nothing strange; the only strange thing about me is my nature, yet even that, as I am always careful to remember, has its foundation in universal dog nature. Now if not even the soaring dogs live in isolation, but invariably manage to encounter their fellows somewhere or other in the great dog world, and even to conjure new generations of themselves out of nothingness, then I too can live in the confidence that I am not quite forlorn. Certainly the fate of types like mine must be a strange one, and the existence of my colleagues can never be of visible help to me, if for no other reason than that I should scarcely ever be able to recognize them. We are the dogs who are crushed by the silence, who long to break through it, literally to get a breath of fresh air; the others seem to thrive on silence: true, that is only so in appearance, as in the case of the musical dogs, who ostensibly were quite calm when they played, but in reality were in a state of intense excitement; nevertheless the illusion is very strong, one tries to make a breach in it, but it mocks every attempt. What help, then, do my colleagues find? What kind of attempts do they make to manage to go on living in spite of everything? These attempts may be of various kinds. My own bout of questioning while

I was young was one. So I thought that perhaps if I as·
sociated with those who asked many questions I might
find my real comrades. Well, I did so for some time,
with great self-control, a self-control made necessary
by the annoyance I felt when I was interrupted by per
petual questions that I mostly could not answer myself:
for the only thing that concerns me is to obtain answers.
Moreover, who but is eager to ask questions when he is
young, and how, when so many questions are going
about, are you to pick out the right questions? One question sounds like another; it is the intention that counts,
but that is often hidden even from the questioner. And
besides it is a peculiarity of dogs to be always asking
questions, they ask them confusedly all together; it is
as if in doing that they were trying to obliterate every
trace of the genuine questions. No, my real colleagues
are not to be found among the youthful questioners,
and just as little among the old and silent, to whom I
now belong. But what good are all these questions, for
they have failed me completely; apparently my colleagues are cleverer dogs than I, and have recourse to
other excellent methods that enable them to bear this
life, methods which, nevertheless, as I can tell from my
own experience, though they may perhaps help at a
pinch, though they may calm, lull to rest, distract, are
yet on the whole as impotent as my own, for, no matter
where I look, I can see no sign of their success. I am
afraid that the last thing by which I can hope to recog-·
nize my real colleagues is their success. But where, then,
are my real colleagues? Yes, that is the burden of my
complaint; that is the kernel of it. Where are they?

Everywhere and nowhere. Perhaps my next-door neighbor, only three jumps away, is one of them; we often
bark across to each other, he calls on me sometimes too,
though I do not call on him. Is he my real colleague? I
do not know, I certainly see no sign of it in him, but it
is possible. It is possible, but all the same nothing is
more improbable. When he is away I can amuse myself,
drawing on my fancy, by discovering in him many things
that have a suspicious resemblance to myself; but once
he stands before me all my fancies become ridiculous.
An old dog, a little smaller even than myself—and I am
hardly medium size—brown, short-haired, with a tired
hang of the head and a shuffling gait; on the top of all
this he trails his left hind leg behind him a little because of some disease. For a long time now I have been
more intimate with him than with anybody else; I am
glad to say that I can still get on tolerably well with
him, and when he goes away I shout the most friendly
greetings after him, though not out of affection, but in
anger at myself; for if I follow him I find him just as
disgusting again, slinking along there with his trailing
leg and his much too low hind-quarters. Sometimes it
seems to me as if I were trying to humiliate myself by
privately calling him my colleague. Nor in our talks does
he betray any trace of similarity of thought; true, he is
clever and cultured enough as these things go here, and
I could learn much from him; but is it for cleverness
and culture that I am looking? We converse usually
about local questions, and I am astonished—my isolation
has made me more clear-sighted in such matters—how
much intelligence is needed even by an ordinary dog,

even in average and not unfavorable circumstances, if
he is to live out his life and defend himself against the
greater of life's customary dangers. True, knowledge
provides the rules one must follow, but even to grasp
them imperfectly and in rough outline is by no means
easy, and when one has actually grasped them the real
difficulty still remains, namely, to apply them to local
conditions—here almost nobody can help, almost every
hour brings new tasks, and every new patch of earth its
specific problems; no one can maintain that he has settled everything for good and that henceforth his life
will go on, so to speak, of itself, not even I myself, though my needs shrink literally from day to day.
And all this ceaseless labor—to what end? Merely to
entomb oneself deeper and deeper in silence, it seems,
so deep that one can never be dragged out of it again
by anybody.

People often cry up the universal progress made by
the dog community throughout the ages, and probably
mean by that more particularly the progress in knowledge. Certainly knowledge is progressing, its advance
is irresistible, it actually progresses at an accelerating
speed, always faster, but what is there to praise in that?
It is as if one were to praise someone because with the
years he grows older, and in consequence comes nearer
and nearer to death with increasing speed. That is a
natural and moreover an ugly process, in which I find
nothing to praise. I can only see decline everywhere,
in saying which, however, I do not mean that earlier
generations were essentially better than ours, but only
younger; that was their great advantage, their memory

was not so overburdened as ours today, it was easier to
get them to speak out, and even if nobody actually succeeded in doing that, the possibility of it was greater,
and it is indeed this greater sense of possibility that
moves us so deeply when we listen to those old and
strangely simple stories. Here and there we catch a
curiously significant phrase and we would almost like
to leap to our feet, if we did not feel the weight of centuries upon us. No, whatever objection I may have to
my age, former generations were not better, indeed
in a sense they were far worse, far weaker. Even in those
days wonders did not openly walk the streets for any
one to seize; but all the same dogs—I cannot put it in
any other way—had not yet become so doggish as today,
the edifice of dogdom was still loosely put together, the
true Word could still have intervened, planning or re-
planning the structure, changing it at will, transforming
it into its opposite; and the Word was there, was very
near at least, on the tip of everybody's tongue, any
one might have hit upon it. And what has become of
it today? Today one may pluck out one's very heart
and not find it. Our generation is lost, it may be, but it
is more blameless than those earlier ones. I can understand the hesitation of my generation, indeed it is no
longer mere hesitation; it is the thousandth forgetting
of a dream dreamt a thousand times and forgotten a
thousand times; and who can damn us merely for forgetting for the thousandth time? But I fancy I understand the hesitation of our forefathers too, we would
probably have acted just as they did; indeed I could
almost say: Well for us that it was not we who had to

take the guilt upon us, that instead we can hasten in almost guiltless silence towards death in a world darkened by others. When our first fathers strayed they had doubtless scarcely any notion that their aberration was to be an endless one, they could still literally see the cross-roads, it seemed an easy matter to turn back whenever they pleased, and if they hesitated to turn back it was merely because they wanted to enjoy a dog's life for a little while longer; it was not yet a genuine dog's life, and already it seemed intoxicatingly beautiful to them, so what must it become in a little while, a very little while, and so they strayed farther. They did not know what we can now guess at, contemplating the course of history: that change begins in the soul before it appears in ordinary existence, and that, when they began to enjoy a dog's life, they must already have possessed real old dogs' souls, and were by no means so near their starting-point as they thought, or as their eyes feasting on all doggish joys tried to persuade them. But who can speak of youth at this time of day? These were the really young dogs, but their sole ambition unfortunately was to become old dogs, truly a thing which they could not fail to achieve, as all succeeding generations show, and ours, the last, most clearly of all.

Naturally I do not talk to my neighbor of these things, but often I cannot but think of them when I am sitting opposite him—that typical old dog—or bury my nose in his coat, which already has a whiff of the smell of cast-off hides. To talk to him, or even to any of the others, about such things, would be pointless. I know what course the conversation would take. He would urge a slight objection now and then, but finally he would agree—agreement is the best weapon of defense —and the matter would be buried: why indeed trouble to exhume it at all? And in spite of this there is a profounder understanding between my neighbor and me, going deeper than mere words. I shall never cease to maintain that, though I have no proof of it and perhaps am merely suffering from an ordinary delusion, caused by the fact that for a long time this dog has been the only one with whom I have held any communication, and so I am bound to cling to him. "Are you after all my colleague in your own fashion? And ashamed because everything has miscarried with you? Look, the same fate has been mine. When I am alone I weep over it; come, it is sweeter to weep in company." I often have such thoughts as these and then I give him a prolonged look. He does not lower his glance, but neither can one read anything from it; he gazes at me dully, wondering why I am silent and why I have broken off the conversation. But perhaps that very glance is his way of questioning me, and I disappoint him just as he disappoints me. In my youth, if other problems had not been more important to me then, and I had not been perfectly satisfied with my own company, I would probably have asked him straight out and received an answer flatly agreeing with me, and that would have been worse even than today's silence. But is not everybody silent exactly in the same way? What is there to prevent me from believing that everyone is my colleague, instead of thinking that I have only one or two fellow-enquirers —lost and forgotten along with their petty achievements,

so that I can never reach them by any road through the
darkness of ages or the confused throng of the present:
why not believe that all dogs from the beginning of
time have been my colleagues, all diligent in their own
way, all unsuccessful in their own way, all silent or
falsely garrulous in their own way, as hopeless research
is apt to make one? But in that case I need not have
severed myself from my fellows at all, I could have remained quietly among the others, I had no need to fight
my way out like a stubborn child through the closed
ranks of the grown-ups, who indeed wanted as much as
I to find a way out, and who seemed incomprehensible
to me simply because of their knowledge, which told
them that nobody could ever escape and that it was
stupid to use force.

Such ideas, however, are definitely due to the influence of my neighbor; he confuses me, he fills me with
dejection; and yet in himself he is happy enough, at
least when he is in his own quarters I often hear him
shouting and singing; it is really unbearable. It would
be a good thing to renounce this last tie also, to cease
giving way to the vague dreams which all contact with
dogs unavoidably provokes, no matter how hardened
one may consider oneself, and to employ the short time
that still remains for me exclusively in prosecuting my
researches. The next time he comes I shall slip away, or
pretend I am asleep, and keep up the pretense until
he stops visiting me.

Also my researches have fallen into desuetude, I relax, I grow weary, I trot mechanically where once I
raced enthusiastically. I think of the time when I be-

gan to enquire into the question: "Whence does the earth procure this food?" Then indeed I really lived among the people, I pushed my way where the crowd was thickest, wanted everybody to know my work and be my audience, and my audience was even more essential to me than my work; I still expected to produce some effect or other, and that naturally gave me a great impetus, which now that I am solitary is gone. But in those days I was so full of strength that I achieved something unprecedented, something at variance with all our principles, and that every contemporary eyewitness assuredly recalls now as an uncanny feat. Our scientific knowledge, which generally makes for an extreme specialization, is remarkably simple in one province. I mean where it teaches that the earth engenders our food, and then, after having laid down this hypothesis, gives the methods by which the different foods may be achieved in their best kinds and greatest abundance. Now it is of course true that the earth brings forth all food, of that there can be no doubt; but as simple as people generally imagine it to be the matter is not; and their belief that it is simple prevents further enquiry. Take an ordinary occurrence that happens every day. If we were to be quite inactive, as I am almost completely now, and after a perfunctory scratching and watering of the soil lie down and wait for what was to come, then we should find the food on the ground, assuming, that is, that a result of some kind is inevitable. Nevertheless that is not what usually happens. Those who have preserved even a little freedom of judgment on scientific matters—and their numbers are truly small, for science draws a wider and wider circle round itself—will easily see, without having to make any specific experiment, that the main part of the food that is discovered on the ground in such cases comes from above; indeed customarily we snap up most of our food, according to our dexterity and greed, before it has reached the ground at all. In saying that, however, I am saying nothing against science; the earth, of course, brings forth this kind of food too. Whether the earth draws one kind of food out of itself and calls down another kind from the skies perhaps makes no essential difference, and science, which has established that in both cases it is necessary to prepare the ground, need not perhaps concern itself with such distinctions, for does it not say: "If you have food in your jaws you have solved all questions for the time being." But it seems to me that science nevertheless takes a veiled interest, at least to some extent, in these matters, inasmuch as it recognizes two chief methods of procuring food; namely the actual preparation of the ground, and secondly the auxiliary perfecting processes of incantation, dance, and song. I find here a distinction in accordance with the one I have myself made; not a definitive distinction, perhaps, but yet clear enough. The scratching and watering of the ground, in my opinion, serves to produce both kinds of food, and remains indispensable; incantation, dance, and song, however, are concerned less with the ground food in the narrower sense, and serve principally to attract the food from above. Tradition fortifies me in this interpretation. The ordinary dogs themselves set science right here without knowing it, and without science being able to venture a word in reply. If, as science claims, these ceremonies minister only to the soil, giving it the potency, let us say, to attract food from the air, then logically they should be directed exclusively to the soil; it is the soil that the incantations must be whispered to, the soil that must be danced to. And to the best of my knowledge science ordains nothing else than this. But now comes the remarkable thing; the people in all their ceremonies gaze upwards. This is no insult to science, since science does not forbid it, but leaves the husbandman complete freedom in this respect; in its teaching it takes only the soil into account, and if the husbandman carries out its instructions concerning the preparation of the ground it is content; yet, in my opinion, it should really demand more than this if it is logical. And, though I have never been deeply initiated into science, I simply cannot conceive how the learned can bear to let our people, unruly and passionate as they are, chant their incantations with their faces turned upwards, wail our ancient folk songs into the air, and spring high in their dances as though, forgetting the ground, they wished to take flight from it forever. I took this contradiction as my starting-point, and whenever, according to the teachings of science, the harvest time was approaching, I restricted my attention to the ground, it was the ground that I scratched in the dance, and I almost gave myself a crick in the neck keeping my head as close to the ground as I could. Later I dug a hole for my nose, and sang and declaimed into it so that only the ground might hear, and nobody else beside or above me.

The results of my experiment were meagre. Sometimes the food did not appear, and I was already preparing to rejoice at this proof, but then the food would appear; it was exactly as if my strange performance had caused some confusion at first, but had shown itself later to possess advantages, so that in my case the usual barking and leaping could be dispensed with. Often, indeed, the food appeared in greater abundance than formerly, but then again it would stay away altogether. With a diligence hitherto unknown in a young dog I drew up exact reports of all my experiments, fancied that here and there I was on a scent that might lead me further, but then it lost itself again in obscurity. My inadequate grounding in science also undoubtedly held me up here. What guarantee had I, for instance, that the absence of the food was not caused by unscientific preparation of the ground rather than by my experiments, and if that should be so, then all my conclusions were invalid. In certain circumstances I might have been able to achieve an almost scrupulously exact experiment; namely, if I had succeeded only once in bringing down food by an upward incantation without preparing the ground at all, and then had failed to extract food by an incantation directed exclusively to the ground. I attempted indeed something of this kind, but without any real belief in it and without the conditions being quite perfect; for it is my fixed opinion that a certain amount of ground-preparation is always necessary, and even if the heretics who deny this are right, their theory can never be proved in any case, seeing that the watering of the ground is done under a kind of compulsion, and within certain limits simply cannot be avoided. An other and somewhat tangential experiment succeeded better and aroused some public attention. Arguing from the customary method of snatching food while still in the air, I decided to allow the food to fall to the ground, but to make no effort to snatch it. Accordingly I always made a small jump in the air when the food appeared, but timed it so that it might always fail of its object; in the majority of instances the food fell dully and indifferently to the ground in spite of this, and I flung myself furiously upon it, with the fury both of hunger and of disappointment. But in isolated cases something else happened, something really strange; the food did not fall but followed me through the air; the food pursued the hungry. That never went on for long, always for only a short stretch, then the food fell after all, or vanished completely, or—the most common case—my greed put a premature end to the experiment and I swallowed down the tempting food. All the same I was happy at that time, a stir of curiosity ran through my neighborhood, I attracted uneasy attention, I found my acquaintances more accessible to my questions, I could see in their eyes a gleam that seemed like an appeal for help; and even if it was only the reflection of my own glance I asked for nothing more, I was satisfied. Until at last I discovered —and the others discovered it simultaneously—that this experiment of mine was a commonplace of science, had already succeeded with others far more brilliantly than with me, and though it had not been attempted for a long time on account of the extreme self-control it required, had also no need to be repeated, for scientifically it had no value at all. It only proved what was already known, that the ground not only attracts food vertically from above, but also at a slant, indeed sometimes in spirals. So there I was left with my experiment, but I was not discouraged, I was too young for that; on the contrary, this disappointment braced me to attempt perhaps the greatest achievement of my life. I did not believe the scientists' depreciations of my experiment, yet belief was of no avail here, but only proof, and I resolved to set about establishing that and thus raise my experiment from its original irrelevance and set it in the very center of the field of research. I wished to prove that when I retreated before the food it was not the ground that attracted it at a slant, but I who drew it after me. This first experiment, it is true, I could not carry any farther; to see the food before one and experiment in a scientific spirit at the same time—one cannot keep that up indefinitely. But I decided to do something else; I resolved to fast completely as long as I could stand it, and at the same time avoid all sight of food, all temptation. If I were to withdraw myself in this manner, remain lying day and night with closed eyes, trouble myself neither to snatch food from the air nor to lift it from the ground, and if, as I dared not expect, yet faintly hoped, without taking any of the customary measures, and merely in response to the un-avoidable irrational watering of the ground and the quiet recitation of the incantations and songs (the dance I wished to omit, so as not weaken my powers) the food were to come of itself from above, and without going near the ground were to knock at my teeth for admit-tance—if that were to happen, then, even *if* science was not confuted, for it has enough elasticity to admit exceptions and isolated cases—I asked myself what would the other dogs say, who fortunately do not possess such extreme elasticity? For this would be no exceptional case like those handed down by history, such as the incident, let us say, of the dog who refuses, because of bodily illness or trouble of mind, to prepare the ground, to track down and seize his food, upon which the whole dog community recite magical formulæ and by this means succeed in making the food deviate from its customary route into the jaws of the invalid. I, on the contrary, was perfectly sound and at the height of my powers, my appetite so splendid that it prevented me all day from thinking of anything but itself; I submitted, moreover, whether it be credited or not, voluntarily to my period of fasting, was myself quite able to conjure down my own supply of food and wished also to do so, and so I asked no assistance from the dog community, and indeed rejected it in the most determined manner.

I sought a suitable place for myself in an outlying clump of bushes, where I would have to listen to no talk of food, no sound of munching jaws and bones being gnawed; I ate my fill for the last time and laid me down. As far as possible I wanted to pass my whole time with closed eyes; until the food came it would be perpetual night for me, even though my vigil might last for days or weeks. During that time, however, I dared not sleep much, better indeed if I did not sleep at all—and that made everything much harder—for I must not only conjure the food down from the air, but

also be on my guard lest I should be asleep when it arrived; yet on the other hand sleep would be very welcome to me, for I would manage to fast much longer
asleep than awake. For those reasons I decided to arrange my time prudently and sleep a great deal, but
always in short snatches. I achieved this by always resting my head while I slept on some frail twig, which
soon snapped and so awoke me. So there I lay, sleeping
or keeping watch, dreaming or singing quietly to myself. My first vigils passed uneventfully; perhaps in the
place whence the food came no one had yet noticed
that I was lying there in resistance to the normal course
of things, and so there was no sign. I was a little disturbed in my concentration by the fear that the other
dogs might miss me, presently find me, and attempt
something or other against me. A second fear was that
at the mere wetting of the ground, though it was un-
fruitful ground according to the findings of science,
some chance nourishment might appear and seduce
me by its smell. But for a time nothing of that kind
happened and I could go on fasting. Apart from such
fears I was more calm during this first stage than I
could remember ever having been before. Although
in reality I was laboring to annul the findings of science, I felt within me a deep reassurance, indeed almost the proverbial serenity of the scientific worker.
In my thoughts I begged forgiveness of science; there
must be room in it for my researches too; consolingly
in my ears rang the assurance that no matter how great
the effect of my enquiries might be, and indeed the
greater the better, I would not be lost to ordinary dog

life; science regarded my attempts with benevolence, it itself would undertake the interpretation of my discoveries, and that promise already meant fulfilment; while until now I had felt outlawed in my innermost heart and had run my head against the traditional walls of my species like a savage, I would now be accepted with great honor, the long-yearned-for warmth of assembled canine bodies would lap me round, I would ride uplifted high on the shoulders of my fellows. Remarkable effects of my first hunger. My achievement seemed so great to me that I began to weep with emotion and self-pity there among the quiet bushes, which it must be confessed was not very understandable, for when I was looking forward to my well-earned reward why should I weep? Probably out of pure happiness. It is always when I am happy, and that is seldom enough, that I weep. After that, however, these feelings soon passed. My beautiful fancies fled one by one before the increasing urgency of my hunger; a little longer and I was, after an abrupt farewell to all my imaginations and my sublime feelings, totally alone with the hunger burning in my entrails. "That is my hunger," I told myself countless times during this stage, as if I wanted to convince myself that my hunger and I were still two things and I could shake it off like a burdensome lover; but in reality we were very painfully óne, and when I explained to myself: "That is my hunger," it was really my hunger that was speaking and having its joke at my expense. A bad, bad time! I still shudder to think of it, and not merely, please note this, on account of the suffering I endured then, but because I know I was insufficiently equipped then and consequently shall have to live through that suffering once more if I am ever to achieve anything; for today I still hold fasting to be the final and most potent weapon of research. The way goes through fasting; the highest, if it is attainable, is attainable only by the highest effort, and the highest effort among us is voluntary fasting. So when I think of those times—and I would gladly pass my life in brooding over them—I cannot help thinking also of the time that still threatens me. It seems to me that it takes almost a lifetime to recuperate from such an attempt; my whole life as an adult lies between me and that fast, and I have not recovered yet. When I begin upon my next fast I shall perhaps have more resolution than the first time, because of my greater experience and deeper insight into the need for the attempt, but my powers are still enfeebled by that first essay, and so I shall probably begin to fail at the mere approach of these familiar horrors. My weaker appetite will not help me; it will reduce the value of the attempt only by a very little, and will, indeed, probably force me to fast longer than was necessary the first time. I think I am clear on these and many other matters, the long interval has not been wanting in trial attempts, often enough I have literally got my teeth into hunger; but I was not still strong enough for the ultimate effort, and now the unspoilt ardor of youth is of course gone forever. It vanished in the great privations of that first fast. All sorts of thoughts tormented me. Our forefathers appeared threateningly before me. True, I held them responsible for everything, even if I dared not say so openly; it was they who involved our dog life in guilt, and so I could easily have responded to their menaces with countermenaces; but I bow before their knowledge, it came from sources of which we know no longer, and for that reason, much as I may feel compelled to oppose them, I shall never actually overstep their laws, but content myself with wriggling out through the gaps, for which I have a particularly good nose. On the question of fasting I appealed to the well-known dialogue in the course of which one of our sages once expressed the intention of forbidding fasting, but was dissuaded by a second with the words: "But who would ever think of fasting?" whereupon the first sage allowed himself to be persuaded and withdrew the prohibition. But now arises the question: "Is not fasting really forbidden after all?" The great majority of commentators deny this and regard fasting as freely permitted, and holding as they think with the second sage do not worry in the least about the evil consequences that may result from erroneous interpretations. I had naturally assured myself on this point before I began my fast. But now that I was twisted with the pangs of hunger, and in my distress of mind sought relief in my own hind legs, despairingly licking and gnawing at them up to the very buttocks, the universal interpretation of this dialogue seemed to me entirely and completely false, I cursed the commentators' science, I cursed myself for having been led astray by it; for the dialogue contained, as any child could see, more than merely one prohibition of fasting; the first sage wished to forbid fasting; what a sage wishes is already done, so fasting was forbidden; as for the second sage, he not only agreed with the first, but actually considered fasting impossible, piled therefore on the first prohibition a second, that of dog nature itself; the first sage saw this and thereupon withdrew the explicit prohibition, that was to say, he imposed upon all dogs, the matter being now settled, the obligation to know themselves and to make their own prohibitions regarding fasting. So here was a threefold prohibition instead of merely one, and I had violated it. Now I could at least have obeyed at this point, though tardily, but in the midst of my pain I felt a longing to go on fasting, and I followed it as greedily as if it were a strange dog. I could not stop; perhaps too I was already too weak to get up and seek safety for myself in familiar scenes. I tossed about on the fallen forest leaves, I could no longer sleep, I heard noises on every side; the world, which had been asleep during my life hitherto, seemed to have been awakened by my fasting, I was tortured by the fancy that I would never be able to eat again, and I must eat so as to reduce to silence this world rioting so noisily round me, and I would never be able to do so; but the greatest noise of all came from my own belly, I often laid my ear against it with startled eyes, for I could hardly believe what I heard. And now that things were becoming unendurable my very nature seemed to be seized by the general frenzy, and made senseless attempts to save itself; the smell of food began to assail me, delicious dainties that I had long since forgotten, delights of my childhood; yes, I could smell the very fragrance of my mother's teats; I forgot my resolution to resist all smells, or rather I did not forget it; I dragged myself to and fro, never for more than a few yards, and sniffed as if that were in accordance with my resolution, as if I were looking for food simply to be on my guard against it. The fact that I found nothing did not disappoint me; the food must be there, only it was always a few steps away, my legs failed me before I could reach it. But simultaneously I knew that nothing was there, and that I made those feeble movements simply out of fear lest I might collapse in this place and never be able to leave it. My last hopes, my last dreams vanished; I would perish here miserably; of what use were my researches?—childish attempts undertaken in childish and far happier days; here and now was the hour of deadly earnest, here my enquiries should have shown their value, but where had they vanished? Only a dog lay here helplessly snapping at the empty air, a dog who, though he still watered the ground with convulsive haste at short intervals and without being aware of it, could not remember even the shortest of the countless incantations stored in his memory, not even the little rhyme which the newly-born puppy says when it snuggles under its mother. It seemed to me as if I were separated from all my fellows, not by a quite short stretch, but by an infinite distance, and as if I would die less of hunger than of neglect. For it was clear that nobody troubled about me, nobody beneath the earth, on it, or above it; I was dying of their indifference; they said indifferently: "He is dying," and it would actually come to pass. And did I not myself assent? Did

I not say the same thing? Had I not wanted to be forsaken like this? Yes, brothers, but not so as to perish
in that place, but to achieve truth and escape from this
world of falsehood, where there is no one from whom
you can learn the truth, not even from me, born as I
am a citizen of falsehood. Perhaps the truth was not so
very far off, and I not so forsaken, therefore, as I
thought; or I may have been forsaken less by my fellows than by myself, in yielding and consenting to die.

But one does not die so easily as a nervous dog im-
agines. I merely fainted, and when I came to and raised
my eyes a strange hound was standing before me. I did
not feel hungry, but rather filled with strength, and my
limbs, it seemed to me, were light and agile, though I
made no attempt to prove this by getting to my feet.
My visual faculties in themselves were no keener than
usual, a beautiful but not at all extraordinary hound
stood before me; I could see that, and that was all, and
yet it seemed to me that I saw something more in him.
There was blood under me, at first I took it for food;
but I recognized it immediately as blood that I had
vomited. I turned my eyes from it to the strange hound.
He was lean, long-legged, brown with a patch of white
here and there, and had a fine, strong, piercing glance.
"What are you doing here?" he asked. "You must leave
this place." "I can't leave it just now," I said, without
trying to explain, for how could I explain everything
to him; besides, he seemed to be in a hurry. "Please go
away," he said, impatiently lifting his feet and setting
them down again. "Let me be," I said, "leave me to
myself and don't worry about me; the others don't."

"I ask you to go for your own sake," he said. "You can ask for any reason you like," I replied. "I can't go even if I wanted to." "You need have no fear of that," he said, smiling. "You can go all right. It's because you seem to be feeble that I ask you to go now, and you can go slowly if you like; if you linger now you'll have to race off later on." "That's my affair," I replied. "It's mine too," he said, saddened by my stubbornness, yet obviously resolved to let me lie for the time being, but at the same time to seize the opportunity of paying court to me. At any other time I would gladly have submitted to the blandishments of such a beautiful creature, but at that moment, why, I cannot tell, the thought filled me with terror. "Get out!" I screamed, and all the louder as I had no other means of protecting myself. "All right, I'll leave you then," he said, slowly retreating. "You're wonderful. Don't I please you?" "You'll please me by going away and leaving me in peace," I said, but I was no longer so sure of myself as I tried to make him think. My senses, sharpened by fasting, suddenly seemed to see or hear something about him; it was just beginning, it was growing, it came nearer, and I knew that this hound had the power to drive me away, even if I could not imagine to myself at the moment how I was ever to get to my feet. And I gazed at him—he had merely shaken his head sadly at my rough answer—with ever-mounting desire. "Who are you?" I asked. "I'm a hunter," he replied. "And why won't you let me lie here?" I asked. "You disturb me," he said. "I can't hunt while you're here." "Try," I said, "perhaps you'll be able to hunt after all." "No,"

he said, "I'm sorry, but you must go." "Don't hunt for
this one day!" I implored him. "No,' he said, "I must
hunt." "I must go; you must hunt," I said, "nothing
but musts. Can you explain to me why we must?" "No,"
he replied, "but there's nothing that needs to be ex·
plained, these are natural, self-evident things." "Not
quite so self-evident as all that," I said, "you're sorry
that you must drive me away, and yet you do it."
"That's so," he replied. "That's so," I echoed him
crossly, "that isn't an answer. Which sacrifice would
you rather make; to give up your hunting, or give up
driving me away?" "To give up my hunting," he said
without hesitation. "There!" said I, "don't you see that
you're contradicting yourself?" "How am I contradicting myself?" he replied. "My dear little dog, can it be
that you really don't understand that I must? Don't
you understand the most self-evident fact?" I made no
answer, for I noticed—and new life ran through me,
life such as terror gives—I noticed from almost invisible indications, which perhaps nobody but myself
could have noticed, that in the depths of his chest the
hound was preparing to upraise a song. "You're going
to sing," I said. "Yes," he replied gravely, "I'm going
to sing, soon, but not yet." "You're beginning already,'
I said. "No," he said, "not yet. But be prepared." "I
can hear it already, though you deny it," I said, trembling. He was silent, and then I thought I saw some·
thing such as no dog before me had ever seen, at least
there is no slightest hint of it in our tradition, and I
hastily bowed my head in infinite fear and shame in
the pool of blood lying before me. I thought I saw that

the hound was already singing without knowing it, nay, more, that the melody, separated from him, was floating on the air in accordance with its own laws, and, as though he had no part in it, was moving towards me, towards me alone. Today, of course, I deny the validity of all such perceptions and ascribe them to my over-excitation at that time, but even if it was an error it had nevertheless a sort of grandeur, and is the sole, even if delusive, reality that I have carried over into this world from my period of fasting, and shows at least how far we can go when we are beyond ourselves. And I was actually quite beyond myself. In ordinary circumstances I would have been very ill, incapable of moving; but the melody, which the hound soon seemed to acknowledge as his, was quite irresistible. It grew stronger and stronger; its waxing power seemed to have no limits, and already almost burst my ear-drums. But the worst was that it seemed to exist solely for my sake, this voice before whose sublimity the woods fell silent to exist solely for my sake; who was I, that I could dare to remain here, lying brazenly before it in my pool of blood and filth. I tottered to my feet and looked down at myself; this wretched body can never run, I still had time to think, but already, spurred on by the melody, I was careering from the spot in splendid style. I said nothing to my friends; probably I could have told them all when I first arrived, but I was too feeble, and later it seemed to me that such things could not be told. Hints which I could not refrain from occasionally dropping were quite lost in the general conversation. For the rest I recovered physically in a few hours, but spiritually I still suffer from the effects of that experiment.

Nevertheless, I next carried my researches into music. True, science had not been idle in this sphere either; the science of music, if I am correctly informed, is perhaps still more comprehensive than that of nurture, and in any case established on a firmer basis. That may be explained by the fact that this province admits of more objective enquiry than the other, and its knowledge is more a matter of pure observation and systematization, while in the province of food the main object is to achieve practical results. That is the reason why the science of music is accorded greater esteem than that of nurture, but also why the former has never penetrated so deeply into the life of the people. I myself felt less attracted to the science of music than to any other until I heard that voice in the forest. My experience with the musical dogs had indeed drawn my attention to music, but I was still too young at that time. Nor is it by any means easy even to come to grips with that science; it is regarded as very esoteric and politely excludes the crowd. Besides, although what struck me most deeply at first about these dogs was their music, their silence seemed to me still more significant; as for their affrighting music, probably it was quite unique, so that I could leave it out of account; but thenceforth their silence confronted me everywhere and in all the dogs I met. So for penetrating into real dog nature research into food seemed to me the best method, calculated to lead me to my goal by the straightest path.

Perhaps I was mistaken. A border region between these two sciences, however, had already attracted my attention. I mean the theory of incantation, by which food is called down. Here again it is very much against me that I have never seriously tackled the science of music and in this sphere cannot even count myself among the half-educated, the class on whom science looks down most of all. This fact I cannot get away from. I could not—I have proof of that, unfortunately—I could not pass even the most elementary scientific examination set by an authority on the subject. Of course, quite apart from the circumstances already mentioned, the reason for that can be found in my incapacity for scientific investigation, my limited powers of thought, my bad memory, but above all in my inability to keep my scientific aim continuously before my eyes. All this I frankly admit, even with a certain degree of pleasure. For the more profound cause of my scientific incapacity seems to me to be an instinct, and indeed by no means a bad one. If I wanted to brag I might say that it was this very instinct that invalidated my scientific capacities, for it would surely be a very extraordinary thing if one who shows a tolerable degree of intelligence in dealing with the ordinary daily business of life, which certainly cannot be called simple, and moreover one whose findings have been checked and verified, where that was possible, by individual scientists if not by science itself, should *a priori* be incapable of planting his paw even on the first rung of the ladder of science. It was this instinct that made me—and perhaps for the sake of science itself, but a different science from that of today, an ultimate science—prize freedom higher than everything else. Freedom! Certainly such freedom as is possible today is a wretched business. But nevertheless freedom, nevertheless a possession.

The Burrow

I HAVE COMPLETED the construction of my burrow and it seems to be successful. All that can be seen from outside is a big hole; that, however, really leads nowhere; if you take a few steps you strike against natural firm rock. I can make no boast of having contrived this ruse intentionally; it is simply the remains of one of my many abortive building attempts, but finally it seemed to me advisable to leave this one hole without filling it in. True, some ruses are so subtle that they defeat themselves, I know that better than any one, and it is certainly a risk to draw attention by this hole to the fact that there may be something in the vicinity worth enquiring into. But you do not know me if you think I am afraid, or that I built my burrow simply out of fear. At a distance of some thousand paces from this hole lies, covered by a movable layer of moss, the real entrance to the burrow; it is secured as safely as anything in this world can be secured; yet some one could step on the moss or break through it, and then my burrow would lie open, and anybody who liked—please note, however, that quite uncommon abilities would also be required —could make his way in and destroy everything for

good. I know that very well, and even now that I am
better off than ever before I can scarcely pass an hour
in complete tranquillity; at that one point in the dark
moss I am vulnerable, and in my dreams I often see a
greedy muzzle sniffing round it persistently. It will be
objected that I could quite well have filled in the entrance too, with a thin layer of hard earth on top and
with loose soil further down, so that it would not cost
me much trouble to dig my way out again whenever I
liked. But that plan is impossible; prudence itself demands that I should have a way of leaving at a moment's notice if necessary, prudence itself demands, as
alas! so often, the element of risk in life. All this involves very laborious calculation, and the sheer pleasure of the mind in its own keenness is often the sole
reason why one keeps it up. I must have a way of leaving at a moment's notice, for, despite all my vigilance,
may I not be attacked from some quite unexpected
quarter? I live in peace in the inmost chamber of my
house, and meanwhile the enemy may be burrowing
his way slowly and stealthily straight towards me. I do
not say that he has a better scent than I; probably he
knows as little about me as I of him. But there are
insatiable robbers who burrow blindly through the
ground, and to whom the very size of my house gives
the hope of hitting by chance on some of its far-flung
passages. I certainly have the advantage of being in my
own house and knowing all the passages and how they
run. A robber may very easily become my victim and a
succulent one too. But I am growing old; I am not as
strong as many others, and my enemies are countless;

it could well happen that in flying from one enemy I might run into the jaws of another. Anything might happen! In any case I must have the confident knowledge that somewhere there is an exit easy to reach and quite free, where I have to do nothing whatever to get out, so that I might never—Heaven shield us!—suddenly feel the teeth of the pursuer in my flank while I am desperately burrowing away, even if it is at loose easy soil. And it is not only by external enemies that I am threatened. There are also enemies in the bowels of the earth. I have never seen them, but legend tells of them and I firmly believe in them. They are creatures of the inner earth; not even legend can describe them. Their very victims can scarcely have seen them; they come, you hear the scratching of their claws just under you in the ground, which is their element, and already you are lost. Here it is of no avail to console yourself with the thought that you are in your own house; far rather are you in theirs. Not even my exit could save me from them; indeed in all probability it would not save me in any case, but rather betray me; yet it is a hope, and I cannot live without it. Apart from this main exit I am also connected with the outer world by quite narrow, tolerably safe passages which provide me with good fresh air to breathe. They are the work of the field mice. I have made judicious use of them, transforming them into an organic part of my burrow. They also give me the possibility of scenting things from afar, and thus serve as a protection. All sorts of small fry, too, come running through them, and I devour these: so I can have a certain amount of subter-

ranean hunting, sufficient for a modest way of life,
without leaving my burrow at all; and that is naturally
a great advantage.

But the most beautiful thing about my burrow is the
stillness. Of course, that is deceitful. At any moment it
may be shattered and then all will be over. For the time
being, however, the silence is still with me. For hours
I can stroll through my passages and hear nothing except the rustling of some little creature, which I immediately reduce to silence between my jaws, or the pat-
tering of soil, which draws my attention to the need for
repair; otherwise all is still. The fragrance of the woods
floats in; the place feels both warm and cool. Sometimes
I lie down and roll about in the passage with pure joy.
When autumn sets in to possess a burrow like mine,
and a roof over your head, is great good fortune for any
one getting on in years. Every hundred yards I have
widened the passages into little round cells; there I can
curl myself up in comfort and lie warm. There I sleep
the sweet sleep of tranquillity, of satisfied desire, of
achieved ambition; for I possess a house. I do not know
whether it is a habit that still persists from former days,
or whether the perils even of this house of mine are
great enough to awaken me; but invariably every now
and then I start up out of profound sleep and listen,
listen into the stillness which reigns here unchanged
day and night, smile contentedly and then sink with
loosened limbs into still profounder sleep. Poor home-
less wanderers in the roads and woods, creeping for
warmth into a heap of leaves or a herd of their comrades, delivered to all the perils of heaven and earth!

I lie here in a room secured on every side—there are more than fifty such rooms in my burrow—and pass as much of my time as I choose between dozing and unconscious sleep.

Not quite in the center of the burrow, carefully chosen to serve as a refuge in case of extreme danger from siege if not from immediate pursuit, lies the chief cell. While all the rest of the burrow is the outcome rather of intense intellectual than of physical labor, this Castle Keep was fashioned by the most arduous labor of my whole body. Several times, in the despair brought on by physical exhaustion, I was on the point of giving up the whole business, flung myself down panting and cursed the burrow, dragged myself outside and left the place lying open to all the world. I could afford to do that, for I had no longer any wish to return to it, until at last, after four hours or days, back I went repentantly, and when I saw that the burrow was unharmed I could almost have raised a hymn of thanksgiving, and in sincere gladness of heart started on the work anew. My labors on the Castle Keep were also made harder, and unnecessarily so (unnecessarily in that the burrow derived no real benefit from those labors) by the fact that just at the place where, according to my calculations, the Castle Keep should be, the soil was very loose and sandy and had literally to be hammered and pounded into a firm state to serve as a wall for the beautifully vaulted chamber. But for such tasks the only tool I possess is my forehead. So I had to run with my forehead thousands and thousands of times, for whole days and nights, against the ground, and I was glad when the blood came, for that was a proof that the walls were beginning to harden; and in that way, as everybody must admit, I richly paid for my Castle Keep.

In the Castle Keep I assemble my stores; everything over and above my daily wants that I capture inside the burrow, and everything I bring back with me from my hunting expeditions outside, I pile up here. The place is so spacious that food for half a year scarcely fills it. Consequently I can divide up my stores, walk about among them, play with them, enjoy their plenty and their various smells, and reckon up exactly how much they represent. That done, I can always arrange accordingly, and make my calculations and hunting plans for the future, taking into account the season of the year. There are times when I am so well provided for that in my indifference to food I never even touch the smaller fry that scuttle about the burrow, which, however, is probably imprudent of me. My constant preoccupation with defensive measures involves a frequent alteration or modification, though within narrow limits, of my views on how the building can best be organized for that end. Then it sometimes seems risky to make the Castle Keep the basis of defense; the ramifications of the burrow present me with manifold possibilities, and it seems more in accordance with prudence to divide up my stores somewhat, and put part of them in certain of the smaller rooms; thereupon I mark off every third room, let us say, as a reserve store-room, or every fourth room as a main and every second as an auxiliary storeroom, and so forth. Or I ignore certain passages

altogether and store no food in them, so as to throw any
enemy off the scent, or I choose quite at random a very
few rooms according to their distance from the main
exit. Each of these new plans involves of course heavy
work; I have to make my calculations and then carry
my stores to their new places. True, I can do that at my
leisure and without any hurry, and it is not at all unpleasant to carry such good food in your jaws, to lie
down and rest whenever you like, and, which is an actual pleasure, to have an occasional nibble. But it is not
so pleasant when, as sometimes happens, you suddenly
fancy, starting up from your sleep, that the present distribution of your stores is completely and totally wrong,
capable of leading to great dangers, and must be set
right at once, no matter how tired or sleepy you may
be; then I rush, then I fly, then I have no time for calculation; as I am burning to execute my perfectly new,
perfectly satisfactory plan, I seize whatever my teeth
hit upon and drag it or carry it away, sighing, groaning,
stumbling, and nothing will content me but some radical alteration of the present state of things, which seems
imminently dangerous. Until little by little full wakefulness sobers me, and I can hardly understand my
panic haste, breathe in deeply the tranquillity of
my house, which I myself have disturbed, return to my
resting-place, fall asleep at once in a new-won exhaustion, and on awakening find hanging from my jaws, say,
a rat, as indubitable proof of night labors which already seem almost unreal. Then again there are times
when the storing of all my food in one place seems the
best plan of all. Of what use to me could my stores in

the smaller rooms be, how much could I store there in any case? And whatever I put there would block the passage, and be a greater hindrance than help to me if I were pursued and had to fly. Besides, it is stupid but true that one's self-conceit suffers if one cannot see all one's stores together, and so at one glance know how much one possesses. And in dividing up my food in those various ways might not a great deal get lost? I can't be always scouring through all my passages and cross-passages so as to make sure that everything is in order. The idea of dividing up my stores is of course a good one, but only if one had several rooms similar to my Castle Keep. Several such rooms! Indeed! And who is to build them? In any case they could not be worked into the general plan of my burrow at this late stage. But I will admit that that is a fault in my burrow; it is always a fault to have only one copy of anything. And I confess too that during the whole time I was constructing the burrow a vague divination that I should have more such cells stirred in my mind, vaguely, yet clearly enough if I had only welcomed it; I did not yield to it, I felt too feeble for the enormous labor it would involve, more, I felt too feeble even to admit to myself the necessity for that labor, and comforted myself as best I could with the vague hope that a building which in any other case would clearly be inadequate, would in my own unique, exceptional, favored case suffice, presumably, because providence was interested in the preservation of my forehead, that unique instrument. So I have only one Castle Keep, but my dark premonitions that one would not suffice have faded. However that may be I must content myself with the one big chamber, the smaller ones are simply no substitute for it, and so, when this conviction has grown on me, I begin once more to haul all my stores back from them to the Castle Keep. For some time afterwards I find a certain comfort in having all the passages and rooms free, in seeing my stores growing in the Castle Keep and emitting their variegated and mingled smells, each of which delights me in its own fashion, and every one of which I can distinguish even at a distance, as far as the very remotest passages. Then I usually enjoy periods of particular tranquillity, in which I change my sleeping-place by stages, always working in towards the center of the burrow, always steeping myself more profoundly in the mingled smells, until at last I can no longer restrain myself and one night rush into the Castle Keep, mightily fling myself upon my stores, and glut myself with the best that I can seize until I am completely gorged. Happy, but dangerous hours; any one who knew how to exploit them could destroy me with ease and without any risk. Here too the absence of a second or third large store-room works to my detriment; for it is the single huge accumulated mass of food that seduces me. I try to guard myself in various ways against this danger; the distribution of my stores in the smaller rooms is really one of these expedients; but unfortunately, like other such expedients, it leads through renunciation to still greater greed, which, overruling my intelligence, makes me arbitrarily alter my plans of defense to suit its ends.

To regain my composure after such lapses I make a

practice of reviewing the burrow, and after the necessary improvements have been carried out, frequently leave it, though only for a short spell. At such moments the hardship of renouncing it for a long time seems too punitive, even to myself, yet I recognize clearly the need for my occasional short excursions. It is always with a certain solemnity that I approach the exit again. During my spells of home life I avoid it, steer clear even of the outer windings of the corridor that leads to it; besides, it is no easy job to wander about there, for I have contrived there a whole little maze of passages; it was there that I began my burrow, at a time when I had no hope of ever completing it according to my plans; I began, half in play, at that corner, and so my first joy in labor found riotous satisfaction there in a labyrinthine burrow which at the time seemed to me the crown of all burrows, but which I judge today, perhaps with more justice, to be too much of an idle *tour de force*, not really worthy of the rest of the burrow, and though perhaps theoretically brilliant—here is my main entrance, I said in those days, ironically addressing my invisible enemies and seeing them all already caught and stifled in the outer labyrinth—is in reality a flimsy piece of jugglery that would hardly withstand a serious attack or the struggles of an enemy fighting for his life. Should I reconstruct this part of my burrow? I keep on postponing the decision, and the labyrinth will probably remain as it is. Apart from the sheer hard work that I should have to face, the task would also be the most dangerous imaginable. When I began the burrow I could work away at it in comparative peace of mind, the risk wasn't much greater than any other risk; but to attempt that today would be to draw the whole world's attention, and gratuitously, to my burrow; today the whole thing is impossible. I am almost glad of that, for I still have a certain sentiment about this first achievement of mine. And if a serious attack were attempted, what pattern of entrance at all would be likely to save me? An entrance can deceive, can lead astray, can give the attacker no end of worry, and the present one too can do that at a pinch. But a really serious attack has to be met by an instantaneous mobilization of all the resources in the burrow and all the forces of my body and soul—that, of course, is self-evident. So this entrance can very well remain where it is. The burrow has so many unavoidable defects imposed by natural causes that it can surely stand this one defect for which I am responsible, and which I recognize as a defect, even if only after the event. In spite of that, however, I do not deny that this fault worries me from time to time, indeed always. If on my customary rounds I avoid this part of the burrow, the fundamental reason is because the sight of it is painful to me, because I don't want to be perpetually reminded of a defect in my house, even if that defect is only too disturbingly present in my mind. Let it continue to exist ineradicably at the entrance; I can at least refuse to look at it as long as that is possible. If I merely walk in the direction of the entrance, even though I may be separated from it by several passages and rooms, I find myself sensing an atmosphere of great danger, actually as if my hair were growing thin and in a moment might fly off and leave

me bare and shivering, exposed to the howls of my enemies. Yes, the mere thought of the door itself brings
such feelings with it, yet it is the labyrinth leading up
to it that torments me most of all. Sometimes I dream
that I have reconstructed it, transformed it completely,
quickly, in a night, with a giant's strength, nobody having noticed, and now it is impregnable; the nights in
which such dreams come to me are the sweetest I know,
tears of joy and deliverance still glisten on my beard
when I awaken.

So I must thread the tormenting complications of this
labyrinth physically as well as mentally whenever I go
out, and I am both exasperated and touched when, as
sometimes happens, I lose myself for a moment in my
own maze, and the work of my hands seems to be still
doing its best to prove its sufficiency to me, its maker,
whose final judgment has long since been passed on it.
But then I find myself beneath the mossy covering,
which has been left untouched for so long—for I stay
for long spells in my house—that it has grown fast to the
soil round it, and now only a little push with my head
is needed and I am in the upper world. For a long time
I do not dare to make that little movement, and if it
were not that I would have to traverse the labyrinth
once more, I would certainly leave the matter for the
time being and turn back again. Just think. Your house
is protected and self-sufficient. You live in peace, warm,
well-nourished, master, sole master of all your manifold
passages and rooms, and all this you are prepared, it
appears, not merely to give up, but actually to abandon;
you nurse the confident hope, certainly, that you will

regain it; yet is it not a dangerous, a far too dangerous stake that you are playing for? Can there be any reasonable grounds for such a step? No, for such acts as these there can be no reasonable grounds. But all the same I then cautiously raise the trap-door and slip outside, let it softly fall back again, and fly as fast as I can from the treacherous spot.

Yet I am not really free. True, I am no longer confined by narrow passages, but rush through the open woods, and feel new powers awakening in my body for which there was no room, as it were, in the burrow, not even in the Castle Keep, though it had been ten times as big. The food too is better up here; though hunting is more difficult, success more rare, the results are more valuable from every point of view; I do not deny all this; I appreciate it and take advantage of it as fully as most animals, and probably more fully, for I do not hunt like a vagrant out of mere idleness or desperation, but calmly and methodically. Also I am not permanently doomed to this free life, for I know that my term is measured, that I do not have to hunt here forever, and that, whenever I am weary of this life and wish to leave it, Someone, whose invitation I shall not be able to withstand, will, so to speak, summon me to him. And so I can pass my time here quite without care and in complete enjoyment, or rather I could, and yet I cannot. My burrow takes up too much of my thoughts. I fled from the entrance fast enough, but soon I am back at it again. I seek out a good hiding-place and keep watch on the entrance of my house—this time from outside—for whole days and nights. Call it foolish if you like; it gives me infinite pleasure and reassures me. At such times it is as if I were not so much looking at my house as at myself sleeping, and had the joy of being in a profound slumber and simultaneously of keeping vigilant guard over myself. I am privileged, as it were, not only to dream about the spectres of the night in all the helplessness and blind trust of sleep, but also at the same time to confront them in actuality with the calm judgment of the fully awake. And strangely enough I discover that my situation is not so bad as I had often thought, and will probably think again when I return to my house. In this connection—it may be in others too, but in this one especially—these excursions of mine are truly indispensable. Carefully as I have chosen an out-of-the-way place for my door, the traffic that passes it is nevertheless, if one takes a week's observation, very great; but so it is, no doubt, in all inhabited regions, and probably it is actually better to hazard the risks of dense traffic, whose very impetus carries it past, than to be delivered in complete solitude to the first persistently searching intruder. Here enemies are numerous and their allies and accomplices still more numerous, but they fight one another, and while thus employed rush past my burrow without noticing it. In all my time I have never seen any one investigating the actual door of my house, which is fortunate both for me and for him, for I would certainly have launched myself at his throat, forgetting everything else in my anxiety for the burrow. True, intruders come in whose neighborhood I dare not remain, and from whom I have to fly as soon as I scent them in the distance; on their attitude to the burrow I really can't pronounce with certainty, but it is at least a reassurance that when I presently return I never find any of them there, and the entrance is undamaged. There have been happy periods in which I could almost assure myself that the enmity of the world towards me had ceased or been assuaged, or that the strength of the burrow had raised me above the destructive struggle of former times. The burrow has probably protected me in more ways than I thought or dared think while I was inside it. This fancy used to have such a hold over me that sometimes I have been seized by the childish desire never to return to the burrow again, but to settle down somewhere close to the entrance, to pass my life watching the entrance, and gloat perpetually upon the reflection—and in that find my happiness—how steadfast a protection my burrow would be if I were inside it. Well, one is soon roughly awakened from childish dreams. What does this protection which I am looking at here from the outside amount to after all? Dare I estimate the danger which I run inside the burrow from observations which I make when outside? Can my enemies, to begin with, have any proper awareness of me if I am not in my burrow? A certain awareness of me they certainly have, but not full awareness. And is not that full awareness the real definition of a state of danger? So the experiments I attempt here are only half-experiments or even less, calculated merely to reassure my fears and by giving me false reassurance to lay me open to great perils. No, I do not watch over my own sleep, as I imagined; rather it is I who sleep, while the destroyer watches.

Perhaps he is one of those who pass the entrance without seeming to notice it, concerned merely to ascertain,
just like myself, that the door is still untouched and
waits for their attack, and only pass because they know
that the master of the house is out, or because they are
quite aware that he is guilelessly lying on the watch in
the bushes close by. And I leave my post of observation
and find I have had enough of this outside life; I feel
that there is nothing more that I can learn here, either
now or at any time. And I long to say a last good-bye to
everything up here, to go down into my burrow never
to return again, let things take their course, and not
try to retard them with my profitless vigils. But spoilt
by seeing for such a long time everything that happened round the entrance, I find great difficulty in summoning the resolution to carry out the actual descent,
which might easily draw anyone's attention, and without knowing what is happening behind my back and
behind the door after it is fastened. I take advantage
of stormy nights to get over the necessary prelimi-
naries, and quickly bundle in my spoil; that seems to
have come off, but whether it has really come off will
only be known when I myself have made the descent;
it will be known, but not by me, or by me, but too late.
So I give up the attempt and do not make the descent.
I dig an experimental burrow, naturally at a good distance from the real entrance, a burrow just as long as
myself, and seal it also with a covering of moss. I creep
into my hole, close it after me, wait patiently, keep
vigil for long or short spells, and at various hours of the
day, then fling off the moss, issue from my hole, and

summarize my observations. These are extremely het-
erogeneous, and both good and bad; but I have never
been able to discover a universal principle or an infallible method of descent. In consequence of all this I have
not yet summoned the resolution to make my actual
descent, and am thrown into despair at the necessity
of doing it soon. I almost screw myself to the point of
deciding to emigrate to distant parts and take up my
old comfortless life again, which had no security whatever, but was one indiscriminate succession of perils,
yet in consequence prevented one from perceiving and
fearing particular perils, as I am constantly reminded
by comparing my secure burrow with ordinary life.
Certainly such a decision would be an arrant piece of
folly, produced simply by living too long in senseless
freedom; the burrow is still mine, I have only to take
a single step and I am safe. And I tear myself free from
all my doubts and by broad daylight rush to the door,
quite resolved to raise it now; but I cannot, I rush past
it and fling myself into a thorn bush, deliberately, as a
punishment, a punishment for some sin I do not know
of. Then, at the last moment, I am forced to admit to
myself that I was right after all, and that it was really
impossible to go down into the burrow without leaving the thing I love best, for a little while at least, at
the disposal of all my enemies, on the ground, in the
trees, in the air. And the danger is by no means a fanci-
ful one, but very real. It need not be any particular enemy that is provoked to pursue me, it may very well be
some chance innocent little creature, some disgusting
little beast which follows me out of curiosity, and thus,

without knowing it, becomes the leader of all the world against me; nor need it be even that, it may be —and that would be just as bad, indeed in some respects worse—it may be some one of my own kind, a connoisseur and prizer of burrows, a hermit, a lover of peace, but all the same a filthy scoundrel who wishes to be housed where he has not built. If he were actually to arrive now, if in his obscene lust he were to discover the entrance and set about working at it, lifting the moss; if he were actually to succeed, if he were actually to wriggle his way in in my stead, until only his hind-quarters still showed; if all this were actually to happen, so that at last, casting all prudence to the winds, I might in my blind rage leap on him, maul him, tear the flesh from his bones, destroy him, drink his blood and fling his corpse among the rest of my spoil, but above all—that is the main thing—were at last back in my burrow once more, I would have it in my heart to greet the labyrinth itself with rapture; but first I would draw the moss covering over me, and I would want to rest, it seems to me, for all the remainder of my life. But nobody comes and I am left to my own resources. Perpetually obsessed by the sheer difficulty of the attempt, I lose much of my timidity, I no longer attempt even to appear to avoid the entrance, but make a hobby of prowling round it; by now it is almost as if I were the enemy spying out a suitable opportunity for successfully breaking in. If I only had someone I could trust to keep watch at my post of observation; then of course I could descend in perfect peace of mind. I would make an agreement with this trusty confederate

of mine that he would keep a careful note of the state
of things during my descent and for quite a long time
afterwards, and if he saw any sign of danger knock on
the moss covering, and if he saw nothing do nothing.
With that a clean sweep would be made of all my fears,
no residue would be left, or at most my confidant. For
would he not demand some counter-service from me;
would he not at last want to see the burrow? That in
itself, to let any one freely into my burrow, would be
exquisitely painful to me. I built it for myself, not for
visitors, and I think I would refuse to admit him; not
even though he alone made it possible for me to get
into the burrow would I let him in. But I simply could
not admit him, for either I must let him go in first by
himself, which is simply unimaginable, or we must both
descend at the same time, in which case the advantage
I am supposed to derive from him, that of being kept
watch over, would be lost. And what trust can I really
put in him? Can I trust one whom I have had under
my eyes just as fully when I can't see him, and the moss
covering separates us? It is comparatively easy to trust
anyone if you are supervising him or at least can su-
pervise him; perhaps it is possible even to trust some
one at a distance; but completely to trust some one
outside the burrow when you are inside the burrow,
that is, in a different world, that, it seems to me, is impossible. But such considerations are not in the least
necessary; the mere reflection is enough that during or
after my descent one of the countless accidents of existence might prevent my confidant from fulfilling his
duty, and what incalculable results might not the small-

est accident of that kind have for me? No, if one takes it by and large, I have no right to complain that I am alone and have nobody that I can trust. I certainly lose nothing by that and probably spare myself trouble. I can only trust myself and my burrow. I should have thought of that before and taken measures to meet the difficulty that worries me so much now. When I began the burrow it would at least have been partly possible. I should have so constructed the first passage that it had two entrances at a moderate distance from each other, so that after descending through the one entrance with that slowness which is unavoidable, I might rush at once through the passage to the second entrance, slightly raise the moss covering, which would be so arranged as to make that easy, and from there keep watch on the position for several days and nights. That would have been the only right way of doing it. True, the two entrances would double the risk, but that consideration need not delay me, for one of the entrances, serving merely as a post of observation, could be quite narrow. And with that I lose myself in a maze of technical speculations, I begin once more to dream my dream of a completely perfect burrow, and that somewhat calms me; with closed eyes I behold with delight perfect or almost perfect structural devices for enabling me to slip out and in unobserved. While I lie there thinking such things I admire these devices very greatly, but only as technical achievements, not as real advantages, for this freedom to slip out and in at will, what does it amount to? It is the mark of a restless nature, of inner uncertainty, disreputable desires, evil propensities that seem still worse when one thinks of the burrow, which is there at one's hand and can flood one with peace if one only remains quite open and receptive to it. For the present, however, I am outside it seeking some possibility of returning, and for that the necessary technical devices would be very desirable. But perhaps not so very desirable after all. Is it not a very grave injustice to the burrow to regard it in moments of nervous panic as a mere hole into which one can creep and be safe? Certainly it is a hole among other things, and a safe one, or should be, and when I picture myself in the midst of danger, then I insist with clenched teeth and all my will that the burrow should be nothing but a hole set apart to save me, and that it should fulfil that clearly defined function with the greatest possible efficiency, and I am ready to absolve it from every other duty. Now the truth of the matter—and one has no eye for that in times of great peril, and only by a great effort even in times when danger is threatening—is that in reality the burrow does provide a considerable degree of security, but by no means enough, for is one ever free from anxieties inside it? These anxieties are different from ordinary ones, prouder, richer in content, often long repressed, but in their destructive effects they are perhaps much the same as the anxieties that existence in the outer world gives rise to. Had I constructed the burrow exclusively to assure my safety I would not have been disappointed, it is true; nevertheless the relation between the enormous labor involved and the actual security it would provide, at least in so far as I could feel it and profit by it, would not have been in my favor. It is extremely painful to have to admit such things to oneself, but one is forced to do it, confronted by that entrance over there which now literally locks and bars itself against me, the builder and possessor. Yet the burrow is not a mere hole for taking refuge in. When I stand in the Castle Keep surrounded by my piled-up stores, surveying the ten passages which begin there, raised and sunken passages, vertical and rounded passages, wide and narrow passages, as the general plan dictates, and all alike still and empty, ready by their various routes to conduct me to all the other rooms, which are also still and empty—then all thought of mere safety is far from my mind, then I know that here is my castle, which I have wrested from the refractory soil with tooth and claw, with pounding and hammering blows, my castle which can never belong to anyone else, and is so essentially mine that I can calmly accept in it even my enemy's mortal stroke at the final hour, for my blood will ebb away here in my own soil and not be lost. And what but that is the meaning of the blissful hours which I pass, now peacefully slumbering, now happily keeping watch, in these passages, these passages which suit me so well, where one can stretch oneself out in comfort, roll about in childish delight, lie and dream, or sink into blissful sleep. And the smaller rooms, each familiar to me, so familiar that in spite of their complete similarity I can clearly distinguish one from the other with my eyes shut by the mere feel of the wall: they enclose me more peacefully and warmly than a bird is enclosed in its nest. And all, all still and empty.

But if that is the case, why do I hang back? Why do I dread the thought of the intruding enemy more than the possibility of never seeing my burrow again? Well, the latter alternative is fortunately an impossibility; there is no need for me even to take thought to know what the burrow means to me; I and the burrow belong so indissolubly together that in spite of all my fears I could make myself quite comfortable out here, and not even need to overcome my repugnance and open the door; I could be quite content to wait here passively, for nothing can part us for long, and somehow or other I shall quite certainly find myself in my burrow again. But on the other hand how much time may pass before then, and how many things may happen in that time, up here no less than down there? And it lies with me solely to curtail that interval and to do what is necessary at once.

And then, too exhausted to be any longer capable of thought, my head hanging, my legs trembling with fatigue, half-asleep, feeling my way rather than walking, I approach the entrance, slowly raise the moss covering, slowly descend, leaving the door open in my distraction for a needlessly long time, and presently remember my omission, and get out again to make it good —but what need was there to get out for that? All that was needed was to draw to the moss covering; right; so I creep in again and now at last draw to the moss covering. Only in this state, and in this state alone, can I achieve my descent.—So at last I lie down beneath the moss on the top of my bloodstained spoil and can now enjoy my longed-for sleep. Nothing disturbs me, no one

has tracked me down, above the moss everything seems
to be quiet thus far at least, but even if it all were not
quiet I question whether I could stop to keep watch
now; I have changed my place, I have left the upper
world and am in my burrow, and I feel its effect at
once. It is a new world, endowing me with new powers,
and what I felt as fatigue up there is no longer that
here. I have returned from a journey, dog-tired with
my wanderings, but the sight of the old house, the
thought of all the things that are waiting to be done,
the necessity at least to cast a glance at all the rooms,
but above all to make my way immediately to the Castle Keep; all this transforms my fatigue into ardent
zeal; it is as though at the moment when I set foot in
the burrow I had wakened from a long and profound
sleep. My first task is a very laborious one and requires
all my attention; I mean getting my spoil through the
narrow and thin-walled passages of the labyrinth. I
shove with all my might, and the work gets done too,
but far too slowly for me; to hasten it I drag part of my
flesh supply back again and push my way over it and
through it; now I have only a portion of my spoil before me and it is easier to make progress; but my road
is so blocked by all this flesh in these narrow passages,
through which it is not always easy for me to make my
way when I am alone, that I could quite easily smother
among my own stores; sometimes I can only rescue myself from their pressure by eating and drinking a clear
space for myself. But the work of transport is successful,
I finish it in quite a reasonable time, the labyrinth is
behind me, I reach an ordinary passage and breathe

freely, push my spoil through a communication passage
into a main passage expressly designed for the purpose,
a passage sloping down steeply to the Castle Keep. What
is left to be done is not really work at all; my whole load
rolls and flows down the passage almost of itself. The
Castle Keep at last! At last I can dare to rest. Everything is unchanged, no great mishap seems to have oc-
curred, the few little defects that I note at a first glance
can soon be repaired; first, however, I must go my long
round of all the passages, but that is no hardship, that
is merely to commune again with friends, as I often did
in the old days or—I am not so very old yet, but my
memory of many things is already quite confused—as I
often did, or as I have often imagined I did. I begin
with the second passage, but break off in the middle
and turn into the third passage and let it take me back
again to the Castle Keep, and now of course I have to
begin at the second passage once more, and so I play
with my task and lengthen it out and smile to myself
and congratulate myself and become quite dazed with
all the work in front of me, but never think of turning
aside from it. It is for your sake, ye passages and rooms,
and you, Castle Keep, above all, that I have come back,
counting my own life as nothing in the balance, after
stupidly trembling for it for so long, and postponing
my return to you. What do I care for danger now that
I am with you? You belong to me, I to you, we are
united; what can harm us? What if my foes should be
assembling even now up above there and their muz-
zles be preparing to break through the moss? And with
its silence and emptiness the burrow answers me, con-

firming my words.—But now a feeling of lassitude over-
comes me and in some favorite room I curl myself up
tentatively, I have not yet surveyed everything by a long
way, though still resolved to examine everything to the
very end, I have no intention of sleeping here, I have
merely yielded to the temptation of making myself
comfortable and pretending I want to sleep, I merely
wish to find out if this is as good a place for sleeping in
as it used to be. It is, but it is a better place for sleep
than for wakening, and I remain lying where I am in
deep slumber.

I must have slept for a long time. I was only wakened
when I had reached the last light sleep which dissolves
of itself, and it must have been very light, for it was an
almost inaudible whistling noise that wakened me. I
recognized what it was immediately; the smaller fry,
whom I had allowed far too much latitude, had burrowed a new channel somewhere during my absence,
this channel must have chanced to intersect an older
one, the air was caught there, and that produced the
whistling noise. What an indefatigably busy lot these
smaller fry are, and what a nuisance their diligence can
be! First I shall have to listen at the walls of my passages and locate the place of disturbance by experimental excavations, and only then will I be able to get
rid of the noise. However, this new channel may be
quite welcome as a further means of ventilation, if it
can be fitted into the plan of the burrow. But after this
I shall keep a much sharper eye on the small fry than I
used to; I shall spare none of them.

As I have a good deal of experience in investigations

of this kind the work probably will not take me long and I can start upon it at once; there are other jobs awaiting me, it is true, but this is the most urgent. I must have silence in my passages. This noise, however, is a comparatively innocent one; I did not hear it at all when I first arrived, although it must certainly have been there; I must first feel quite at home before I could hear it; it is, so to speak, audible only to the ear of the householder. And it is not even constant, as such noises usually are; there are long pauses, obviously caused by stoppages of the current of air. I start on my investigations, but I can't find the right place to begin at, and though I cut a few trenches I do it at random; naturally that has no effect, and the hard work of digging and the still harder work of filling the trenches up again and beating the earth firm is so much labor lost. I don't seem to be getting any nearer to the place where the noise is, it goes on always on the same thin note, with regular pauses, now a sort of whistling, but again like a kind of piping. Now I could leave it to itself for the time being; it is very disturbing, certainly, but there can hardly be any doubt that its origin is what I took it to be at first; so it can scarcely become louder, on the contrary such noises may quite well—though until now I have never had to wait so long for that to happen— may quite well vanish of themselves in the course of time through the continued labors of these little bur- rowers; and apart from that often chance itself puts one on the track of the disturbance, where systematic in- vestigation has failed for a long time. In such ways I comfort myself, and resolve simply to continue my tour of the passages, and visit the rooms, many of which I have not even seen yet since my return, and enjoy myself contemplating the Castle Keep now and then between times; but my anxiety will not let me, and I must go on with my search. These little creatures take up much, far too much, time that could be better employed. In such cases as the present it is usually the technical problem that attracts me; for example, from the noise, which my ear can distinguish in all its finest shades, so that it has a perfectly clear outline to me, I deduce its cause, and now I am on fire to discover whether my conclusion is valid. And with good reason, for as long as that is not established I cannot feel safe, even if it were merely a matter of discovering where a grain of sand that had fallen from one of the walls had rolled to. And even a noise such as this is by no means a trifling matter, regarded from that angle. But whether trifling or important, I can find nothing, no matter how hard I search, or it may be that I find too much. This had to happen just in my favorite room, I think to myself, and I walk a fair good distance away from it, almost half-way along the passage leading to the next room; but I do this merely as a joke, pretending to myself that my favorite room is not alone to blame, but that there are disturbances elsewhere as well, and with a smile on my face I begin to listen; but soon I stop smiling, for, right enough, the same whistling meets me here too. It is really nothing to worry about; sometimes I think that nobody but myself would hear it; it is true, I hear it now more and more distinctly, for my ear has grown keener through practice; though in reality it is exactly the same noise wherever I may hear it, as I have convinced myself by comparing my impressions. Nor is it growing louder; I recognize this when I listen in the middle of the passage instead of pressing my ear against the wall. Then it is only by straining my ears, indeed by lowering my head as well, that I can more guess at than hear the merest trace of a noise now and then. But it is this very uniformity of the noise everywhere that disturbs me most, for it cannot be made to agree with my original assumption. Had I rightly divined the cause of the noise, then it must have issued with greatest force from some given place, which it would be my task to discover, and after that have grown fainter and fainter. But if my hypothesis does not meet the case, what can the explanation be? There still remains the possibility that there are two noises, that up to now I have been listening at a good distance from the two centers, and that while its noise increases, when I draw near to one of them, the total result remains approximately the same for the ear in consequence of the lessening volume of sound from the other center. Already I have almost fancied sometimes, when I have listened carefully, that I could distinguish, if very indistinctly, differences of tone which support this new assumption. In any case I must extend my sphere of investigation far further than I have done. Accordingly I descend the passage to the Castle Keep and begin to listen there. Strange, the same noise there too. Now it is a noise produced by the burrowing of some species of small fry who have infamously exploited my absence; in any case they have no intention of doing me harm, they are simply busied with their own work, and so long as no obstacle comes in their way they will keep on in the direction they have taken: I know all this, yet that they should have dared to approach the very Castle Keep itself is incomprehensible to me and fills me with agitation, and confuses the faculties which I need so urgently for the work before me. Here I have no wish to discover whether it is the unusual depth at which the Castle Keep lies, or its great extent and correspondingly powerful air suction, calculated to scare burrowing creatures away, or the mere fact that it is the Castle Keep, that by some channel or other has penetrated to their dull minds. In any case I have never noticed any sign of burrowing in the walls of the Castle Keep until now. Crowds of little beasts have come here, it is true, attracted by the powerful smells; here I have had a constant hunting-ground, but my quarry has always burrowed a way through in the upper passages, and come running down here, somewhat fearfully, but unable to withstand such a temptation. But now, it seems, they are burrowing in all the passages. If I had only carried out the best of the grand plans I thought out in my youth and early manhood, or rather, if I had only had the strength to carry them out, for there would have been no lack of will. One of these favorite plans of mine was to isolate the Castle Keep from its surroundings, that is to say, to restrict the thickness of its walls to about my own height, and leave a free space of about the same width all round the Castle Keep, except for a narrow foundation, which unfortunately would have to be left to bear up the whole. I had always pictured this

free space, and not without reason, as the loveliest imaginable haunt. What a joy to lie pressed against the
rounded outer wall, pull oneself up, let oneself slide
down again, miss one's footing and find oneself on firm
earth, and play all those games literally upon the Castle
Keep and not inside it; to avoid the Castle Keep, to rest
one's eyes from it whenever one wanted, to postpone
the joy of seeing it until later and yet not have to
do without it, but literally hold it safe between one's
claws, a thing that is impossible if you have only an
ordinary open entrance to it; but above all to be able to
stand guard over it, and in that way to be so completely
compensated for renouncing the actual sight of it that,
if one had to choose between staying all one's life in the
Castle Keep or in the free space outside it, one would
choose the latter, content to wander up and down there
all one's days and keep guard over the Castle Keep.
Then there would be no noises in the walls, no insolent
burrowing up to the very Keep itself; then peace would
be assured there and I would be its guardian; then I
would not have to listen with loathing to the burrowing of the small fry, but with delight to something that
I cannot hear now at all: the murmurous silence of the
Castle Keep.

But that beautiful dream is past and I must set
to work, almost glad that now my work has a direct
connection with the Castle Keep, for that wings it.
Certainly, as I can see more and more clearly, I need
all my energies for this task, which at first seemed quite
a trifling one. I listen now at the walls of the Castle
Keep, and wherever I listen, high or low, at the roof or

the floor, at the entrance or in the corners, everywhere, everywhere, I hear the same noise. And how much time, how much care must be wasted in listening to that noise, with its regular pauses. One can, if one wishes, find a tiny deceitful comfort in the fact that here in the Castle Keep, because of its vastness, one hears nothing at all, as distinguished from the passages, when one stands back from the walls. Simply as a rest and a means to regain my composure I often make this experiment, listen intently and am overjoyed when I hear nothing. But the question still remains, what can have happened? Confronted with this phenomenon my original explanation completely falls to the ground. But I must also reject other explanations which present themselves to me. One could assume, for instance, that the noise I hear is simply that of the small fry themselves at their work. But all my experience contradicts this; I cannot suddenly begin to hear now a thing that I have never heard before though it was always there. My sensitiveness to disturbances in the burrow has perhaps become greater with the years, yet my hearing has by no means grown keener. It is of the very nature of small fry not to be heard. Would I have tolerated them otherwise? Even at the risk of starvation I would have exterminated them. But perhaps—this idea now insinuates itself—I am concerned here with some animal unknown to me. That is possible. True, I have observed the life down here long and carefully enough, but the world is full of diversity and is never wanting in painful surprises. Yet it cannot be a single animal, it must be a whole swarm that has suddenly fallen upon my do-

main, a huge swarm of little creatures, which as they
are audible, must certainly be bigger than the small
fry, but yet cannot be very much bigger, for the sound
of their labors is itself very faint. It may be, then, a
swarm of unknown creatures on their wanderings, who
happen to be passing by my way, who disturb me, but
will presently cease to do so. So I could really wait for
them to pass, and need not put myself to the trouble of
work that will be needless in the end. Yet if these creatures are strangers, why is it that I never see any of
them? I have already dug a host of trenches, hoping to
catch one of them, but I can find not a single one. Then
it occurs to me that they may be quite tiny creatures,
far tinier than any I am acquainted with, and that it is
only the noise they make that is greater. Accordingly I
investigate the soil I have dug up, I cast the lumps into
the air so that they break into quite small particles, but
the noise-makers are not among them. Slowly I come to
realize that by digging such small fortuitous trenches I
achieve nothing; in doing that I merely disfigure the
walls of my burrow, scratching hastily here and there
without taking time to fill up the holes again; at many
places already there are heaps of earth which block my
way and my view. Still, that is only a secondary worry;
for now I can neither wander about my house, nor review it, nor rest; often already I have fallen asleep at
my work in some hole or other, with one paw clutching
the soil above me, from which in a semi-stupor I have
been trying to tear a lump. I intend now to alter my
methods. I shall dig a wide and carefully constructed
trench in the direction of the noise and not cease from

digging until, independent of all theories, I find the real cause of the noise. Then I shall eradicate it, if that is within my power, and if it is not, at least I shall know the truth. That truth will bring me either peace or despair, but whether the one or the other, it will be beyond doubt or question. This decision strengthens me. All that I have done till now seems to me far too hasty; in the excitement of my return, while I had not yet shaken myself free from the cares of the upper world, and was not yet completely penetrated by the peace of the burrow, but rather hypersensitive at having had to renounce it for such a long time, I was thrown into complete confusion of mind by an unfamiliar noise. And what was it? A faint whistling, audible only at long intervals, a mere nothing to which I don't say that one could actually get used, for no one could get used to it, but which one could, without actually doing anything about it at once, observe for a while; that is, listen every two hours, let us say, and patiently register the results, instead of, as I had done, keeping one's ear fixed to the wall and at every hint of noise tearing out a lump of earth, not really hoping to find anything, but simply so as to do something to give expression to one's inward agitation. All that will be changed now, I hope. And then, with furious shut eyes, I have to admit to myself that I hope nothing of the kind, for I am still trembling with agitation just as I was hours ago, and if my reason did not restrain me I would probably like nothing better than to start stubbornly and defiantly digging, simply for the sake of digging, at some place or other, whether I heard anything there or not; almost like the small fry, who bur-row either without any object at all or simply because they eat the soil. My new and reasonable plan both tempts me and leaves me cold. There is nothing in it to object to, I at least know of no objection; it is bound, so far as I can see, to achieve my aim. And yet at bottom I do not believe in it; I believe in it so little that I do not even fear the terrors which its success may well bring, I do not believe even in a dreadful denouément; in-deed it seems to me that I have been thinking ever since the first appearance of the noise of such a methodical trench, and have not begun upon it until now simply because I put no trust in it. In spite of that I shall of course start on the trench; I have no other alternative; but I shall not start at once, but postpone the task for a little while. If reason is to be reinstated on the throne again, it must be completely reinstated; I shall not rush blindly into my task. In any case I shall first repair the damage that I have done to the burrow with my wild digging; that will take a good long time, but it is neces-sary; if the new trench is really to reach its goal it will probably be long, and if it should lead to nothing at all it will be endless; in any case this task means a longish absence from the burrow, though an absence by no means so painful as an absence in the upper world, for I can interrupt my work whenever I like and pay a visit to my house; and even if I should not do that the air of the Castle Keep will be wafted to me and surround me while I work; nevertheless it means leaving the burrow and surrendering myself to an uncertain fate, and con-sequently I want to leave the burrow in good order behind me; it shall not be said that I, who am fighting for its peace, have myself destroyed that peace without reinstating it at once. So I begin by shovelling the soil back into the holes from which it was taken, a kind of work I am familiar with, that I have done countless times almost without regarding it as work, and at which, particularly as regards the final pressing and smoothing down—and this is no empty boast, but the simple truth—I am unbeatable. But this time everything seems difficult, I am too distracted, every now and then, in the middle of my work, I press my ear to the wall and listen, and without taking any notice let the soil that I have just lifted trickle back into the passage again. The final embellishments, which demand a stricter attention, I can hardly achieve at all. Hideous protuberances, disturbing cracks remain, not to speak of the fact that the old buoyancy simply cannot be restored again to a wall patched up in such a way. I try to comfort myself with the reflection that my present work is only temporary. When I return after peace has been restored I shall repair everything properly: work will be mere play to me then. Oh, yes, work is mere play in fairy tales, and this comfort of mine belongs to the realm of fairy tales too. It would be far better to do the work thoroughly now, at once, far more reasonable than perpetually to interrupt it and wander off through the passages to discover new sources of noise, which is easy enough, all that is needed being to stop at any point one likes and listen. And that is not the end of my useless discoveries. Sometimes I fancy that the noise has stopped, for it makes long pauses; sometimes such a

faint whistling escapes one, one's own blood is pounding all too loudly in one's ears; then two pauses come
one after another, and for a while one thinks that the
whistling has stopped forever. I listen no longer, I
jump up, all life is transfigured; it is as if the fountains
from which flows the silence of the burrow were un-
sealed. I refrain from verifying my discovery at once, I
want first to find some one to whom in all good faith I
can confide it, so I rush to the Castle Keep, I remember,
for I and everything in me has awakened to new life,
that I have eaten nothing for a long time, I snatch something or other from among my store of food half buried
under debris and hurriedly begin to swallow it while I
hurry back to the place where I made my incredible
discovery, I only want to assure myself about it inci-
dentally, perfunctorily, while I am eating; I listen, but
the most perfunctory listening shows at once that I was
shamefully deceived: away there in the distance the
whistling still remains unshaken. And I spit out my
food, and would like to trample it underfoot, and go
back to my task, not caring which I take up; any place
where it seems to be needed, and there are enough
places like that, I mechanically start on something or
other, just as if the overseer had appeared and I must
make a pretense of working for his benefit. But hardly
have I well begun in this fashion when it may happen
that I make a new discovery. The noise seems to have
become louder, not much louder, of course—here it is
always a matter of the subtlest shades—but all the same
sufficiently louder for the ear to recognize it clearly.
And his growing-louder is like a coming-nearer; still

more distinctly than you hear the increasing loudness
of the noise, you can literally see the step that brings it
closer to you. You leap back from the wall, you try to
grasp at once all the possible consequences that this discovery will bring with it. You feel as if you had never
really organized the burrow for defense against attack;
you had intended to do so, but despite all your experience of life the danger of an attack, and consequently
the need to organize the place for defense, seemed remote—or rather not remote (how could it possibly be!)
—but infinitely less important than the need to put it in
a state where one could live peacefully; and so that consideration was given priority in everything relating to
the burrow. Many things in this direction might have
been done without affecting the plan of the whole;
most incomprehensibly they have been neglected. I
have had a great deal of luck all those years, luck has
spoilt me; I have had anxieties, but anxiety leads to
nothing when you have luck to back you.

The thing to do, really to do now, would be to go
carefully over the burrow and consider every possible
means of defending it, work out a plan of defense and a
corresponding plan of construction, and then start on
the work at once with the vigor of youth. That is the
work that would really be needed, for which, I need not
say, it is now far too late in the day; yet that is what
would really be needed, and not the digging of a grand
experimental trench, whose only real result would be
to deliver me hand and foot to the search for danger,
out of the foolish fear that it will not arrive quickly
enough of itself. Suddenly I cannot comprehend my

former plan. I can find no slightest trace of reason in what had seemed so reasonable; once more I lay aside my work and even my listening; I have no wish to discover any further signs that the noise is growing louder; I have had enough of discoveries; I let everything slide; I would be quite content if I could only still the conflict going on within me. Once more I let my passages lead me where they will, I come to more and more remote ones that I have not yet seen since my return, and that are quite unsullied by my scratching paws, and whose silence rises up to meet me and sinks into me. I do not surrender to it, I hurry on, I do not know what I want, probably simply to put off the hour. I stray so far that I find myself at the labyrinth; the idea of listening beneath the moss covering tempts me; such distant things, distant for the moment, chain my interest. I push my way up and listen. Deep stillness; how lovely it is here, outside there nobody troubles about my burrow, everybody has his own affairs, which have no connection with me; how have I managed to achieve this state of things with all my calculations? Here under the moss covering is perhaps the only place in my burrow now where I can listen for hours and hear nothing. A complete reversal of things in the burrow; what was once the place of danger has become a place of tranquillity, while the Castle Keep has been plunged into the mêlée of the world and all its perils. Still worse, even here there is no peace in reality, here nothing has changed; silent or vociferous, danger lies in ambush as before above the moss, but I have grown insensitive to it, my mind is far too much taken up with the whistling in my walls. Is my mind really taken up with it? It grows louder, it comes nearer, but I wriggle my way through the labyrinth and make a couch for myself up here under the moss; it is almost as if I were already leaving the house to the whistler, content if I can only have a little peace up here. To the whistler? Have I come, then, to a new conclusion concerning the cause of the noise? But surely the noise is caused by the channels bored by the small fry? Is not that my considered opinion? It seems to me that I have not retreated from it thus far. And if the noise is not caused directly by these channels, it is indirectly. And even if it should have no connection with them what-ever, one is not at liberty to make *a priori* assumptions, but must wait until one finds the cause, or it reveals it-self. One could play with hypotheses, of course, even at this stage; for instance it is possible that there has been a water burst at some distance away, and that what seems a piping or whistling to me is in reality a gur-gling. But apart from the fact that I have no experience in that sphere—the groundwater that I found at the start I drained away at once, and in this sandy soil it has never returned—apart from this fact the noise is undeniably a whistling and simply not to be translated into a gurgling. But what avail all exhortations to be calm; my imagination will not rest, and I have actually come to believe—it is useless to deny it to myself—that the whistling is made by some beast, and moreover not by a great many small ones, but by a single great one. Many signs contradict this. The noise can be heard everywhere and always at the same strength, and more-over uniformly, both by day and night. At first, therefore, one cannot but incline to the hypothesis of a great number of little animals; but as I must have found some of them during my digging and I have found nothing, it only remains for me to assume the existence of a great beast, especially as the things that seem to contradict the hypothesis are merely things which make the beast, not so much impossible, as merely dangerous beyond all one's powers of conception. For that reason alone have I stuck out against this hypothesis. I shall cease from this self-deception. For a long time already I have played with the idea that the beast can be heard at such a great distance because it works so furiously; it burrows as fast through the ground as another animal can walk on the open road; the ground still trembles at its burrowing when it has ceased; this reverberation and the noise of the boring itself unite into one sound at such a great distance, and I, as I hear only the last dying ebb of that sound, hear it always at the same uniform strength. It follows from this also that the beast is not making for me, seeing that the noise never changes; more likely it has a plan in view whose purpose I cannot decipher; I merely assume that the beast—and I make no claim whatever that it knows of my existence—is encircling me; it has probably made several circles round my burrow already since I began to observe it. The nature of the noise, the piping or whistling, gives me much food for thought. When I scratch and scrape in the soil in my own fashion the sound is quite different. I can explain the whistling only in this way: that the beast's chief means of burrowing is not its claws, which it probably employs merely as a secondary resource, but its

snout or its muzzle, which, of course, apart from its
enormous strength, must also be fairly sharp at the
point. It probably bores its snout into the earth with
one mighty push and tears out a great lump; while it is
doing that I hear nothing; that is the pause; but then it
draws in the air for a new push. This indrawal of its
breath, which must be an earth-shaking noise, not only
because of the beast's strength, but of its haste, its furious lust for work as well: this noise I hear then as a faint
whistling. But quite incomprehensible remains the
beast's capacity to work without stopping; perhaps the
short pauses provide also the opportunity of snatching
a moment's rest; but apparently the beast has never yet
allowed itself a really long rest, day and night it goes
on burrowing, always with the same freshness and vig-
or, always thinking of its object, which must be
achieved with the utmost expedition, and which it has
the ability to achieve with ease. Now I could not have
foreseen such an opponent. But apart altogether from
the beast's peculiar characteristics, what is happening
now is only something which I should really have
feared all the time, something against which I should
have been constantly prepared; the fact that someone
would come. By what chance can everything have flowed
on so quietly and happily for such a long time? Who can
have diverted my enemies from their path, and forced
them to make a wide detour round my property? Why
have I been spared for so long, only to be delivered to
such terrors now? Compared with this, what are all the
petty dangers in brooding over which I have spent my
life! As owner of the burrow I had hoped to be in a

stronger position than any enemy who might chance to appear. But simply by virtue of being owner of this great vulnerable edifice I am obviously defenseless against any serious attack. The joy of possessing it has spoilt me, the vulnerability of the burrow has made me vulnerable; any wound to it hurts me as I myself were hit. It is precisely this that I should have foreseen; instead of thinking only of my own defense—and how perfunctorily and vainly I have done even that—I should have thought of the defense of the burrow. Above all, provision should have been made for cutting off sections of the burrow, and as many as possible of them, from the endangered sections when they are attacked; this should have been done by means of improvised land-slides, calculated to operate at a moment's notice; moreover these should have been so thick, and have provided such an effectual barrier, that the attacker would not even guess that the real burrow only began at the other side. More, these land-slides should have been so devised that they not only concealed the burrow, but also entombed the attacker. Not the slightest attempt have I made to carry out such a plan, nothing at all has been done in this direction, I have been as thoughtless as a child, I have passed my manhood's years in childish games, I have done nothing but play even with the thought of danger, I have shirked really taking thought for actual danger. And there has been no lack of warning.

Nothing, of course, approaching the present situation has happened before; nevertheless there was an incident not unlike it when the burrow was only beginning.

The main difference between that time and this is simply that the burrow was only beginning then. . . . In
those days I was literally nothing more than a humble
apprentice in his first year, the labyrinth was only
sketched out in rough outline, I had already dug a little
room, but the proportions and the execution of the walls
were sadly bungled; in short everything was so tentative that it could only be regarded as an experiment, as
something which, if one lost patience some day, one
could leave lying as it was without much regret. Then
one day as I lay on a heap of earth resting from my
labors—I have rested far too often from my labors
all my life—suddenly I heard a noise in the distance.
Being young at the time, I was less frightened than curious. I left my work to look after itself and set myself to
listen; I listened and listened, and had no wish to fly up
to my moss covering and stretch myself out there so that
I might not hear. I did listen, at least. I could clearly
recognize that the noise came from some kind of burrowing similar to my own; it was somewhat fainter, of
course, but how much of that might be put down to the
distance one could not tell. I was intensely interested,
but otherwise calm and cool. Perhaps I am in somebody else's burrow, I thought to myself, and now the
owner is boring his way towards me. If that assumption
had proved to be correct I would have gone away, for I
have never had any desire for conquest or bloodshed,
and begun building somewhere else. But after all I was
still young and still without a burrow, so I could remain
quite cool. Besides, the further course of the noise
brought no real cause for apprehension, except that it

was not easy to explain. If whoever was boring there was really making for me, because he had heard me boring, then if he changed his direction, as now actually happened, it could not be told whether he did this because my pause for rest had deprived him of any definite point to make towards, or because—which was more plausible—he had himself changed his plans. But perhaps I had been deceived altogether, and he had never been actually making in my direction; at any rate the noise grew louder for a while as if he were drawing nearer, and being young at that time I probably would not have been displeased to see the burrower suddenly rising from the ground; but nothing of that kind happened, at a certain point the sound of boring began to weaken, it grew fainter and fainter, as if the burrower were gradually diverging from his first route, and suddenly it broke off altogether, as if he had decided now to take the diametrically opposite direction and were making straight away from me into the distance. For a long time I still went on listening for him in the silence, before I returned once more to my work. Now that warning was definite enough, but I soon forgot it, and it scarcely influenced my building plans.

Between that day and this lie my years of maturity, but is it not as if there were no interval at all between them? I still take long rests from my labors and listen at the wall, and the burrower has changed his intention anew, he has turned back, he is returning from his journey, thinking he has given me ample time in the interval to prepare for his reception. But on my side everything is worse prepared for than it was then; the great burrow stands defenseless, and I am no longer a young apprentice, but an old architect and the powers I still have fail me when the decisive hour comes; yet old as I am it seems to me that I would gladly be still older, so old that I should never be able to rise again from my resting-place under the moss. For to be honest I cannot endure the place, I rise up and rush, as if I had filled myself up there with new anxieties instead of peace, down into the house again.—What was the state of things the last time I was here? Had the whistling grown fainter? No, it had grown louder. I listen at ten places chosen at random and definitely note my own disappointment; the whistling is just the same as ever, nothing has altered. Up there under the moss no change touches one, there one is at peace, uplifted above time; but here every instant frets and gnaws at the listener. I go once more the long road to the Castle Keep, all my surroundings seem filled with agitation, seem to be looking at me, and then look away again so as not to annoy me, yet cannot refrain the very next moment from trying to read the saving solution from my expression. I shake my head, I have not yet found any solution. Nor do I go to the Castle Keep in pursuance of any plan. I pass the spot where I had intended to begin the experimental trench, I look it over once more, it would have been an admirable place to begin at, the trench's course would have been in the direction where lay the majority of the tiny ventilation holes, which would have greatly lightened my labors; perhaps I should not have had to dig very far, should not even have had to dig to the source of the noise; perhaps if I had listened at the ven-

tilation holes it would have been enough. But no consideration is potent enough to animate me to this labor of digging. This trench will bring me certainty,
you say? I have reached the stage where I no longer wish
to have certainty. In the Castle Keep I choose a lovely
piece of flayed red flesh and creep with it into one of
the heaps of earth; there I shall have silence at least,
such silence, at any rate, as still can be said to exist here.
I munch and nibble at the flesh, think of the strange
beast going its own road in the distance, and then again
that I should enjoy my store of food as fully as possible,
while I still have the chance. This last is probably the
sole plan I have left that I can carry out. For the rest I
try to unriddle the beast's plans. Is it on its wanderings,
or is it working on its own burrow? If it is on its wanderings then perhaps an understanding with it might be
possible. If it should really break through to the burrow I shall give it some of my store and it will go on its
way again. It will go its way again, a fine story! Lying
on my heap of earth I can naturally dream of all
sorts of things, even of an understanding with the
beast, though I know well enough that no such thing
can happen, and that at the instant when we see each
other, more, at the moment when we merely guess at
each other's presence, we shall both blindly bare our
claws and teeth, neither of us a second before or after
the other, both of us filled with a new and different
hunger, even if we should already be gorged to bursting. And with entire justice, for who, even if he were
merely on his wanderings, would not change his itiner-
ary and his plans for the future on catching sight of the

burrow? But perhaps the beast is digging in its own burrow, in which case I cannot even dream of an understanding. Even if it should be such a peculiar beast as
to be able to tolerate a neighbor near its burrow, it
could not tolerate my burrow, it would not tolerate in
any case a neighbor who could be clearly heard. Now
actually the beast seems to be a great distance away; if
it would only withdraw a little farther the noise too
would probably disappear; perhaps in that case everything would be peaceful again as in the old days; all
this would then become a painful but salutary lesson,
spurring me on to make the most diverse improvements
on the burrow; if I have peace, and danger does not
immediately threaten me, I am still quite fit for all sorts
of hard work; perhaps, considering the enormous possibilities which its powers of work open before it, the
beast has given up the idea of extending its burrow in
my direction, and is compensating itself for that in some
other one. That consummation also cannot, of course,
be brought about by negotiation, but only by the beast
itself, or by some compulsion exercised from my side.
In both cases the decisive factor will be whether the
beast knows about me, and if so what it knows. The
more I reflect upon it the more improbable does it seem
to me that the beast has even heard of me; it is possible,
though unimaginable, that it can have received news of
me through some other channel, but it has certainly
never heard me. So long as I still knew nothing about
it, it simply cannot have heard me, for at that time I
kept very quiet, nothing could be more quiet than my
return to the burrow; afterwards, when I dug the ex-

perimental trenches, perhaps it could have heard me, though my style of digging makes very little noise; but if it had heard me I must have noticed some sign of it, the beast must at least have stopped its work every now and then to listen. But all remained unchanged.

Josephine the Singer, or the Mouse Folk

OUR SINGER is called Josephine. Anyone who has not heard her does not know the power of song. There is no one but is carried away by her singing, a tribute all the greater as we are not in general a music-loving race. Tranquil peace is the music we love best; our life is hard, we are no longer able, even on occasions when we have tried to shake off the cares of daily life, to rise to anything so high and remote from our usual routine as music. But we do not much lament that; we do not get even so far; a certain practical cunning, which admittedly we stand greatly in need of, we hold to be our greatest distinction, and with a smile born of such cunning we are wont to console ourselves for all shortcomings, even supposing—only it does not happen—that we were to yearn once in a way for the kind of bliss which music may provide. Josephine is the sole exception; she has a love for music and knows too how to transmit it; she is the only one; when she dies, music—who knows for how long—will vanish from our lives.

I have often thought about what this music of hers really means. For we are quite unmusical; how is it that we understand Josephine's singing or, since Josephine denies that, at least think we can understand it? The simplest answer would be that the beauty of her singing is so great that even the most insensitive cannot be deaf to it, but this answer is not satisfactory. If it were really so, her singing would have to give one an immediate and lasting feeling of being something out of the ordinary, a feeling that from her throat something is sounding which we have never heard before and which we are not even capable of hearing, something that Josephine alone and no one else can enable us to hear. But in my opinion that is just what does not happen, I do not feel this and have never observed that others feel anything of the kind. Among intimates we admit freely to one another that Josephine's singing, as singing, is nothing out of the ordinary.

Is it in fact singing at all? Although we are unmusical we have a tradition of singing; in the old days our people did sing; this is mentioned in legends and some songs have actually survived, which, it is true, no one can now sing. Thus we have an inkling of what singing is, and Josephine's art does not really correspond to it. So is it singing at all? Is it not perhaps just a piping? And piping is something we all know about, it is the real artistic accomplishment of our people, or rather no mere accomplishment but a characteristic expression of our life. We all pipe, but of course no one dreams of making out that our piping is an art, we pipe without thinking of it, indeed without noticing it, and there are even many among us who are quite unaware that piping is one of our characteristics. So if it were true that

Josephine does not sing but only pipes and perhaps, as it seems to me at least, hardly rises above the level of our usual piping—yet, perhaps her strength is not even quite equal to our usual piping, whereas an ordinary farmhand can keep it up effortlessly all day long, besides doing his work—if that were all true, then indeed Josephine's alleged vocal skill might be disproved, but that would merely clear the ground for the real riddle which needs solving, the enormous influence she has.

After all, it is only a kind of piping that she produces. If you post yourself quite far away from her and listen, or, still better, put your judgment to the test, whenever she happens to be singing along with others, by trying to identify her voice, you will undoubtedly distinguish nothing but a quite ordinary piping tone, which at most differs a little from the others through being delicate or weak. Yet if you sit down before her, it is not merely a piping; to comprehend her art it is necessary not only to hear but to see her. Even if hers were only our usual workaday piping, there is first of all this peculiarity to consider, that here is someone making a ceremonial performance out of doing the usual thing. To crack a nut is truly no feat, so no one would ever dare to collect an audience in order to entertain it with nut-cracking. But if all the same one does do that and succeeds in entertaining the public, then it cannot be a matter of simple nut-cracking. Or it is a matter of nut-cracking, but it turns out that we have overlooked the art of cracking nuts because we were too skilled in it and that this newcomer to it first shows us its real nature, even finding it useful in making his effects to be rather less expert in nut-cracking than most of us.

Perhaps it is much the same with Josephine's singing; we admire in her what we do not at all admire in ourselves; in this respect, I may say, she is of one mind with us. I was once present when someone, as of course often happens, drew her attention to the folk piping everywhere going on, making only a modest reference to it, yet for Josephine that was more than enough. A smile so sarcastic and arrogant as she then assumed I have never seen; she, who in appearance is delicacy itself, conspicuously so even among our people who are prolific in such feminine types, seemed at that moment actually vulgar; she was at once aware of it herself, by the way, with her extreme sensibility, and controlled herself. At any rate she denies any connection between her art and ordinary piping. For those who are of the contrary opinion she has only contempt and probably unacknowledged hatred. This is not simple vanity, for the opposition, with which I too am half in sympathy, certainly admires her no less than the crowd does, but Josephine does not want mere admiration, she wants to be admired exactly in the way she prescribes, mere admiration leaves her cold. And when you take a seat before her, you understand her; opposition is possible only at a distance, when you sit before her, you know: this piping of hers is no piping.

Since piping is one of our thoughtless habits, one might think that people would pipe up in Josephine's audience too; her art makes us feel happy, and when we are happy we pipe; but her audience never pipes, it sits in mouselike stillness; as if we had become partakers in the peace we long for, from which our own piping at the very least holds us back, we make no sound. Is it her singing that enchants us or is it not rather the solemn stillness enclosing her frail little voice? Once it happened while Josephine was singing that some silly little thing in all innocence began to pipe up too. Now it was just the same as what we were hearing from Josephine; in front of us the piping sound that despite all rehearsal was still tentative and here in the audience the unself-conscious piping of a child; it would have been impossible to define the difference; but yet at once we hissed and whistled the interrupter down, although it would not really have been necessary, for in any case she would certainly have crawled away in fear and shame, whereas Josephine struck up her most triumphal notes and was quite beyond herself, spreading her arms wide and stretching her throat as high as it could reach.

That is what she is like always, every trifle, every casual incident, every nuisance, a creaking in the parquet, a grinding of teeth, a failure in the lighting incites her to heighten the effectiveness of her song; she believes anyhow that she is singing to deaf ears; there is no lack of enthusiasm and applause, but she has long learned not to expect real understanding, as she conceives it. So all disturbance is very welcome to her; whatever intervenes from outside to hinder the purity of her song, to be overcome with a slight effort, even with no effort at all, merely by confronting it, can help

to awaken the masses, to teach them not perhaps understanding but awed respect.

And if small events do her such service, how much
more do great ones. Our life is very uneasy, every day
brings surprises, apprehensions, hopes and terrors, so
that it would be impossible for a single individual to
bear it all did he not always have by day and night the
support of his fellows; but even so it often becomes very
difficult; frequently as many as a thousand shoulders
are trembling under a burden that was really meant
only for one pair. Then Josephine holds that her time
has come. So there she stands, the delicate creature,
shaken by vibrations especially below the breastbone,
so that one feels anxious for her, it is as if she has con-
centrated all her strength on her song, as if from everything in her that does not directly subserve her singing
all strength has been withdrawn, almost all power of
life, as if she were laid bare, abandoned, committed
merely to the care of good angels, as if while she is so
wholly withdrawn and living only in her song a cold
breath blowing upon her might kill her. But just when
she makes such an appearance, we who are supposed to
be her opponents are in the habit of saying: "She can't
even pipe; she has to put such a terrible strain on herself to force out not a song—we can't call it song—but
some approximation to our usual customary piping."
So it seems to us, but this impression although, as I
said, inevitable is yet fleeting and transient. We too are
soon sunk in the feeling of the mass, that, warmly
pressed body to body, listens with indrawn breath.

And to gather around her this mass of our people

who are almost always on the run and scurrying hither
and thither for reasons that are often not very clear,
Josephine mostly needs to do nothing else than take up
her stand, head thrown back, mouth half open, eyes
turned upwards, in the position that indicates her in
tention to sing. She can do this where she likes, it need
not be a place visible a long way off, any secluded corner pitched on in a moment's caprice will serve as well.
The news that she is going to sing flies round at once
and soon whole processions are on the way there. Now,
sometimes, all the same, obstacles intervene, Josephine
likes best to sing just when things are most upset, many
worries and dangers force us then to take devious ways,
with the best will in the world we cannot assemble ourselves as quickly as Josephine wants, and on occasion
she stands there in ceremonial state for quite a time
without a sufficient audience—then indeed she turns
furious, then she stamps her feet, swearing in most un-
maidenly fashion; she actually bites. But even such
behavior does no harm to her reputation; instead of
curbing a little her excessive demands, people exert
themselves to meet them; messengers are sent out to
summon fresh hearers; she is kept in ignorance of the
fact that this is being done; on the roads all around sen-
tries can be seen posted who wave on newcomers and
urge them to hurry; this goes on until at last a tolerably
large audience is gathered.

What drives the people to make such exertions for
Josephine's sake? This is no easier to answer than the
first question about Josephine's singing, with which it
is closely connected. One could eliminate that and com-

bine them both in the second question, if it were possible to assert that because of her singing our people are
unconditionally devoted to Josephine. But this is simply
not the case; unconditional devotion is hardly known
among us; ours are people who love slyness beyond
everything, without any malice, to be sure, and childish
whispering and chatter, innocent, superficial chatter, to
be sure, but people of such a kind cannot go in for unconditional devotion, and that Josephine herself certainly feels, that is what she is fighting against with all
the force of her feeble throat.

In making such generalized pronouncements, of
course, one should not go too far, our people are all the
same devoted to Josephine, only not unconditionally.
For instance, they would not be capable of laughing at
Josephine. It can be admitted: in Josephine there is
much to make one laugh; and laughter for its own sake
is never far away from us; in spite of all the misery of
our lives quiet laughter is always, so to speak, at our
elbows; but we do not laugh at Josephine. Many a time
I have had the impression that our people interpret
their relationship to Josephine in this way, that she,
this frail creature, needing protection and in some way
remarkable, in her own opinion remarkable for her gift
of song, is entrusted to their care and they must look
after her; the reason for this is not clear to anyone, only
the fact seems to be established. But what is entrusted
to one's care one does not laugh at; to laugh would be a
breach of duty; the utmost malice which the most malicious of us wreak on Josephine is to say now and then:

"The sight of Josephine is enough to make one stop laughing."

So the people look after Josephine much as a father takes into his care a child whose little hand—one cannot tell whether in appeal or command—is stretched out to him. One might think that our people are not fitted to exercise such paternal duties, but in reality they discharge them, at least in this case, admirably; no single individual could do what in this respect the people as a whole are capable of doing. To be sure, the difference in strength between the people and the individual is so enormous that it is enough for the nursling to be drawn into the warmth of their nearness and he is sufficiently protected. To Josephine, certainly, one does not dare mention such ideas. "Your protection isn't worth an old song," she says then. Sure, sure, old song, we think. And besides her protest is no real contradiction, it is rather a thoroughly childish way of doing, and childish gratitude, while a father's way of doing is to pay no attention to it.

Yet there is something else behind it which is not so easy to explain by this relationship between the people and Josephine. Josephine, that is to say, thinks just the opposite, she believes it is she who protects the people. When we are in a bad way politically or economically, her singing is supposed to save us, nothing less than that, and if it does not drive away the evil, at least gives us the strength to bear it. She does not put it in these words or in any other, she says very little anyhow, she is silent among the chatterers, but it flashes from her eyes, on her closed lips—few among us can keep their lips closed, but she can—it is plainly legible. Whenever we get bad news—and on many days bad news comes thick and fast at once, lies and half-truths included—she rises up at once, whereas usually she sits listlessly on the ground, she rises up and stretches her neck and tries to see over the heads of her flock like a shepherd before a thunderstorm. It is certainly a habit of children, in their wild, impulsive fashion, to make such claims, but Josephine's are not quite so unfounded as children's. True, she does not save us and she gives us no strength; it is easy to stage oneself as a savior of our people, in- ured as they are to suffering, not sparing themselves, swift in decision, well acquainted with death, timorous only to the eye in the atmosphere of reckless daring which they constantly breathe, and as prolific besides as they are bold—it is easy, I say, to stage oneself after the event as the savior of our people, who have always somehow managed to save themselves, although at the cost of sacrifices which make historians—generally speaking we ignore historical research entirely—quite horror-struck. And yet it is true that just in emergencies we hearken better than at other times to Josephine's voice. The menaces that loom over us make us quieter, more humble, more submissive to Josephine's domina- tion; we like to come together, we like to huddle close to each other, especially on an occasion set apart from the troubles preoccupying us; it is as if we were drink- ing in all haste—yes, haste is necessary, Josephine too often forgets that—from a cup of peace in common be- fore the battle. It is not so much a performance of songs as an assembly of the people, and an assembly where except for the small piping voice in front there is complete stillness; the hour is much too grave for us to waste it in chatter.

A relationship of this kind, of course, would never content Josephine. Despite all the nervous uneasiness that fills Josephine because her position has never been quite defined, there is still much that she does not see, blinded by her self-conceit, and she can be brought fairly easily to overlook much more, a swarm of flatterers is always busy about her to this end, thus really doing a public service—and yet to be only an incidental, unnoticed performer in a corner of an assembly of the people, for that, although in itself it would be no small thing, she would certainly not make us the sacrifice of her singing.

Nor does she need to, for her art does not go unnoticed. Although we are at bottom preoccupied with quite other things and it is by no means only for the sake of her singing that stillness prevails and many a listener does not even look up but buries his face in his neighbor's fur, so that Josephine up in front seems to be exerting herself to no purpose, there is yet something—it cannot be denied—that irresistibly makes its way into us from Josephine's piping. This piping, which rises up where everyone else is pledged to silence, comes almost like a message from the whole people to each individual; Josephine's thin piping amidst grave decisions is almost like our people's precarious existence amidst the tumult of a hostile world. Josephine exerts herself, a mere nothing in voice, a mere nothing in execution, she asserts herself and gets across to us; it does us good to think of that. A really trained singer, if ever such a one should be found among us, we could certainly not endure at such a time and we should unanimously turn away from the senselessness of any such performance. May Josephine be spared from perceiving that the mere fact of our listening to her is proof that she is no singer. An intuition of it she must have, else why does she so passionately deny that we do listen, only she keeps on singing and piping her intuition away.

But there are other things she could take comfort from: we do really listen to her in a sense, probably much as one listens to a trained singer; she gets effects which a trained singer would try in vain to achieve among us and which are only produced precisely because her means are so inadequate. For this, doubtless, our way of life is mainly responsible.

Among our people there is no age of youth, scarcely the briefest childhood. Regularly, it is true, demands are put forward that the children should be granted a special freedom, a special protection, that their right to be a little carefree, to have a little senseless giddiness, a little play, that this right should be respected and the exercise of it encouraged; such demands are put forward and nearly everyone approves them, there is nothing one could approve more, but there is also nothing, in the reality of our daily life, that is less likely to be granted, one approves these demands, one makes attempts to meet them, but soon all the old ways are back again. Our life happens to be such that a child, as soon as it can run about a little and a little distinguish one thing from another, must look after itself just like an adult; the areas on which, for economic reasons, we have to live in dispersion are too wide, our enemies too numerous, the dangers lying everywhere in wait for us too incalculable—we cannot shelter our children from the struggle for existence, if we did so, it would bring them to an early grave. These depressing considerations are reinforced by another, which is not depressing: the fertility of our race. One generation—and each is numerous—treads on the heels of another, the children have no time to be children. Other races may foster their children carefully, schools may be erected for their little ones, out of these schools the children may come pouring daily, the future of the race, yet among them it is always the same children that come out day after day for a long time. We have no schools, but from our race come pouring at the briefest intervals the innumerable swarms of our children, merrily lisping or chirping so long as they cannot yet pipe, rolling or tumbling along by sheer impetus so long as they cannot yet run, clumsily carrying everything before them by mass weight so long as they cannot yet see, our children! And not the same children, as in those schools, no, always new children again and again, without end, without a break, hardly does a child appear than it is no more a child, while behind it new childish faces are already crowding so fast and so thick that they are indistinguishable, rosy with happiness. Truly, however delightful this may be and however much others may envy us for it, and rightly, we simply cannot give a real childhood to our children. And that has its consequences. A kind of unexpended, ineradicable childishness pervades our people; in direct opposition to what is best in us, our infallible practical common sense, we often behave with the utmost foolishness, with exactly the same foolishness as children, senselessly, wastefully, grandiosely, irresponsibly, and all that often for the sake of some trivial amusement. And although our enjoyment of it cannot of course be so wholehearted as a child's enjoyment, something of this survives in it without a doubt. From this childishness of our people Josephine too has profited since the beginning.

Yet our people are not only childish, we are also in a sense prematurely old. Childhood and old age come upon us not as upon others. We have no youth, we are all at once grown-up, and then we stay grown-up too long, a certain weariness and hopelessness spreading from that leaves a broad trail through our people's nature, tough and strong in hope that it is in general. Our lack of musical gifts has surely some connection with this; we are too old for music, its excitement, its rapture do not suit our heaviness, wearily we wave it away; we content ourselves with piping; a little piping here and there, that is enough for us. Who knows, there may be talents for music among us; but if there were, the character of our people would suppress them before they could unfold. Josephine on the other hand can pipe as much as she will, or sing or whatever she likes to call it, that does not disturb us, that suits us, that we can well put up with; any music there may be in it is reduced to the least possible trace; a certain tradition of music is preserved, yet without making the slightest demand upon us.

But our people, being what they are, get still more than this from Josephine. At her concerts, especially in times of stress, it is only the very young who are interested in her singing as singing, they alone gaze in astonishment as she purses her lips, expels the air between her pretty front teeth, swoons in sheer wonderment at the sounds she herself is producing and after such a lying away swells her performance to new and more incredible heights, whereas the real mass of the people —this is plain to see—are quite withdrawn into themselves. Here in the brief intervals between their struggles our people dream, it is as if the limbs of each were loosened, as if the harried individual once in a while could relax and stretch himself at ease in the great, warm bed of the community. And into these dreams Josephine's piping drops note by note; she calls it pearl-like, we call it staccato; but at any rate here it is in its right place, as nowhere else, finding the moment wait for it as music scarcely ever does. Something of our poor brief childhood is in it, something of lost happiness that can never be found again, but also something of activ' daily life, of its small gaieties, unaccountable and yet springing up and not to be obliterated. And indeed this is all expressed not in full round tones but softly, in whispers, confidentially, sometimes a little hoarsely. Of course it is a kind of piping. Why not? Piping is our people's daily speech, only many a one pipes his whole life long and does not know it, where here piping is set free from the fetters of daily life and it sets us free too for a little while. We certainly should not want to do without these performances.

But from that point it is a long, long way to Josephine's claim that she gives us new strength and so on and so forth. For ordinary people, at least, not for her train of flatterers. "What other explanation could there be"—they say with quite shameless sauciness—"how else could you explain the great audiences, especially when danger is most imminent, which have even often enough hindered proper precautions being taken in time to avert danger?" Now, this last statement is unfortunately true, but can hardly be counted as one of Josephine's titles to fame, especially considering that when such large gatherings have been unexpectedly flushed by the enemy and many of our people left lying for dead, Josephine, who was responsible for it all, and indeed perhaps attracted the enemy by her piping, has always occupied the safest place and was always the first to whisk away quietly and speedily under cover of her escort. Still, everyone really knows that, and yet people keep running to whatever place Josephine decides on next, at whatever time she rises up to sing. One could argue from this that Josephine stands almost beyond the law, that she can do what she pleases, at the risk of actually endangering the community, and will be forgiven for everything. If this were so, even Josephine's claims would be entirely comprehensible, yes, in this freedom to be allowed her, this extraordinary gift granted to her and to no one else in direct contravention of the laws, one could see an admission of the fact that the people do not understand Josephine, just as she alleges, that they marvel helplessly at her art, feel themselves unworthy of it, try to assuage the pity she rouses in them by making really desperate sacrifices for her and, to the same extent that her art is beyond their comprehension, consider her personality and her wishes to lie beyond their jurisdiction. Well, that is simply not true at all, perhaps as individuals the people may surrender too easily to Josephine, but as a whole they surrender unconditionally to no one, and not to her either.

For a long time back, perhaps since the very beginning of her artistic career, Josephine has been fighting for exemption from all daily work on account of her singing; she should be relieved of all responsibility for earning her daily bread and being involved in the general struggle for existence, which—apparently—should be transferred on her behalf to the people as a whole. A facile enthusiast—and there have been such—might argue from the mere unusualness of this demand, from the spiritual attitude needed to frame such a demand, that it has an inner justification. But our people draw other conclusions and quietly refuse it. Nor do they trouble much about disproving the assumptions on which it is based. Josephine argues, for instance, that the strain of working is bad for her voice, that the strain of working is of course nothing to the strain of singing, but it prevents her from being able to rest sufficiently after singing and to recuperate for more singing, she has to exhaust her strength completely and yet, in these circumstances, can never rise to the peak of her abilities.

The people listen to her arguments and pay no atten-tion. Our people, so easily moved, sometimes cannot be moved at all. Their refusal is sometimes so decided that even Josephine is taken aback, she appears to sub-mit, does her proper share of work, sings as best she can, but all only for a time, then with renewed strength —for this purpose her strength seems inexhaustible— she takes up the fight again.

Now it is clear that what Josephine really wants is not what she puts into words. She is honorable, she is not work-shy, shirking in any case is quite unknown among us, if her petition were granted she would certainly live the same life as before, her work would not at all get in the way of her singing nor would her singing grow any better—what she wants is public, unambiguous, per-manent recognition of her art, going far beyond any precedent so far known. But while almost everything else seems within her reach, this eludes her persistently. Perhaps she should have taken a different line of attack from the beginning, perhaps she herself sees that her approach was wrong, but now she cannot draw back, retreat would be self-betrayal, now she must stand or fall by her petition.

If she really had enemies, as she avers, they could get much amusement from watching this struggle, without having to lift a finger. But she has no enemies, and even though she is often criticized here and there, no one finds this struggle of hers amusing. Just because of the fact that the people show themselves here in their cold, judicial aspect, which is otherwise rarely seen among us. And however one may approve it in this case, the very idea that such an aspect might be turned upon oneself some day prevents amusement from breaking in. The important thing, both in the people's refusal and in Josephine's petition, is not the action itself, but the fact that the people are capable of presenting a stony, impenetrable front to one of their own, and that it is all the more impenetrable because in other respects they show an anxious paternal care, and more than paternal care, for this very member of the people.

Suppose that instead of the people one had an individual to deal with: one might imagine that this man had been giving in to Josephine all the time while nursing a wild desire to put an end to his submissiveness one fine day; that he had made superhuman sacrifices for Josephine in the firm belief that there was a natural limit to his capacity for sacrifice; yes, that he had sacrificed more than was needful merely to hasten the process, merely to spoil Josephine and encourage her to ask for more and more until she did indeed reach the limit with this last petition of hers; and that he then cut her off with a final refusal which was curt because long held in reserve. Now, this is certainly not how the matter stands, the people have no need of such guile, besides, their respect for Josephine is well tried and genuine, and Josephine's demands are after all so far-reaching that any simple child could have told her what the outcome would be; yet it may be that such considerations enter into Josephine's way of taking the matter and so add a certain bitterness to the pain of being refused.

But whatever her ideas on the subject, she does not

let them deter her from pursuing the campaign. Re cently she has even intensified her attack; hitherto she has used only words as her weapons but now she is beginning to have recourse to other means, which she thinks will prove more efficacious but which we think will run her into greater dangers.

Many believe that Josephine is becoming so insistent because she feels herself growing old and her voice falling off, and so she thinks it high time to wage the last battle for recognition. I do not believe it. Josephine would not be Josephine if that were true. For her there is no growing old and no falling off in her voice. If she makes demands it is not because of outward circumstances but because of an inner logic. She reaches for the highest garland not because it is momentarily hanging a little lower but because it is the highest; if she had any say in the matter she would have it still higher.

This contempt for external difficulties, to be sure, does not hinder her from using the most unworthy methods. Her rights seem beyond question to her; so what does it matter how she secures them; especially since in this world, as she sees it, honest methods are bound to fail. Perhaps that is why she has transferred the battle for her rights from the field of song to another which she cares little about. Her supporters have let it be known that, according to herself, she feels quite capable of singing in such a way that all levels of the populace, even to the remotest corners of the opposition, would find it a real delight, a real delight not by popular standards, for the people affirm that they have always delighted in her singing, but a delight by her

own standards. However, she adds, since she cannot fal-
sify the highest standards nor pander to the lowest, her
singing will have to stay as it is. But when it comes to
her campaign for exemption from work, we get a different story; it is of course also a campaign on behalf of
her singing, yet she is not fighting directly with the
priceless weapon of her song, so any instrument she uses
is good enough. Thus, for instance, the rumor went
round that Josephine meant to cut short her grace notes
if her petition were not granted. I know nothing about
grace notes, and have never noticed any in Josephine's
singing. But Josephine is going to cut short her grace
notes, not, for the present, to cut them out entirely, only
to cut them short. Presumably she has carried out her
threat, although I for one have observed no difference
in her performance. The people as a whole listened in
the usual way without making any pronouncement on
the grace notes, nor did their response to her petition
vary by a jot. It must be admitted that Josephine's way
of thinking, like her figure, is often very charming.
And so, for instance, after that performance, just as if
her decision about the grace notes had been too severe
or too sudden a move against the people, she announced
that next time she would put in all the grace notes
again. Yet after the next concert she changed her mind
once more, there was to be definitely an end of these
great arias with the grace notes, and until her petition
was favorably regarded they would never recur. Well,
the people let all these announcements, decisions and
counterdecisions go in at one ear and out at the other,
like a grown-up person deep in thought turning a deaf

ear to a child's babble, fundamentally well disposed but not accessible.

Josephine, however, does not give in. The other day, for instance, she claimed that she had hurt her foot at work, so that it was difficult for her to stand up to sing; but since she could not sing except standing up, her songs would now have to be cut short. Although she limps and leans on her supporters, no one believes that she is really hurt. Granted that her frail body is extra sensitive, she is yet one of us and we are a race of workers; if we were to start limping every time we got a scratch, the whole people would never be done limping. Yet though she lets herself be led about like a cripple, though she shows herself in this pathetic condition oftener than usual, the people all the same listen to her singing thankfully and appreciatively as before, but do not bother much about the shortening of her songs.

Since she cannot very well go on limping forever, she thinks of something else, she pleads that she is tired, not in the mood for singing, feeling faint. And so we get a theatrical performance as well as a concert. We see Josephine's supporters in the background begging and imploring her to sing. She would be glad to oblige, but she cannot. They comfort and caress her with flatteries, they almost carry her to the selected spot where she is supposed to sing. At last, bursting inexplicably into tears, she gives way, but when she stands up to sing, obviously at the end of her resources, weary, her arms not widespread as usual but hanging lifelessly down, so that one gets the impression that they are perhaps a little too short—just as she is about to strike up, there, she cannot do it after all, an unwilling shake of the head tells us so and she breaks down before our eyes. To be sure, she pulls herself together again and sings, I fancy, much as usual; perhaps, if one has an ear for the finer shades of expression, one can hear that she is singing with unusual feeling, which is, however, all to the good. And in the end she is actually less tired than before, with a firm tread, if one can use such a term for her trip-ping gait, she moves off, refusing all help from her sup-porters and measuring with cold eyes the crowd which respectfully makes way for her.

That happened a day or two ago; but the latest is that she has disappeared, just at a time when she was supposed to sing. It is not only her supporters who are looking for her, many are devoting themselves to the search, but all in vain; Josephine has vanished, she will not sing; she will not even be cajoled into singing, this time she has deserted us entirely.

Curious, how mistaken she is in her calculations, the clever creature, so mistaken that one might fancy she has made no calculations at all but is only being driven on by her destiny, which in our world cannot be any-thing but a sad one. Of her own accord she abandons her singing, of her own accord she destroys the power she has gained over people's hearts. How could she ever have gained that power, since she knows so little about these hearts of ours? She hides herself and does not sing, but our people, quietly, without visible disappoint-ment, a self-confident mass in perfect equilibrium, so constituted, even although appearances are misleading, that they can only bestow gifts and not receive them, even from Josephine, our people continue on their way.

Josephine's road, however, must go downhill. The time will soon come when her last notes sound and die into silence. She is a small episode in the eternal history of our people, and the people will get over the loss of her. Not that it will be easy for us; how can our gatherings take place in utter silence? Still, were they not silent even when Josephine was present? Was her actual piping notably louder and more alive than the memory of it will be? Was it even in her lifetime more than a simple memory? Was it not rather because Josephine's singing was already past losing in this way that our people in their wisdom prized it so highly?

So perhaps we shall not miss so very much after all, while Josephine, redeemed from the earthly sorrows which to her thinking lay in wait for all chosen spirits, will happily lose herself in the numberless throng of the heroes of our people, and soon, since we are no historians, will rise to the heights of redemption and be forgotten like all her brothers.

MODERN LIBRARY GIANTS

A series of sturdily bound and handsomely printed, full-sized library editions of books formerly available only in expensive sets. These volumes contain from 600 to 1,400 pages each.

THE MODERN LIBRARY GIANTS REPRESENT A
SELECTION OF THE WORLD'S GREATEST BOOKS